SERENA'S GRACE

ALSO BY SIBERIA JOHNSON

Lovesick (Contemporary Romance)

Nia's Resolve

Ivory's Ruin

Serena's Grace

Riley's Inferno

The Monster's Mate (Paranormal Erotica)

Sin, Secrets, and Summoning

Alpha Affinity

Crimson Vow

Embers of Eternity

Omnibus - 2027

& more TBA

SERENA'S GRACE

A COWBOY CURE

SIBERIA JOHNSON

A LOVESICK NOVEL

This book contains topics that may be sensitive to some readers, including explicit sexual content, profanity, attempted assault, and implied racism.

To find out more about Siberia's books, visit her website (https://beacons.ai/siberia) and join her exclusive reader group (www.facebook.com/groups/sweetsinners).

Sensitivity Edit by Dee Hudson at Tessera Editorial
Editing by Shawsome Reads Editing Services
Proofreading by Lindsey Clarke

ISBN: 978-1-963206-13-5

*Dedicated to country sunrises, grey sweatpants,
and girls who just wanna have fun.*

CONTENTS

Chapter 1	1
Chapter 2	7
Chapter 3	13
Chapter 4	19
Chapter 5	25
Chapter 6	31
Chapter 7	41
Chapter 8	49
24 Days Left	55
Chapter 9	57
Chapter 10	65
Chapter 11	71
Chapter 12	77
Chapter 13	83
Chapter 14	91
Chapter 15	97
Chapter 16	105
Chapter 17	113
Chapter 18	119
15 Days Left	125
Chapter 19	127
Chapter 20	133
Chapter 21	143
Chapter 22	151
Chapter 23	157
Chapter 24	163
Chapter 25	171
Chapter 26	177
Chapter 27	183
Chapter 28	189
Chapter 29	195
8 Days Left	203
Chapter 30	205

Chapter 31   213
Chapter 32   219
Chapter 33   227
Chapter 34   233
Chapter 35   241
Chapter 36   247
Chapter 37   253
Chapter 38   259
Chapter 39   267
Epilogue   275

Acknowledgments   285
About the Author   287

Hollow Oak Ranch

ONE

Serena

Wild. Rough and unapologetic. Jagged mountains on the horizon cut into a sky so big and blue it could drown the ocean.

She'd never seen anything like it. Photos, sure, but nothing compared to the presence of untouched nature. The permanence of something timeless and powerful. It took her breath away, but didn't stop a pit from forming in her gut.

This summer was going to be nothing like she planned.

No frat parties, no laid-back job on campus, and certainly no trips to the mall. A long trail of dust churned outside the window as they sped down the lonely highway, dirt and bugs smattering across the black paint of their family's Audi.

Serena wrinkled her nose and tried to calculate if the car wash would be open by the time her sister got home to the city. Lexi had just gotten her learner's permit and was more than eager to get out of the house for a trip out here and back. Unfortunately, their drive had been anything but entertaining. At least the company wasn't bad.

"Hey, I know I said you could go over the speed limit, but keep it below seventy-five, all right?" Serena glanced at her younger sister, who took after her in one too many ways. Honey-blonde hair. Warm chestnut eyes. A rebellious side that meant she was intent on testing her limits even when they'd been all but lifted.

Lexi rolled her eyes. "You sound like mom."

Serena scoffed. Static crackled on the radio, interrupting her second-favorite pop song. She reached over to turn down the volume. "I got in enough trouble for the both of us. You don't need to pile more on."

With an exaggerated exhale, Lexi eased off on the gas. "I can't believe you'll be stuck out here for a whole month."

"I know," Serena echoed her little sister's sigh. "It's fucked up."

She turned to look out the passenger window, tired of seeing those intimidating mountains tower over miles of nothing but tumbleweeds and dry amber grass. "Do you think they even know what fast food is out here?"

Lexi shook her head with a laugh. "Not unless by fast, you mean over an hour delivery time."

Serena huffed and adjusted her feet on the dash. As they drove into the heart of literal nowhere, fields of open land met with sloping foothills. The only sign of humanity had been a bare wooden fence or two, and even those looked worn and neglected. There were probably more cows out here than people.

For the moment, she tried to enjoy the luxury of air conditioning and patchy radio. Who knew if basic commodities would be too modern for where they were headed. Her first year away from home was supposed to be filled with shameless college hook-ups and generally not giving a fuck. And she'd done a pretty good job of doing just that.

Until now.

Instead of relaxing while classes were out, she'd been

saddled with one hundred hours of court-ordered community service, stretched over four weeks at some ranch in the middle of the desert. It wasn't even located on the same map as the nearest shopping center. Why the judge had such a hard-on for this place, she'd never be able to figure out.

She also wasn't a delinquent. Running a stop sign and getting caught with an open beer can shouldn't be a crime. Not that she was old enough to drink legally, and it wasn't the only questionable substance she'd ingested, but no one else cared because she wasn't a damn shut-in. Everybody bent the rules.

However, she'd been in the wrong place at the wrong time —with the wrong fucking asshole—and ended up paying for it with her last month of summer.

It was better than what her so-called friend got charged with: possession of controlled substances and an ongoing sexual assault case. The drugs she knew about, but assault? But maybe she had turned a blind eye for too long. It wasn't like the culture on campus made it hard to get whatever you wanted. She would know.

Serena pursed her lips and tried to ignore the nagging thoughts, winding a strand of blonde hair around a manicured fingernail—her last tie to civilization. Okay, so she needed better friends, but from the looks of it, she wasn't going to find any out here.

"What's the place called again?" Lexi asked, turning off the radio and adjusting her sunglasses. "I think we lost service, but our GPS said it should be coming up soon."

"Hollow Oak Ranch." The words tasted stale on her tongue.

She didn't need their stupid pamphlet to know what it was all about—turning troubled teens into upstanding, model citizens. The promotional material said the ranch was a residential treatment program to provide guidance for young adults struggling in school or at home. Looked good on paper, but who knew if anyone went away changed. Maybe all they did was wear people out and call it old-fashioned discipline.

Since she wasn't a youth, she hadn't been qualified for the program, but the judge pulled some strings and got her in as an extra staff member. Woo-fucking-hoo. They were bullshitting themselves if they thought she'd be of actual use. She wasn't made for hard labor, and getting her hands dirty was reserved for things that held her interest, not farm work or whatever they thought she needed. Besides, she didn't want someone else to tell her how to live or who to be.

"If you can't find it, we'll just have to turn around and say we tried our best." Serena shrugged and made a face at her sister.

Lexi didn't look so amused. "What was that about not piling on more trouble? Mom and Dad are already pissed at you for the fine."

"It's not like they can't afford it. Hasn't Dad been working overtime all summer?"

"That's not the point." Lexi leaned forward and slowed down. "Ah, there it is. Hard to miss the first sign that's existed for miles." She flicked on the turn signal—to warn the cows—and they veered onto a long dirt road lined with a barbed wire fence.

Above them, a sign with the ranch's brand hung from a thick, sturdy beam. Serena sat up to inspect her new surroundings. The road took them into a valley backed against a ridge, where a thick grove of trees provided a fair amount of shade for the buildings nestled in the center.

The estate must be huge. Its fence extended as far as she could see, originating at a big barn on the left. Two smaller buildings settled on the right, the windows open and cream curtains flowing out in the breeze. True to aesthetic, the main house was built out of large round planks, like a cozy cabin but at ten times the scale. Several floor-to-ceiling windows at the front reflected a panoramic view of the mountain range.

For such a large structure that rose out of undeveloped ground, it had a charming feel. Quaint in an almost nostalgic way, except she'd never been anywhere that resembled this. At least it looked hospitable enough. She wouldn't know how to survive if they expected her to brave the wilderness.

But as peaceful as it was, someone else had silently been watching as they pulled in. A man followed them with dark, twinkling eyes, propped against one of the smaller houses like a part of the scenery. He might have looked youthful if it wasn't for his impressive height and physique. His bare, tan chest glistened in the sun, throat moving as he brought a water bottle to his lips and swallowed in long gulps. When he finished, he wiped his mouth with the back of his hand and effortlessly crunched the plastic in his palm.

They made eye contact, and he tipped his head down, his shoulders hunching as his face disappeared under a dusty brown cowboy hat. She knew it'd be hot outside, but damn, this guy turned up the heat all on his own. There wasn't a muscle on his body that didn't look like it could be put to good use— and it wasn't the kind of bulk that guys could get from going to the gym once or twice a week. No, this was the build of a real man, one who'd been formed from the rugged outdoors and could toss her around like a rag doll.

One who could give her the ride of her life.

She chewed her lip. Exactly the kind of man she liked. Maybe this place wouldn't be so bad. It shouldn't take too much effort to earn a few favors.

Lexi made a poor attempt at a low whistle. "I think I just found myself a new type—do you see that? I guess it's true they grow 'em different out here."

"Chill, you're too young to mess around. Much less with guys like him," Serena chided. Her sister was off-limits. But for her, it might as well be open season. She smoothed her hair and gave him a small wave as they pulled to a stop.

The cowboy replied with a touch of his fingers to his hat, barely hiding a dimpled grin as he pushed off the wall.

Her lips curled into a smile. "Looks like going to the country won't be as bad as I thought."

TWO

Grant

MID-SUMMER HEAT DESCENDED ON HOLLOW OAK LIKE A BIBLICAL plague. A few clouds bordered the mountain peaks, teasing a promise of shade and a sprinkle of rain the grass desperately needed.

He stopped for a break and leaned against the open doorway, cracking the seal on a cold bottle of water. After a decade of use and a stellar turn-around rate that brought in much-needed funding, he thought they'd put air conditioning into the guesthouses. Apparently not.

More than a few success stories had come out of this place, but he doubted a lack of cold air was the key factor. If sweating could change a man, he'd have evolved into a superhuman by now. Instead, all he got was a drenched shirt that had long ago been abandoned on the fence line.

Between airing out a year's worth of dust and making sure all the guest rooms were stocked with fresh supplies, he'd run around the ranch more than a dozen times. They were short-staffed this summer, not that he minded, but it meant he had to put in twice as much work. He'd been the only one to come back a second year in a row, and though everyone kept bringing up college like it might change his mind, he didn't have plans to go anywhere else. He didn't belong anywhere else.

Besides, Hollow Oak needed workers who cared, and he needed something good to spend his energy on. Better than mingling with a bunch of preppy new adults his age who thought getting a piece of paper meant they'd made an important contribution to society. Living out here required a true work ethic.

A breeze dried the sweat rolling down his chest, and he relished the taste of cool spring water, guzzling a whole bottle in one go. The rumble of an engine broke through the silent countryside, and he looked up to see a black Audi barreling down the gravel drive. Guests weren't supposed to arrive until tomorrow, and that vehicle didn't belong to anyone from town.

In the front, two blondes with sunglasses as big as their foreheads craned their necks like this was some sort of petting zoo. One of them waved, her pink nails flashing in a little arc that was meant to be cute and flirtatious.

He sighed and returned her greeting. Sure, it might be cute, but she looked so out of place that he had to dip his head and hide a chuckle under the brim of his hat. The only animal he'd consider letting her near was the one between his legs. But he doubted she could handle that, either.

In any case, his Ma raised a gentleman, so he pushed off the wall and went to give them directions to the closest Starbucks.

The vehicle rolled to a stop, and the one with pink nails stepped out, lifting her glasses to reveal rich brown eyes framed by long lashes. Her attention lingered over his abdomen, and despite the high-heeled ankle boots and impressive legs, she had to tip her head to meet his gaze. He held back a smirk as she put on a sultry smile that came across as more than a little suggestive. "This place has quite the view, doesn't it?"

He ignored her insinuation. "Can I help you?"

She turned to observe the ranch house, wind playing with

strands of her hair and twirling them like golden fairy silk. "Well, this is where I'm supposed to be staying for the next month."

This time, his laugh echoed out loud. "Ma'am, I'm sure you have the wrong address."

She arched a thin blonde eyebrow, pursing her lips like the joke was on him. No way would a dolled-up city girl like her want to spend a month out here.

The front door of the main house swung open and shattered their moment. Or whatever that was. He turned as Mrs. Weston stepped out, on point as always, followed by her husband. The elderly couple trekked across the lawn to greet Miss Lost And Confused.

Both had been his mentors at some point or another, and they'd grown close enough to be honorary grandparents. They may have graying hairs on their head, but they kept a gait as swift and energetic as any pair of troublemakers. It made sense that they'd be full of energy when he took care of all the heavy lifting.

"Hello, dear. You must be Serena." Mrs. Weston slipped between their awkward stand-off and quickly broke the ice.

The blonde nodded and motioned inside the car. "And this is Lexi, my sister. She offered to drive me out here." Serena stuffed a hand in the back pocket of her shorts and pushed out her hips, accentuating the curve of her ass.

Wait. He forced his attention back to her conversation with Mrs. Weston.

So, she *hadn't* been kidding?

"We're glad to have you," Mrs. Weston was saying. "My husband and I run Hollow Oak." They exchanged handshakes. "We should have everything you need, but if something comes up, just let us know."

Mrs. Weston turned to him, the corners of her eyes crinkled with a smile. "Or you can ask Grant. I see you've already met.

He's our best worker, and I'm sure he'd love to help you get settled in."

Calling on his better judgment, he nodded and kept any additional commentary to himself. He slid his eyes over Serena a second time. This was the girl he'd be working with? He hadn't heard much, but he knew they'd gotten someone else to come up as an extra assistant for the month.

She wore booty shorts and a crop top. That was about as far from work attire as one could get. Her tan stomach had probably seen the inside of a salon more than the sun, and the only thing those shoes would be good for was strutting around and looking pretty. They were made of *suede,* for heaven's sake, not practical leather that could handle a bit of mud. He didn't even want to think about her qualifications for working with the guests.

What the hell had everyone been thinking when they gave her this job?

"Would your sister like to come in for a bit?" Mrs. Weston asked. "She's more than welcome to rest and get some food before making the drive back."

"I'll ask, but I'm sure she wants to head back before it gets late." Serena went to open the car door again.

He cleared his throat. Best to make himself busy before he got roped into being the entertainment. "I'll take your bags to the room if you'd like."

Serena gave him a saccharine smile. "That would be great. I'll have Lexi open the trunk."

He sauntered around the car while the ladies continued talking, and Mr. Weston conveniently excused himself to go check on a vague something 'out back.'

The trunk hatch opened with a click, then he let out a muffled groan. Somehow, those girls had managed to stuff three suitcases in here. Maybe that chick had some skills after all, because such a small space was *not* meant to hold this much. He was surprised she didn't come with a personal attendant at this rate.

He leaned over to catch Serena's attention. "All of these?"

"Yep." Her lips popped around the 'p,' full and glossy.

He made sure to hide his head before rolling his eyes. She wouldn't last a week.

But if she wanted to put that cute mouth of hers to good use, he might let her. The only thing he'd likely get out of this whole ordeal was a blow job, anyway.

Grabbing a suitcase in each hand, he heaved them out of the trunk and disappeared into the ladies' guesthouse.

The ranch's layout was simple enough: one house for the boys and another for the ladies. A large common room spread out on the main floor of each, along with the assistant's bedroom, private bath, laundry, and a utility closet. The other bedrooms were all upstairs, with two beds apiece and a shared shower and toilet. The Westons lived in the main house, where everyone gathered for meal times and evening meetings when the summer program was in session.

Grateful he didn't have to carry these things up any stairs, he lumbered into what would be Serena's room and dropped the suitcases next to the bed. They hit the floor with a rattling thud. Her window looked out directly across from where he'd be with the guys, but he didn't plan on taking advantage of their proximity. Didn't need her pretty head thinking he was desperate for some action. Even if she would win first prize in a wet t-shirt contest.

When he left to get the third suitcase, the Westons had both disappeared, and Serena was busy talking to her sister inside the car. Wordlessly, he took the last bag—which must have been full of bricks—and shut the back hatch. That earned him a glare from the front seat, but he brushed it off and went inside.

He heard the engine turn on, and gravel crunched as the

car pulled out of the drive. Then, the clack of heels echoed across the wood flooring. He dropped the suitcase and braced himself before turning around.

Serena had stopped at the open door, arms crossed over her chest. She met his eyes with a hard stare.

Great, he'd already managed to piss her off.

THREE

Serena

ALL SHE WANTED WAS A GOOD TIME. AND IT LOOKED LIKE HE didn't mind getting down and dirty—but he could show off his masculinity without being so abrasive about it.

Grant dropped her suitcase on the floor, and it abruptly toppled onto its side.

"Gosh, maybe you could be a little rougher with my stuff? Might not have broken everything in there." She leveled her eyes as he turned to face her, then crossed her arms and pretended he didn't affect her as much as he did.

The strain of his muscles when he picked up those bags had been enough to make her thighs squeeze, and even now, that clench in his jaw had heat crawling up her neck. It didn't mean he had to go around rolling his eyes behind her back and slamming doors like she'd become the biggest pain in his ass— all within five minutes of meeting each other.

If he had a problem, then he needed to say it to her face.

"My bad. Wasn't aware name-brand clothes were so fragile, but sure," he scoffed, giving her a forced grin with matching dimples. "I could chuck it out the window if you'd like."

"Really?" She deadpanned. It took a monumental amount

of restraint not to roll her eyes back at him, but she wasn't about to stoop to his level.

She could handle an attitude; her ex had a temper ten times worse, and she knew firsthand that a disagreement or two served its purpose—a little angry sex went a long way—but she and Grant were ages away from that. If she ever cared to get to that stage with anyone again.

Cynical jokes and personal history aside, if they'd be working together for the next month, they had to at least get over the communication issues. She'd seen enough not to ignore signs of hidden animosity.

Maybe if she'd learned that sooner, she wouldn't be in this mess to begin with.

She sighed and took the edge of irritation out of her voice. "You didn't have to slam the trunk."

Grant's smile fell as he sucked in a breath and leaned back on his heels, making her glad these boots gave her an extra three inches. Every part of him bulged with sinew and hard muscle as he towered above her, but he didn't mirror her stance. If anything, it looked like he was trying to make himself less intimidating. Which was pointless because this guy might as well be a giant.

He pinned her with a matter-of-fact expression. "Could you explain how else it was gonna get closed?"

"There's a button. Hopefully, you didn't break it."

He snorted. The green of his eyes flashed with sardonic amusement, so vibrant that it felt like all the color of summer had been extracted from the trees and poured into his irises.

If he put on a damn shirt, it would be a lot easier to stay mad. Or maybe not.

She fanned herself and looked away, eternally grateful the windows had been opened. Warm sunlight poured in with a cool breeze and energized the small space. Light linens softened dark hardwood floors, while antique furniture with a full-length mirror stood against the wall. It was exactly the kind of chic decor she'd seen in a modern country magazine.

The subtle scent of fabric softener wafted through the air, and a new candle had been placed on the nightstand. Grant must've been working hard to get everything in order—she hadn't seen anyone else around besides the Westons.

Her gaze returned to his, and he ran a hand over the back of his neck. A sheen of sweat reflected on his forehead under the brim of his hat. "Look, I apologize if I messed up your car. I can pay for any repairs." He shuffled on his feet. "I'm just not used to fancy things."

Or welcoming new coworkers.

Dropping her arms, she stepped away from the door into a stray beam of light. Fresh air from outside whisked the heat off her skin. The sun somehow felt different than usual. Like out here it brought renewal, instead of smoldering the asphalt like it did in the city.

"Well, at least you know for next time," she relented. "I do appreciate the hospitality, if that's what it was. But I could have done it myself. I got the suitcases in the trunk on my own, and I'm more than capable of taking them out."

He pressed his full lips in a line, which only accentuated their curve. She bet he made for one hell of a kisser.

"We wouldn't want you to chip a nail, would we?" he replied.

She narrowed her eyes. "You *do* have a problem with me."

He shook his head, that dimple flashing briefly before he sobered. "It's nothing personal. We don't know each other, and I don't know why you came all this way, but it's clear you have no experience working on a ranch. Things are different out here than in the city. Don't expect me to hold your hand through everything that needs to get done. If you came out to try something new, that's great, but know it's gonna be a sharp learning curve." He blew out a slow breath. "We could use the help, though."

She deflated against the wall, and her voice dropped to a low mutter. "I know I'm out of my element. It's not like I wanted to be here."

He looked at her with surprise, raising a thick eyebrow. "You signed up for the job, didn't you?"

Now it was her turn to be surprised. "They didn't tell you why I'm here? I'm not getting paid—it's community service. For a court order."

He stared at her for a moment, as if he couldn't look away. Then he dipped his head and waved a hand. "That's none of my business. I should go and finish up before dinner."

Grant made a move to step around her, but she caught his arm and curled her fingers around a sturdy bicep. "Not so fast, cowboy."

She trailed her eyes up his massive shoulder, smirking at how easily it'd been to get under his skin. He hadn't been mean or rude on purpose, and she knew she'd dressed this way with the intention of not looking fit for the job. If they really did need her help, then she wasn't going to be a stick in the mud about it. After all, she could do more than look pretty, and getting closer to him was a decent enough incentive to roll up her metaphorical sleeves.

"I'm not asking for pity or a full course on the Wild West," she continued. "But I think we can figure out a way to make this month worth both of our time." She tipped her head to catch the sun with her eyelashes. Putting on an easy smile, she swiped the hat off his head and placed it on hers. "Aren't you going to give me a tour?"

Tousled sandy hair fell over his forehead as Grant's face froze. Then he broke into a low chuckle. "You got good game, I'll give you that. But don't think I haven't caught onto you."

Leaving one arm captive in her grip, he brought his other

hand beside her head and boxed her against the wall. The toe of their boots touched—his brown leather to her black suede. She stared at the strong lines of his jaw as he smirked. Shit, now she had his *full* attention, and it was nothing short of overwhelming.

"You haven't caught me yet," she breathed, inhaling the scent of leather and musk.

"Uh-huh," he hummed, dragging his hot gaze over her chest. Then pinned her with a searing intensity that made her heart stutter. "Don't get me wrong, I appreciate a girl who knows what she wants."

"And I like a man who can give it to me," she whispered.

His eyes twinkled, half hooded in shadow and the other half a bright bottle green—splintered like broken glass and sharp enough to cut the air between them. "Oh, sunflower, you think you can woo me into going easy on you. You think your uptown style and expensive perfume will have me wrapped around your little finger, but..."

He leaned in so close that their lips almost touched. Faint traces of licorice sweetened his breath, and his body heat seeped into her skin. Her hand tightened around his arm, feeling just how hard his muscle was as it pressed into her palm.

He hummed as her eyes flicked down to his mouth. "If you want a piece of this, then you're the one who's going to have to work for it."

Taking his hat back, he strode away as if he hadn't melted through her panties without so much as touching her. She pulled her lip between her teeth and watched him take the steps two at a time to the upper floor, his ass filling out a pair of dark denim jeans.

Well, then. Guess it was time to get to work.

FOUR

Grant

Fuck. Nothing could have prepared him for that. This woman had no business stepping onto *his* ranch and then negotiating to do things *her* way.

And his heart had no business reacting to her the way it did.

It'd almost leapt out of his chest at the gentle slide of her fingers up his arm. The pull of those tiny dagger-like nails still lingered on his skin, as if she'd transformed into some sort of demonic angel. Equally devious and unbearably beautiful. That low rasp in her voice had all his blood rushing south, and the way her hair shone brighter than the sun itself drew him in like a moth to a flame.

It'd been years since he'd felt anything so potent. Since he'd glimpsed color outside of the monotone gray that settled over his world.

Since before the accident.

Maybe that only meant he needed to get out and let off some steam—hit up the bar or reach out to one of the few women who hadn't moved away from this town. Even if he knew they wouldn't satisfy him in the end.

Dry grass crunched beneath their boots as he led Serena across the front yard. After she got settled in and he finished the guest rooms on the second floor, he decided to entertain her request for a tour. Test if she'd meant what she said about helping. If she ran for the hills on the first day, then he'd tell the Westons she just wasn't cut out for it. Maybe they could find something easy for her to do, like staying locked indoors on desk duty.

The clouds moved overhead and granted them a respite of shade, which he appreciated all the more after putting back on his white t-shirt. If he'd known she was coming this early, he would've been more presentable—and a few extra barriers between them wouldn't hurt at this point. But that hadn't stopped Serena from casting unashamed glances in his direction. Likewise, he watched her through his peripheral vision. One of them had to be discreet about it.

He wondered how long her attraction would last. For the time being, he didn't mind the view. Her long legs easily kept up with his strides, and she should be banned from wearing any kind of denim because the way those shorts hugged her ass was downright criminal.

Dammit. He shouldn't have brought up why she came here. Community service from a court order? That had to be something she didn't want to talk about. If Hollow Oak could help her, then the last thing he wanted to do was push her away. Lord knew he had his own history that he didn't want out in the open.

People came out here to get rid of their problems, and although that often meant facing them, it had to be on their terms. The ranch could facilitate the right atmosphere for reflection, but it was up to the individual to open up. Not that it was his place to judge what she needed.

"Ever been around horses, sunflower?" he asked, distracting himself from heavier thoughts.

Just like it had before, his endearment seemed to catch her off guard. Serena tried to cover her reaction and locked her inquisitive brown eyes on the mountains in the distance. She casually rubbed her arms, though it wasn't nearly cold enough for goosebumps.

"No. We had a puppy once, but no one wanted to take care of it after a few months." She tucked back a strand of shiny hair, the trace of a frown appearing on her lips. "Why do you keep calling me that?"

He waited until she turned to face him and met her gaze. "You mean sunflower?"

There it was again, the smallest flush in her cheeks and a dart of her tongue to wet her bottom lip. Nothing about her demeanor came off as meek, but in this moment she almost appeared shy. Like she'd never had someone compliment her without giving in to her advances. Like she wasn't used to a man who could appreciate her beauty and challenge her as an equal at the same time.

"Does it bother you?" he asked.

"Not really." She shrugged and looked away again. "Just wanted to know where it came from. Do you always give girls silly flower names?"

He grinned. "Only when it makes them blush."

She scoffed and bumped into him with her hip. "Wow, I bet you're such a player. Do you keep count of how many you've deflowered?"

That smile of hers had started to make his world spin. He took in a breath of fresh air and followed her gaze to the mountains. "No, I'm a simple ranch hand who can't close a car hatch, remember? I can probably only count so high." She opened her mouth to reply, but he finished before she got the chance. "And for the record, the number I've 'deflowered' would be zero."

The barely healed scar on his heart began to fester, but he'd long ago mastered the art of ignoring it. Nothing a glass of whiskey from Mr. Weston's not-so-secret stash wouldn't fix.

Serena's smile fell. "Hey, I didn't mean to insult you earlier. I wasn't thrilled at being all the way out here, and I think we got off on the wrong foot. Can we call a truce?" She blew out a breath and added in a mumble, "Even if you are the one who started it."

He barked out a laugh and walked close enough to let their shoulders brush. A rush of heat shot through his veins. "Offer declined."

She snapped her eyes to his with an exasperated expression that only made him laugh harder. "Then fuck you."

He shook his head in disbelief. Wasn't she the one who'd gotten on his case for being impolite? He'd never be able to keep up with her mood swings at this rate.

"Where's the fun in acting all nice?" he teased, recognizing her words for what they were—a reaction he'd purposely drawn out. "Haven't seen this much drama since Mrs. Weston's favorite soap opera ended."

Serena stared at him for a beat, then breathed out a laugh and turned to the horizon. For someone who claimed to dislike it here, she sure seemed to enjoy looking around. He knew the view was impressive—had spent his fair share of days wanting to be alone with his thoughts under the sky—but from the way it sucked her in, one would think she'd never seen the outdoors.

The longer they interacted, the more he realized she was more complicated than she wanted him to believe.

"First stop is the main barn," he said, changing the subject as they reached the building.

White trim stood out against deep red siding, bright from the fresh coat of paint he'd put on last year. "We lease most of the land to cattle ranchers who house their livestock in a barn a couple miles down the road, but keep a few acres for recreation and pastures for the horses."

"Who counts as 'we'?" Serena asked, waiting while he opened the side door.

"Ah, the Westons, I mean," he corrected as they stepped inside. Heat saturated the air as the tail of a thin breeze ruffled the leaves outside. Low rays of sun filtered through the windows over the loft and a few of the open stalls, creating slanted highlights along the boarded walls and concrete floor.

"I've officially worked here for three years, but I've known them almost my whole life, so it feels a lot longer. They hire workers for the summer—and volunteers," he added, remembering Serena's situation, "but I'm the only one who sticks around all year."

A delicate, fresh scent wafted past as she walked behind him. It was much lighter than the warm, rich undertones of hay and manure he'd grown accustomed to. He had to stop himself from breathing in too deeply—her perfume was gonna stink up the whole barn.

Serena took to wandering about the space, reading the name slots in front of each stall and looking around curiously at the grain and tack room. He could tell by her tentative movements that this was all new to her, but she didn't hover in the corner like he thought she would.

A few horses poked in their heads, hoping for a snack. They usually got fed after dinner, but it was gonna be their lucky day. Might as well get it out of the way early.

"The Westons don't ride much anymore. We have a few boarders who don't mind us using their hoses for the program," he continued, climbing to the loft as he spoke. "Our policy is that everyone pitches in. The technical term is equine therapy, but it's more caretaking than telling them your sob stories."

Serena tracked his movements as he tossed down a new bale of hay. "Guests enrolled in equine therapy will work with the horses here and sometimes the birds out back. Anyone who's uncomfortable with the animals can take an alternative life skills course." He climbed down and shook out a few pieces of hay from his shirt.

Serena walked over as he separated the new bale, her boots clicking on the cement floor. "Birds?"

"Chickens, actually," he said. "We tried ducks a few years ago. And goats. Both ended in a total mess. Although Mrs. Weston still insists the goats were cute."

"Goats *are* cute," she agreed. "Especially the little ones."

He grimaced. Typical opinion for someone who'd never been around one in real life. "Yeah, until they head-butt you every time you try to feed 'em."

She brought a hand up to her mouth and broke out in a fit of laughter.

Guess it was kinda funny if you weren't the one who had to deal with the bruises. And fixing the fence every other day. And a million other problems.

"Don't get me started on trying to milk them," he added.

She doubled over, bracing a hand on the wall between tangled bridles and lead ropes. "Don't tell me you—*milked*—a goat?"

He raised his eyebrows. "It's pretty common, actually."

"All right, all right." She sucked in a long breath. "I'd pay to see a video of that."

"And I'd pay to see *you* do it," he grumbled, smiling despite himself. She didn't need to know that there probably was a video of it somewhere.

"Here." He held out a bucket full of grain and a scoop. "There's no better introduction than being the one to serve dinner."

FIVE

Serena

"I CAN'T GET THE FEED IN WHEN ITS HEAD IS IN THE WAY," SHE huffed.

The black horse snorted and stared at her with large brown eyes. All the others had behaved as she dished out their grains, but this one came right up to the front of the stall and refused to move. This was exactly the kind of thing she *hadn't* signed up for.

She hovered a step out of reach. The creature looked more than twice her size, though they were about the same height. Probably weighed about ten times more than she did. Quite frankly, she didn't want to get any closer than necessary.

Grant grinned at her struggle, but he didn't laugh this time. "Hey now, Lucy, you gotta move over." Taking the horse's head in his hands, he guided her away from the feeding bin.

Lucy's ears twitched, and she lowered her nose so he could scratch under her chin.

"I know, you just want attention, don't you?" he murmured. Grant ran his hands over Lucy's nose, rubbing the white stripe between her eyes and down the pink patch on her nostrils. His palms were large and calloused, nails lined with dirt.

Something about his gentle movements felt soothing, even without experiencing them herself.

Lucy's eyes slid closed. Serena took advantage of the moment and stepped forward to dump out the grain. Making a swift retreat, she dropped the scoop back into the bucket and wiped the dust off her hands.

That hadn't been so bad. But she wasn't going to ask to do it without him.

Lucy turned as Grant let go and began to munch happily on her food. He seemed like a different person with the animals than the one she met in the guesthouse. Like he knew and trusted them on a personal level, and they knew him even better.

Something inside her twisted. She wondered if she'd ever find a bond like that—human or otherwise. Her parents and siblings interacted with each other only when it served their own self-interest. When they did manage a decent conversation, there were things they just couldn't help with. And a few things she'd been too prideful to admit.

"Is this one yours?" she asked, glancing over at Grant. It'd be fitting if the most difficult horse was his.

He shook his head and leaned against the outside of the stall, crossing his arms. His biceps strained under the white t-shirt, the fabric making his tan all the more apparent. "Sold mine a few years back."

"Why?" Even if she'd only known him a few hours, that didn't add up. She couldn't imagine what could make him give up something he cared so much about.

"Had to focus on other things." He shrugged, watching as Lucy ate. "Besides, it was time I moved on from junior rodeo."

She mirrored his position on the other side of the door and watched from her peripheral vision to make sure Lucy didn't move too close. "Were you any good?"

Grant raised his eyes to hers, the shadow of that damn

cowboy hat making it hard to read his expression. "Would it matter to you whether I was or not?"

She shrugged. "I think it matters that you don't want to tell me."

He gave her a slanted grin. "Maybe I don't think you'll appreciate the answer. How much do you know about rodeo, anyway?"

She pursed her lips. They both knew that was a big fat zero. Fine, she could figure it out on her own. He already had enough fuel to tease her with, so she filed her questions away for later.

"What's Lucy's story?" She nodded to the horse, whose ears swiveled to attention. "I noticed the door isn't open on the other side of her stall."

"Yeah, she got injured a while back. Can't go out to pasture yet," he explained. "Tore a tendon while practicing in the spring, and the owner asked us to look after her. Poor thing's been on stall rest since."

Then, he hadn't stopped for a break but to check on the horse's injury. Grant seemed to do a lot of things that way—reserved and purposeful. He wasn't one to wear his accomplishments on his sleeve or boast to whoever would listen, like the guys she knew at college. She'd gotten so used to their toxic testosterone levels that she almost forgotten how immature it all was. Grant couldn't have been much older than any of the frat boys, but he acted leagues apart.

"Will she make a full recovery?" she asked. Being cooped up in that tiny stall didn't sound fun at all.

"Hope so." His eyes creased at the edges. "Looks like her leg isn't bothering her as much, and if everything goes well with the vet next week, then she'll be able to go out on her own."

Lucy stopped eating and poked her head over the door. Serena stepped out of reach.

"I think she has cabin fever," Grant said as Lucy nuzzled his shoulder. "I try to walk her outside every day, but she's only allowed twenty minutes or so."

Lucy shuffled, hooves clicking on the floor. A thick black mane hung over her neck and flew into the air as she shook her head.

Grant turned back to Serena. "Also, she can sense when you're nervous."

"I'm not nervous," she protested. "I put the feed in, didn't I?" She raised her eyebrows and dared him to argue otherwise. That was no trivial accomplishment.

He grinned, a dimpled cheek pushing out over full lips and a hard jawline.

Lucy snorted and lowered her head, no doubt wanting more scratches. Grant obliged.

"She's got the softest nose," he murmured. His voice dropped into a low whisper, churning the warm air between them and making her want to lean in closer. "What do you say?" he asked. "Want to make a new friend?"

Was he talking to her or the horse? She couldn't tell.

He rubbed Lucy's cheek, and her eyes fell half-lidded again. Then he gave Serena an inquiring glance. Thick golden lashes fanned over his dark green eyes, glinting under the brim of his hat.

She raised her chin and stepped forward. She *wasn't* nervous. Not about touching the horse or looking like a fool in front of Grant. She could do this.

His smile widened. "Use the back of your hand, like this." He brushed his knuckles over the pink patch on Lucy's nose. The horse's nostrils flared, but she held still as if she wanted to be extra nice. Like they were kids learning how to play together for the first time.

Serena raised a hand and mimicked Grant's movements. A slow breath passed through her lips. "Wow, she is really soft."

Grant hummed beside her.

She relaxed as Lucy's warm breath blew over her skin. How could a creature this big seem so...calm? Yet so powerful and intelligent at the same time? Contentment shone in Lucy's big brown eyes, the same expression she'd seen in them earlier. Then again, if Grant's hands had been on her, she'd probably feel the same way.

She ran her fingers over Lucy's cheek, the velvet skin blending into coarse hair and firm muscle.

"Here," Grant said, covering her hand with his and guided her to scratch under Lucy's mane.

Her heart skipped a beat, having forgotten how close he'd been standing—forgotten how his proximity made everything inside her warm and molten, even though she'd been hot and miserable all afternoon.

Well...maybe not so miserable.

His palm radiated heat, rough and worn in several places, but steady. She held her breath, afraid to break the moment. Lucy blinked as she scratched along the horse's neck.

"It's her favorite spot," Grant murmured. His voice sounded thicker than usual. Or maybe she was imagining it.

She hummed in response and tried to clear her head before he caught on to how he affected her. He'd already won their first encounter. She needed to make herself worth the chase—someone who could beat him at his own game—if she was ever going to make the most out of this month.

"Want to give her a treat?" Grant asked.

She cast a wary glance at the horse's mouth. Despite Grant's talent at convincing her to try new things, she'd about reached her daily limit. "Maybe next time."

He chuckled under his breath and took a step back. "Alright. We should get washed up for dinner. Trust me, you don't want to be late for Mrs. Weston's cooking."

The disappointment in Lucy's eyes resonated a little too clearly with her own. Not letting herself dwell on the feeling, she snapped back into balance and caught up with Grant as he turned to the exit.

But before he reached the door, she hooked her arm around his and put on a flirtatious smile. "Does this mean I've worked hard enough to earn my keep?" Batting her eyes a few times, she coated her voice with honeyed sarcasm and did her best to look the part of an innocent damsel.

Much to her pleasure, his next step faltered the smallest amount.

"Hardly," he scoffed and shook his head. "But if you help me collect eggs, we'll call it even."

She played along with an exaggerated sigh. "Hey, for real though. Thanks for showing me around, even though I'm a snobby city dweller and all." She added a wink for his benefit, but heat simmered in her own belly. "I guess you aren't so intolerable, after all."

Grant paused with a hand on the door and bit his lip. "Guess you're not so bad yourself, sunflower."

SIX

Serena

GRANT HAD BEEN RIGHT ABOUT MRS. WESTON'S COOKING. IT filled a pit she didn't know she had and then some. She'd never eaten so much in her life. Turned out that being crammed in a car half the day and then getting dragged around outside for the other half built up quite an appetite.

At dinner, the Westons introduced her to more of the staff: a librarian who oversaw a small computer lab donated by the school district, a handful of social workers who assisted with the workshops, and a neighboring rancher who stopped by to help care for the animals.

Several returning graduates were also planning to visit on the last weekend when the ranch offered an overnight horseback ride. It was supposed to be the highlight of the program, but to her, it sounded like the worst part of the whole thing. The minute she learned it was optional, she decided to start packing the night everyone else headed out. By then, they'd probably be as sick of her as she already was of this miserable charade.

Even so, they all seemed like good people. People who came out of respect for the program and for the Westons. But they acted like she was one of them—that she wanted to be here to help troubled teens—and that couldn't be further from the truth.

She was in no position to mentor someone else. If anything, her mandatory participation in this was proof that she barely knew how to navigate her own life, much less help a stranger do it. None of them seemed to know about her community service, and she wasn't about to break the ice.

Why couldn't she be assigned to clean up trash on the side of the highway? Collect donations for a random charity? Any of it would have been better than this.

At least her job didn't sound that hard. She could manage to keep a handful of teenage girls on schedule between meals and workshops. If anything came up, there would always be another adult to ask for help. It felt kinda like being a chaperone for a school field trip, except none of the kids wanted to be there. The most she could hope for was to get through the next month without screwing up.

Dinner stretched on and on. For the first time in her life, she was at a loss for what to say. Instead, she listened for interesting tidbits about Grant, and learned that he had two brothers, one in college and the other in high school. It felt like everyone purposely spoke in vague terms about his situation. They didn't bring up details about his future or his past—almost like they were avoiding a certain topic.

She'd been surprised to find out it was his first year as an assistant in the program, so they were both new in a way. Although, from what she'd gathered, he'd lived on the ranch full-time for more than a few years.

It'd been a long time since she felt like such an outsider. Even in college, she'd known how to make her way to the top of the social ladder. Getting attention had never been hard, and she enjoyed the spontaneous antics of frat parties. She could drink and dance and pretend to be interested in some guy's random story all night long.

But here, none of that mattered. She didn't know a thing about life outside of her social circle, and until now, she hadn't needed to. She had nothing to offer these people. And as kind as they were, she didn't want anything from them, either.

When she grew tired of listening to everyone's excitement, she excused herself to go back to the guesthouse. On her way, she spotted Mrs. Weston tackling a stack of dishes and leftovers covering a polished countertop. The kitchen's layout was large and spacious, with a long granite island in the middle and several windows overlooking the backyard. Through the glass, a darkening sky blended into a thicket of dense woods. They'd had a full table, but it looked like Mrs. Weston cooked enough for a buffet. Why was she in here all alone?

"You didn't hire anyone to help with this?" Serena asked, announcing her presence and stepping into the room.

Mrs. Weston glanced up and gave a light-hearted sigh. "Oh, I can manage. We use paper plates when all the guests arrive, but it does wear me down a little more every year. Might have to find someone who can take the job, eventually." She gestured to a bowl covered in plastic wrap. "Since you're here, mind putting this on the bottom shelf in the fridge?"

Serena held in a sigh of her own. "Sure."

Coming from a family of six and then living in a house full of irresponsible frat boys, she'd gotten used to cleaning up after meals. Of course, she'd pawn the job off on someone else as often as possible, but she also knew how much of a pain it would be to take care of all this alone. And not helping an old woman felt like a worse crime than getting caught drinking when she shouldn't have been.

Serena took the bowl and carried it to a double-door stainless steel fridge. "How long have you been running the program?" she asked.

"Let's see..." Mrs. Weston hummed. "We started a few years after we moved here, so about twenty years, I think. Somewhere around there, anyway."

Based on the dates in the pamphlet, that meant the Westons started the program themselves. Kinda impressive that they grew it from scratch into a place so renowned for its success that it caught a judge's attention from all the way across the state. Why would the Westons let her work here when she had nothing to offer?

"You really like living out here?" she wondered aloud.

Mrs. Weston chuckled at her skepticism. "It's not for everyone, but you get used to it. I prefer to carve out my own space rather than trying to fit in where I don't want to be. And it's been a decent place to raise a family. I got pregnant young, so we had to make the most out of what we had at the time. Didn't imagine it would turn into this."

"You were with Mr. Weston from back then?" Serena asked.

"Mhm." Mrs. Weston nodded as she put the plastic wrap away in the stained wood cabinet. "We hadn't even graduated high school when I had our first kid. Getting married with a big round belly was *quite* the controversy in those days."

Serena stared at her. Guess not everyone here had the perfect life story she'd imagined. "How long have you been married?"

Mrs. Weston smiled. "Coming up on forty-five years. Wouldn't change a thing." She rolled up her sleeves and started running water in the sink. "Here, why don't you put the dishes in the washer while I rinse?"

It wasn't like there was anything better to do. Serena opened the dishwasher and pulled out the bottom drawer. "I can't imagine living with someone else for so long," she admitted.

Mrs. Weston's smile stretched as if she had some insider secret about relationships that could only be learned after decades of being in one. "It's not your job to imagine it right now. First, you gotta find the right person, and then you learn to live with them."

Serena fell silent as she stacked plates in the dishwasher. Marriage had always felt like a lost relic of society. Something she didn't know how to begin searching for, or if she wanted it in the first place. She'd spent enough of her life with younger siblings to know she didn't want kids anytime soon, and living with her ex had been the worst mistake she'd ever made.

Sneaking away just to get a night in her own bed had been one of the lowest moments of her life...right beside going back to his place the next night because he had something she wanted. If she ever got into a serious relationship, it would have to be with someone she didn't have to hide from. And someone who didn't make her want to hide from herself.

"How was your first day on the ranch?" Mrs. Weston asked, interrupting her thoughts. "I noticed that Grant showing you around."

Serena let out a sarcastic scoff, though she was grateful for the change of topic. "Not sure we got off the best start. I think I gave him a harder time than he expected."

Mrs. Weston shook her head. "Oh, to be young again. Grant can handle a challenge every now and then. Been a while since I've seen him talk to someone new for so long."

Really? Grant hadn't come off as the anti-social type. Maybe not socially refined, but he didn't seem to have trouble taking the lead in their conversations.

Serena paused. "He didn't know anything about my community service. Why didn't you tell him why I'm here?"

"Ah, that." Mrs. Weston gathered the dishes in the sink. "Because it's your story to tell." She finished rinsing a few glasses and handed them over. "I've learned the people who come here have already been told what's wrong with them. Doesn't seem to fix any problems. So, we try to see what's right with them instead. We don't disclose why guests come here for treatment—Hollow Oak is a place for people to heal and reconnect. What and how much our guests wish to share is up to them."

Serene pursed her lips. The unspoken truth was that people were sent here precisely because something had gone wrong. In any case, she appreciated her story not being turned into the town's newest gossip. "That's not a bad approach," she replied.

Her initial skepticism about the so-called success of this place hadn't disappeared, but interacting with everyone proved they weren't drill sergeants or better-than-thou preachers as she anticipated.

"I know you weren't planning on spending the summer here," Mrs. Weston continued, handing Serena some silverware and meeting her eyes. "And we're grateful you came. But if you find the job doesn't suit you, then we'll figure something else out."

Serena hesitated, caught off guard by her reluctance to accept the offer. For weeks, she'd been looking for an excuse to get out of this...but Grant did mention the ranch needed extra workers, and none of the others who came to dinner had been available to help full-time.

She shrugged. "I'm already here, so I might as well see what I can do."

"Glad to hear it." Mrs. Weston looked away and continued to rinse what was left in the sink.

Getting through it all hadn't taken too long with the both of them. But before they finished, Serena had to ask one more thing. "Grant mentioned he used to compete in the rodeo, but I don't know anything about it. Could you tell me what he did, exactly?"

"Oh, yes," Mrs. Weston hummed. "He used to ride a lot. I think he'd explain it better than I can."

Serena frowned. There was a fat chance of that. He'd acted like explaining to her would be a waste of breath.

"Have you seen the display case out in the dining room?" Mrs. Weston suddenly asked, drying off her hands with a towel. "It was passed down from my grandmother. Maybe you could take a closer look tomorrow morning at breakfast."

Serena took the towel with a questioning glance. "Um... okay." The house seemed to be full of antiques. She hadn't noticed any that stood out in particular. But then she caught the sparkle in Mrs. Weston's eyes and realized she hadn't been talking about the furniture. "I'll do that, thanks."

❁

When they finished, the sky had grown black and the house had fallen silent. Grant wasn't around when she left the kitchen, so she headed straight for her room and got ready for bed.

The guesthouse finally cooled down, her room dark and still. Cricket songs filled the quiet countryside as a breeze drifted through her cracked window. She should've been knocked out as soon as her head hit the pillow, but if anything, her mind felt as full as her stomach.

Nighttime looked both darker and brighter out here than in the city. Shadowy tree tops stretched into glimmering stars, and the moon shone with such clarity that she could see across the entire yard. The wilderness seemed all the more foreboding without streetlights, yet none of it made her uneasy—quite the opposite. She'd witnessed real danger. Gotten way too close to it, and it looked nothing like this.

When she shut her eyes, the thump of bass still resonated in her chest. Fresh beer fizzed on her tongue, and she could smell a thick cloud of smoke filling the Mercedes. Heard her boyfriend at the time, Jace, barking to turn off the music, then shouting in a different language over the phone. His older cousin casting withering glares through the rear-view mirror and, consequently, missing a stop sign at the corner.

Lights flashing behind them. The officer's stern tone as he asked them to step out of the vehicle. Standing by herself while the cops tore through the inside. Them restraining Jace as he blamed it all on her. Spending the rest of the night at the station, cold and numb.

But now that was all in the past.

Through her window, she watched a single light click on in the lower bedroom of the boy's guesthouse. Grant must've finally turned in for the night.

It wasn't like her to pine over a guy. Sure, he'd given her something to look forward to, but she had no reason to get attached. No reason to care about his secrets. He'd be an entertaining distraction while she got this service out of the way, and then they could both move on.

Not that she had anything to move on to. Not anymore.

After the incident with the police, Jace had broken up with her on the spot. The strange part was she hadn't been upset, hadn't even felt a twinge of regret. She'd dealt with his volatile temperament for long enough and was almost relieved to get rid of him.

He'd often spiral into fits of rage when things didn't go his way, leaving her behind without notice or when he didn't, giving her bruises that would last for days. But he came from an influential family and was president of the fraternity Beta Rho, which meant she'd been the envy of everyone on campus. He'd given her access to things no one else did—drugs, parties, you name it. He had everything she'd ever wanted.

Or what she thought she'd wanted.

The same people who spent countless hours playing drinking games with her turned their backs without a second thought. None of them cared about a girl foolish enough to get into a mess like this, who would dare to smear Jace or his family's reputation, least of all by involving the cops. All it took was one mistake, and they'd wiped her from their memories.

She only had herself to rely on now.

Blowing out a long breath, she sank into the mattress and watched Grant's silhouette move behind closed curtains. Maybe that wasn't entirely true.

Whatever tomorrow brought, she wouldn't have to face it completely alone.

SEVEN

Grant

"Rise and shine!"

The clang of the cowbell reverberated through the guesthouse—it was obnoxious as hell, and he knew it. This was also the customary wake-up routine, so Serena might as well get used to it.

Just because she got a glimpse at his soft side in the barn didn't mean he was gonna let her off the hook. They had work to do.

A loud *thwack* sounded on the other side of her door, followed by a string of curses that would put any hardened rancher to shame. He broke into a chuckle and decided to spare her a few minutes of peace. Walking outside, he tried not to imagine what she looked like getting out of bed—if her hair would be rumpled or if her nipples poked out of her pajamas after leaving the window open all night.

Shit. So much for not thinking about it. He blinked out into the brightening hues of dawn, grateful for a blast of fresh air. They might have gotten over the edge of hating each other, but he wasn't done testing her patience or the extent of her rehearsed charm. Especially when he noticed she'd gone out of her comfort zone to try and impress him.

Not that she needed to. He didn't want her attempting to be a country gal, nor did he need her flirtatious smiles or not-so-casual touches. The ranch gave people enough space to be themselves—and if she took anything away from her stay, then he hoped that would be it. For his own selfish reasons, that was. Maybe a few carnal ones.

Every time they interacted, it only left him wanting more. Not strictly more of her sex appeal, though that had been on his mind. More of her genuine expressions, more of what made her decide to go through with the job instead of actually acting like the pain in the ass she threatened to be.

More of the depth that played behind her eyes when she thought he wasn't looking. A depth he hoped she hadn't seen in him.

He shook his head, already having committed to memory the priceless horror on her face when he'd made her stick a hand under a fluffy chicken butt to check for eggs. If she thought she had enough willpower to hold out for the whole month, then she'd woefully underestimated the lengths he would go.

He'd crack that shallow facade of hers one way or another. Sure, *trouble* might as well be stamped across her forehead, and he wasn't foolish enough to think she was innocent in any sense of the word, but that didn't make her one-dimensional. He knew better than anyone else that people could be both good and evil, that they could sow love and hate in the same breath.

He'd tried to just be one or the other. It hadn't worked.

Everyone said he'd done everything right. But the one person he thought he would love forever had still lied to him. She still got in a car she never should have been in, still ended up at the hospital fighting for her life because the person driving had been drunk. Yet when he tried to push aside the betrayal of her cheating, she decided to leave a second time. Telling the truth had been too much, or maybe everything else had been a lie. Maybe there wasn't a difference.

Afterward, it'd made him want to do everything wrong. Grief and anger and hate had ripped through his chest like he'd been held together with frayed twine. He'd tried all the usual suspects—sneaking out with his old friends, nursing a bottle of hard liquor alone in the middle of a field, picking up all the girls he'd turned down over the years—but in her absence, nothing could fill the void. And his soul had been empty ever since.

His body still worked, though. His muscles burned after a long day, and he could taste the salt on his skin when heat saturated his veins. So now, the only thing he cared for was helping run the ranch, and in return, his heart wouldn't be broken a third time.

Looking over the pastures, he took in the flare of the sun as it floated above the hills and fanned horizontal rays of light across dew-covered grass. The peak of dawn carried a certain magic with it, when birdsong filled the sky, and the air was cold and sharp after night's embrace. Today, it felt particularly energizing. Or maybe he'd just started to notice it again. Life became calm, and he didn't dare ask for anything more.

Without realizing, he discovered he'd taken his usual path to the barn, even though it wasn't necessary to get to feeding right away. Extra ranch hands came to Hollow Oak for the month, so his primary focus could be on the program guests. But he needed something to do, and muscle memory had already taken over. So he got to work and let his thoughts fade into the background.

Half an hour later, he pulled out a chair in the dining room and plopped next to a stoic Mr. Weston, sipping his morning coffee in the typical attire of stained jeans, a polo shirt, and a baseball cap to cover a growing bald spot.

"Ready to wrangle another crew?" Grant broke into a smile as Mr. Weston's cool amber eyes slid over him in acknowledgment

"I should be askin' you the same thing," Mr. Weston muttered around the rim of his mug. "But it seems you've got enough entertainment already."

Grant laughed a little too loud and clapped Mr. Weston on the shoulder. "Haven't got a clue what you're talking about."

The old man knew him too well.

On cue, Serena came out from the kitchen and promptly glared at him from the doorway. Figured she wouldn't be one to hide her opinion of being woken up early. Even so, he couldn't help but appreciate her morning appearance—a light coat of make-up over rich brown eyes and glossy lips, long white-gold hair straightened instead of curled, and a pink tank top cut off above the dark denim hugging her hips.

"Mornin' sunflower," he greeted with an extra cheery tone, just to piss her off. "Sleep well?"

She scowled. "I left the window open. Woke up in a fucking ice box to the most ungodly sound I've ever heard."

Mr. Weston's impassive exterior cracked as he chuckled. "Now, that's an honest statement if I've ever heard one."

Grant shook his head. If he left it up to these two, mornings would be purgatory.

Mr. Weston took another sip of coffee and then got to his feet. "Caffeine's finally kickin' in, so I'm gonna see if the Missus needs any help before guests start showin' up."

"Let us know if you need extra hands," Grant offered.

Mr. Weston paused, looked between him and Serena, and raised his eyebrows. "And *you* let me know if someone needs to come back an' supervise."

Grant groaned. "What's that? Is Mrs. Weston calling your name?"

Mr. Weston grinned. "You need to get your ears checked, son." Eyes dancing with mirth, he tipped his head to Serena as he passed by on his way to the kitchen.

As soon as they were alone, Serena's glare intensified. "You could've mentioned how cold it gets at night. After sweating my ass off most of the day, I didn't expect to wake up half-frozen."

His lips twitched, and he fought back a laugh. "Well, now you know. The days are hot and the nights cold, but that doesn't mean you can't work up a sweat in both." He ended the sentence with a wink to give her a taste of her own medicine.

She huffed, then her composure shifted, as if she decided going back and forth was no longer worth her time. A delicate pink nail flicked the front of her hair behind her ear, and she smiled. "Would you like some coffee?"

Well, that mood shift came out of nowhere.

"Yeah, but I can get it." He started to stand.

"Let me," Serena insisted, pushing him back down in the chair. "After all, you woke me up so I could be useful, right?"

Her smile sweetened unnaturally, and his processing mechanisms couldn't quite keep up. "Uh..."

Not waiting for his response, she turned and disappeared into the kitchen. A minute later, she returned with two steaming mugs and set one in front of him.

"Thanks," he mumbled, wary of her kindness.

"My pleasure," she hummed, sitting across from him with her own cup. Her glossy, rose-colored lips puckered as she blew on her coffee.

His eyes flicked between her and the mug. When she didn't say anything else, he brought the coffee to his mouth—and immediately spewed out the first sip.

"What the hell did you do to this?" he sputtered. Fuck, that was intense. He looked around for something to wash away the taste but found nothing.

Serena smirked and took a long sip from her cup. "I added some extra sugar. Or"—she tapped a finger on her pouty lips—"was that the salt? I'm sorry, I'm a little sleep deprived..."

"Ten bucks you didn't mix up the salt and sugar in *your* coffee," he muttered.

Her smile returned as she lowered the mug from her lips, then rotated it so he could see the shiny impression of her lip gloss on the rim. "This coffee is just as contaminated as yours."

He scoffed. "Don't patronize me."

If she wanted to play dirty, then she better be prepared for the consequences. Cause he'd toss her over his shoulder and wrestle her in the mud if he had to. In fact, that wasn't a half-bad idea...but first, he had to drink something and get the horrid aftertaste out of his mouth.

Holding her gaze, he reached across the table and picked up her mug, placed his lips directly over where hers had been, and downed half the cup.

Not what he was used to, but it was better than whatever the hell she'd given him.

"A bit too sweet, if you ask me," he muttered and poured out some of his coffee to refill her cup. "This outta even it out."

Her jaw dropped open, and she gasped. "I can't believe you'd be that petty."

He grinned. "There's a lotta things about me you wouldn't believe."

She shook her head, then something caught her attention behind him. It didn't take a full turn for him to realize what it was. That antique case where Mrs. Weston insisted on keeping his medallions and buckles.

"Those are all yours?" she asked, scanning the shelves.

"Yeah," he mumbled.

Nearly a decade's worth of rodeo events. His parents had a few mementos at their place, too.

Serena stood up and walked around the table to get a closer look. Her perfume blended with the rich tones of coffee beans, and he fiddled with the rim of her mug.

"That's her?" she asked from behind him.

Tension iced over his muscles. He knew every photo in that case—and more importantly, all the photos he'd taken out of it. But his ex had been at almost every event with him, and he couldn't completely remove her from his life history. Even though she'd had no issues erasing him.

"The yellow one, she was your horse?" Serena clarified. "The one you sold?"

He exhaled, hating how the thought of *her* still made him hold his breath. It wasn't like he'd take her back even if she crawled and begged for it.

"Marigold," he answered, turning to face Serena. "The best palomino on planet earth. She'd go stir-crazy sitting in a barn, so I gave her to someone who loved to ride as much as she did. How'd you know she was a mare?"

Serena shrugged. "Call it a lucky guess. Maybe I was just hoping it'd be a girl for feminism's sake, seeing as she helped you win so much."

Grant snorted, about to reply, but the low hum of an engine came from around the front.

He glanced up to see a car pull into the drive. Mrs. Weston emerged from the kitchen and clapped her hands. "I see the first guest has arrived! Alrighty folks, let's get this show on the road."

EIGHT

Serena

THE COUNTRYSIDE WARMED WITH THE RISING SUN. WAVES OF DRY heat rippled on the horizon, as if in defiance to the cool blue mountain vista presiding over the ranch. A cloudless sky expanded across fields of tall grass and grazing livestock, but unlike yesterday, she didn't have time to appreciate the view.

Yet another door slammed as she made her way downstairs. Serena sighed and glanced out the common room window, watching as Grant led a boy with short, curly hair and brown skin into the adjacent guesthouse. Meanwhile, a family with three young kids that resembled hers headed toward the main house. A few parents stayed to check out the ranch, but most were prompt to drop off their kids and leave.

After the guests signed in and filled out all the necessary paperwork, she and Grant showed them to their rooms and made sure they hadn't brought any contraband. Needless to say, the general mood had been *fuck this, I don't want to be here.*

Not like she'd been any better yesterday.

She understood wanting to keep out drugs and video games, but did they have to ban cell phones, too? The ranch required all personal electronics to be left at home, with the only exception being for medical devices. Mrs. Weston had explained the program included replacing virtual reality with the real one. No one would be cut off from family—both phones and computers were available for anyone to use in the main house, plus an emergency line in each cabin.

Still, she'd been glad not to run into any issues so far. Kids wouldn't be eligible if they were a danger to themselves or others, so at least she didn't need to worry about weapons. But asking each guest to go through their bags in front of her felt way too invasive.

Serena found the newest guest waiting on the porch, a young woman named Renae, who said she'd arrived with her twin brother, Richard. That must have been the kid she saw earlier with Grant. If anything, Renae looked like an average teenager. Her sneakers were tied with colored laces, jeans ripped to match the latest trend—probably self-made—and her shirt displayed a slogan Serena recognized from one of her siblings' favorite streamers.

Even so, appearances didn't mean anything in a place like this. True to Mrs. Weston's philosophy, Serena had no idea why Renae enrolled.

After a quick greeting, she led Renae through the rustic wood furniture in the common area and upstairs to the next available guest room. "This is where you'll be staying." She opened a new door and stepped aside. "You'll have one roommate and share the bathroom with the adjoining room. I'm staying right downstairs if you need anything, and there's a phone next to my door you can use anytime."

"Got it." Renae nodded and walked in, her gaze tentative as she took in the space. Similar to Serena's room, antique furniture and a cozy twin bed basked in natural light pouring in from outside.

Serena pursed her lips. Is that what she looked like yesterday—skeptical of old rugs and open windows? "Okay then," she continued, swinging her arms. "The last thing we need to do is the bag check."

This part got harder every time she had to do it. But she had promised to do her job. And maybe a tiny part of her cared to make sure these kids didn't get involved in anything they shouldn't be.

Renae turned and raised her eyebrows. "You really gotta go through my stuff?"

"I'm sorry, but it's protocol," Serena pointed out with a half-hearted shrug. "I've had to drag everyone else through the same process. If you're uncomfortable with me, I can ask someone else to come."

Renae shook her head. "You're okay. I'm sure they'd say the same thing, anyway."

Serena deflated. Last night, she'd gotten her own taste of feeling out of place—as if the invasion of privacy and unfamiliar atmosphere wasn't enough. "I'm not here to make you feel judged or take your stuff," she added softly. "Trust me, I don't want to be doing this any more than you do."

Renae gave a doubtful hum and heaved her suitcase up on the bed with surprising strength. Then she proceeded to dump out her small handbag on the quilt. "You want to confiscate my lipstick?"

Serena fought to maintain her composure. If she couldn't keep a mature attitude, how could she ask that of Renae? "You know that's not what this is for."

Renae huffed and pulled open the zipper on her suitcase, stopping mid-way. "Isn't this kind of ineffective? I mean...if people wanted to hide something, do you really think they'd just show you?"

Serena shrugged. Having to pretend this whole thing wasn't bullshit had gotten exhausting. "I wouldn't."

"Then why do it?" Renae tilted her head, and the small braids of her hair slid over one shoulder.

Serena sat next to the suitcase; if only she knew the answer. "Well, I have to do what I can. It could be worse. What if we had to do pat-downs or install ugly metal detectors?"

Renae looked away and fiddled with the zipper. "I guess there are worse places to be. Metal detectors would ruin the whole outdoorsy vibe."

"You never know—it might be the new trend. We'll call it prison-chic."

Renae snorted. "Don't jinx it."

"Yeah, on second thought, I don't think they fit the aesthetic here," Serena added dryly.

"They don't fit the aesthetic anywhere." Renae rolled her eyes.

"All I need to know is that you won't be a threat to yourself or anyone else. Then I'll let you have some space," Serena offered.

Renae sighed and finished unzipping her bag. After she'd opened the side pockets and pretended to rummage around a stack of folded clothes and silk bedding, she looked up. "We good?"

"Yep, that should do it." Serena nodded, eager to leave. "You're free to get settled in. When you're done, head over to the main house to go over the rest of orientation." She stood and took a step toward the door.

Then something clattered onto the wood floor. Something that sounded a lot like a cellphone.

"Dammit," Renae cursed under her breath.

For half a second, Serena considered not turning around. This had been difficult enough, and she wasn't about to become the same tyrant she'd expected to find when she came here.

But when she looked down, the iPod that had skittered across the floor happened to land next to her feet. Ignoring it wasn't an option.

Serena bent to pick up the worn device, turning it over to make sure the screen hadn't cracked. "I didn't know people still used these."

"They don't," Renae said, looking at her defensively. "I knew phones weren't allowed, so I thought this would be easier to hide."

"Makes sense." Serena extended her arm to hand it back.

"You're not gonna take it?" Renae eyed the bright pink iPod and black earbuds dangling between them.

Serena shook her head, then she breathed out a laugh. "Girl, if all you got is an iPod, I'm not going to punish you. Hell, even I've grown sick of hearing one radio station out here." She leveled her eyes with Renae. "Just don't let me see it outside this room, 'kay? Or else you're not the only one who will get in trouble."

For the first time, Renae's lips slanted into something resembling a smile. "All right, you got a deal."

Accepting their truce, Renae began to untangle her headphones, then looked up. "Wait, are you not allowed a phone, either?"

Serena hesitated. For the purposes of her 'service,' she'd been given the same rules as the guests. She'd have to use the ranch phone to make any personal calls. "It's better if the guests and workers are treated equally," she replied, then nodded toward the iPod. "What kinda music you got on there, anyway?"

"All kinds." Renae turned it on and swiped a few times with her thumb. "But this one is my favorite." She held up the screen to show an album cover Serena immediately recognized.

"My little sister is a huge fan of that one," Serena said.

Renae's eyes widened. "Really? You know them?"

"What can I say? My sister's unique." Serena shrugged. "For the record, I don't mind their stuff, but I'm not about to cover my bedroom in posters."

Renae laughed. "I wouldn't go the poster route, either. My parents would kill me."

"Trust me, mine have all but threatened to ban the mere mention of them," Serena chuckled.

"What's it like living out here?" Renae asked.

Serena paused. "I wouldn't know. I'm from the city." When Renae shot her a questioning look, she continued. "It's a summer job that gets me far enough away from home."

After a moment, Renae nodded. "I get that." She placed the iPod back in her suitcase. "Thanks for this."

Serena returned her smile. "Don't mention it."

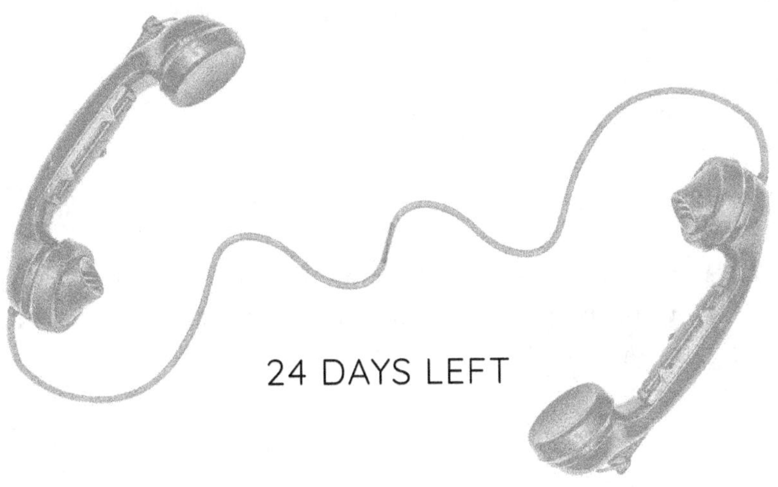

24 DAYS LEFT

Lexi:
"Nine-one-one, what's your emergency?"

Serena:
"Ha. I don't think I've gotten to that point yet."

"Well, it's only been a few days. We'll see if you survive the rest."

"I'll do my best."

"Speaking of...how's it going with that hottie in a hat?"

"You mean Grant?"

"Ooh, *Grant.* I suppose it's moan-able enough."

"Shush. You better not let Mom hear you talking like that. And the landline is in the common room, so I can't let anyone hear you on my end, either."

"Fine, fine."

"How is everyone back home?"

"Kids are either on a sugar high from pool parties or nagging me about being bored. Nothing out of the ordinary. But don't dodge my question."

"He's a pain in my ass."

"Ew, kinky."

"Not like that. You get to do anything outside of babysitting duty?"

"Does locking myself in my room count?"

"When I get back, let's go on a girl's date. Just you and me."

"Deal. I'll hold you to it."

NINE

Grant

Five days in, and she hadn't quit. He was a little surprised. If Serena really didn't want to stay, he knew the Westons would help find another way to fulfill her obligations. They were understanding like that.

But here she was, rummaging through piles of old riding gear like a mad woman. He was glad she decided to stick around. Even though, from the looks of it, she'd tangled up more bridles than she'd sorted out.

Watching from under the brim of his hat, he stood just outside the tack room and hoped to get in a few more minutes of peace before announcing his presence.

Her tempered curiosity on their tour had evolved into tentative contentment, and he even caught moments when she appeared relaxed. Like now, sitting cross-legged in a disheveled tack room and humming along with the radio. Somehow, she'd managed to find the one pop station that got a signal and cranked it on full blast.

Maybe Serena would enjoy her time here, after all.

Days at Hollow Oak were divided into three segments. Following morning exercise and breakfast, guests went to

Workshop A, which involved either summer classes or individual-driven research projects. In the afternoon, they were divided into specialized groups: either applied arts and sciences or equestrian therapy. Everyone gathered after dinner for Workshop B, a group discussion used to reflect on their day.

Serena followed a modified regiment. Most of the time, she shadowed the guests to get the same experience, but in the mornings, she had the same job as him—chores.

It didn't take him more than an hour to finish the daily tasks, and in his free time, he'd gotten into the habit of spying on Serena. Which quickly turned into figuring out new ways to get on her nerves.

And admiring her more than he wanted to admit. Watching as she improvised her way through things she'd never done in her life proved to be quite entertaining. He'd even caught her slipping Lucy a treat once.

Grant clicked his tongue and stepped into the tack room, walking over to tug on one of Serena's braided pigtails. "This is new," he noted, and dodged when she took a swipe at him. "What?" He chuckled at her unamused expression. "They're cute."

"They're to keep all the damn dust out of my hair," she muttered. "If you're gonna bother me, you'll have to help out while you do it."

"Oh, look who's finally catching on to how things work around here." He broke out in a dimpled grin when she rolled her eyes and then plopped next to her in the pile of tangled gear and cleaning supplies.

The Westons tasked Serena with re-organizing the barn, which had needed a good, thorough sweep for a while now. But at this point, he wasn't sure which needed more washing—Serena or the equipment.

"What even are these things?" She held up a thick rope, jumbled in a series of messy knots, and wrinkled her nose.

"And why does it smell like they haven't been used in a decade?"

He shook his head and took the lead rope. "It's been a while since any of us actively rode, and we have about three extra of everything." Pausing, he looked over at her. "You really don't know anything about this life, do you?"

She huffed. "I didn't grow up under a rock like you."

He hummed and slipped the rope through his fingers. Old memories wound through the frayed edges of his mind as he picked apart the knots. "Then what do you call those blocks of steel and cement that cover the view of the sky out where you're from?"

"I guess you'd call them the great mountains of Babylon or something." A hint of a smile pulled at one corner of her lips.

He laughed and finished working on the rope. His hands were almost as rough as the woven fabric, palms calloused from years of tying and untying, of roping and training. A result of practicing day after day, even when he wasn't gearing up to compete, because he loved it.

When loving things hadn't hurt.

"Well, better to learn late than never," he said on an exhale. "This is a lead rope." He picked up a halter from the pile and held it around his hand, showing how it would fit on a horse's head. "You clip it on like a leash."

"So, horses are just big dogs?" she asked.

He snorted. "A horse can do a lot more than a dog."

Making a loop, he reached for Serena's hand, then wound the rope around her wrists and pulled the end through the loophole. "When you're competing, you and the horse learn to speak the same language. Notice the same cues. Work as a team without words. Sometimes, I think horses like winning as much as humans do."

He met her gaze, then wrapped the rope around her other wrist and cinched them together with a flick of his hands. His breath caught at the smoothness of her skin, the softness so opposite of his. Her manicure had chipped at the ends, bright pink giving way to her natural tone and a flush just under the surface.

"Show off." Serena's words came off as an insult, but her eyes glimmered as she tested the integrity of his work.

He didn't need her demonstration to know his knots held true, though the lead rope was a far cry from piggin string. It'd been almost a full year since he'd practiced for any competitions, let alone remembered how much he used to enjoy it.

He let her go and put away the rope. "How long have you been at this?"

"Two days."

He chuckled. "And you've only gotten this far?"

"Hey!" She shoved him sideways, which made him laugh harder. "It's more than you would've gotten done without me."

He hung his head in mock defeat. "Looks like you won't finish anytime soon." Then he bit his lip. Maybe it was the sudden rush in his blood, or maybe the feeling lingering in his subconscious had finally decided to take form. "Come on, let's take a break."

Serena scoffed. "Excuse me, you've been working for a total of five minutes, and you already want a break?"

"You wanna sneak away with me or not?" He looked up at her under his eyelashes and raised his eyebrows.

"Better watch yourself, or you'll start to sound like you don't hate me," she said through a grin that finally broke free.

He got to his feet and held out a hand to help her up. "I never hated you, sunflower."

A blush colored her face as she took his hand. "What's your idea of a break, anyway?"

He only grinned in response. Then walked out the door and waited for her to follow.

The guests were currently occupied inside the media room at the main house, so no one would be outside to see them sneak off behind the barn. The air smelled fresh, like pollen and dry dirt baking under the sun, and leaves rustled as flecks of light danced along the overgrown path.

"Still upset at being stuck all the way out here?" he asked, walking alongside her through the woods at the back of the property.

"I don't dislike the ranch specifically," she replied. "Maybe I strongly doubted my survival, but I can handle a challenge."

"So, you disliked me, specifically."

She arched a brow. "I can handle you."

"Don't be so sure." He gave her a sideways glance as they stepped through a thicker patch and held aside a tree branch. Her choice of shoes had improved to sneakers and a full-length top covering her belly, but those jean shorts still exposed her long legs. "You know I wouldn't let anything happen to you, right?"

"That's what they all say," Serena hummed. "Until you get me alone in the woods and tie me up with your fancy rope tricks." She swayed her hips and pressed her ass into him as she slid past. "Although you do make for a handsome lumberjack."

He shook his head as his dick stirred. For once, he didn't fight the subconscious thoughts he'd been suppressing all week. "Sunflower...you really shouldn't bring up all the things I'd like to do to you alone in the woods."

She shrugged and flashed a coy smile. "Threats like that don't work on me."

"Not a threat." He grinned. "A promise."

One he intended to keep sooner rather than later.

Looking into the maze of tree trunks and whispering leaves, he spotted what he'd come for. "We're here."

Serena stopped beside him and spun in a circle, searching aimlessly through the oak trees. "Here?"

He tipped his head toward the old brick-and-mortar well nestled in the woods. Vines crawled up the rusted metal hand pump, twisting around the iron and wedging their feelers into cracks between the stones. It'd never been in service while he worked at the ranch, but through his own adventures, he discovered a pool of thick mud at the bottom.

Serena followed his gaze and wandered over to the well. He turned his back to give her privacy and took a deep breath. Her sweet perfume mingled with pine on the breeze, and he closed his eyes to appreciate the titillating blend. "It's a place you can go to think. I know being outdoors isn't your thing, and it's probably a waste to bring you all the way out here...but I thought it was worth a shot."

"Thanks," she whispered instead of tossing out her usual jab.

Twigs snapped under her footsteps. He didn't have to look to know her hair gleamed in the sun, that the light passing through her irises gave them an amber hue while she took it all in, or that she'd nibble her lip when she decided she liked this place more than she'd admit.

He'd always known flowers bloomed better outdoors.

"The ranch isn't all about work, you know," he added, unable to keep himself from turning to look at her. "If you want to get away for a few hours, this way I'll know where to find you."

Her gaze broke from the well, and she glanced at him with an amused quirk of her lips. "Why wait to find me when I'm already here? I don't have any reason to hide from you."

He took a step closer. His own reasons for hiding had begun to fade, lost down a dark, deep well that he'd wallowed in for far too long. "Not even if I brought you here so we could be alone?"

"How audacious—are you flirting with me, cowboy?"

"If I was flirting, I would have brought the rope."

"Too bad you didn't."

"There's always next time."

She closed the gap between them and trailed a finger up his chest, drawing out his pulse. "I've played by your rules, cowboy." Her gaze lingered over his jaw before finally meeting his eyes. "I got my hands dirty. So, don't I get my reward?"

"What would you like?" he murmured, voice husky and low.

She smirked. "Each time you call me sunflower, I want you to remember how I look on my knees."

God *damn*. If he wasn't hard enough before, he sure as hell was now. "Then show me, sunflower. Let's see just how much you can take."

TEN

THE WOODS WERE DENSE—DEEP AND GREEN. MOSS COVERED ONE side of the thick tree trunks and camouflaged the old well, reclaiming it as nature's own.

Grant's eyes were greener. Deeper.

His hands found her hips, hot and steady, as he walked them away from the main path. She didn't care if anyone saw, but he made sure to block her from the view of potential wanderers.

Such a gentleman.

One with viridian fire in his eyes, a reflection of the summer heat that held secrets she no longer wanted to leave unspoken. Something about his desire felt different—it scorched her from the inside out, burning its way through the shield of casual flirtation they'd grown accustomed to.

It felt like the embers had been sizzling inside him, waiting to ignite, and she'd given them their first breath of oxygen.

"Sure you're not the one who isn't ready for me?" she teased.

He scoffed. "We'll see how well you can talk in a few minutes. It's about time I put that mouth of yours to good use."

He pushed aside some twigs with his foot, then tipped his

head to the side as if to question if she would follow through. A breathless chuckle left her lips. He thought he was the one challenging her?

Such a typical man. But she wasn't fooled.

She held all the control. His breaths had become shallow, a flush had crept up his neck, and the bulge in his pants spoke for itself—which had thoroughly captured her attention. *Impressive* would be an understatement.

Her mouth began to water as she locked their gazes and sunk to her knees. She rolled her shoulders and let her breasts push out, knowing the neckline of her top dipped low enough for him to see the blush of her areolas.

Grant kept his glances discreet before, but now he wasn't shy about where he looked—or for how long. His unashamed appraisal sent a flood of arousal through her veins. And she didn't mind taking a lingering glance for herself.

He was every bit the rough-and-tumble man she'd seen on her first day. His stance was one of strength, his posture confident and strong. The fabric of his cotton shirt clung to the hard lines of his muscles, and he towered above her like a marble statue carved by the gods. He'd been built to contend with the forces of nature, made to bend but not break.

She'd seen the power inside him on her first day, and smiled as he embraced it now—but she wanted more. He *fit* into the ranch, belonged here as much as any other part of the valley. And even if only for a moment, she wanted to pretend that she fit here, too. In a place where nothing came polished or perfect but it all had a purpose.

Grant broke their silent stare with a low hum and ran his fingers down the length of her braids. He brought one end over her shoulder, brushing it along her jaw and then tracing her bottom lip. "You're even more beautiful like this than I imagined."

For a split second, she forgot how to respond.

Beautiful.

Guys had called her quite a few names before she'd sucked them off—pretty, hot, a good slut—but not that. Not a word meant for things you leave untouched, for things to put in a glass case for fear of them getting ruined. Her cheeks grew hot with a blush.

"Did you only want to look?" She found her voice and ran her hands up his thighs. His muscles contracted at her touch, dick straining against the zipper.

"Impatient as usual," he chuckled. "I'll let you get away with it because, at the moment, I can't wait either." His hands went to work on his belt, a large western buckle depicting the head of a steer surrounded by scrawling embellishments made of polished brass. It came undone with a click, and his jeans fell apart to reveal what she'd been waiting for.

Holy mother of cocks.

His dick all but freed itself, pushing through his boxers and bobbing against his stomach. The head looked angry and flared, a bright red with precum glistening at the slit. He'd definitely been blessed with the elite package.

She licked her lips at the sight. "It's a damn crime to have kept this to yourself for so long."

He smirked at her. "Then you better prove that showing you was worth my time."

Her smile widened as she took him into her mouth. The crown alone made her jaw ache, but she didn't stop until he hit the back of her throat. A strangled groan from Grant's clenched jaw as she buried her nose in his golden locks.

"Shit," he mumbled. "I've never had someone take it all like that."

That wasn't hard to believe. She struggled to keep him in so deep, but that only made her want him more. She hummed around his cock, squeezing it tight, then licked the underside and sucked until he left her lips with a *pop*. "You've never had me before."

The look he gave her could've sparked a wildfire, the combustion of awe and agony enough to devour every last acre.

So she swallowed him again.

He tipped his head and rocked his hips into her mouth. His taste bloomed over her tongue, a warm and rich scent that mingled with salty traces of sweat along his navel. She let out a soft moan of her own and worked him harder, but not fast enough to end their fun too soon.

He'd made her wait a week for this, and for that, he was going to suffer for what would feel like an eternity before she gave him what he wanted.

"Dammit, sunflower." Grant's voice had deteriorated to something between a growl and broken grunts. "I should've known you'd be a dirty girl. Fuck, you're too good at this."

Glancing up through watery eyes, she all but glowed with satisfaction at seeing his clenched jaw and the rapid tick of his pulse on his neck. Lust consumed his features as he fought to keep his composure.

Nothing was better than watching a man unravel. Of being the reason for his guttural sounds and feeling him strain against the tension. Knowing you could make him break.

She smiled and slowed her pace, dragging her teeth along his base.

"Mm, that's how you want it?" he growled. "Gonna make me work for it?"

She pressed her tongue to the sensitive spot under his crown and lapped at his precum with a devious grin.

His eyes narrowed, a dark expression etched on his face. "Careful what you ask for."

Then he fisted his hands in her braid and thrust himself down her throat, hips jerking with barely contained tremors.

She moaned again, sending vibrations along his shaft, which had gotten impossibly harder, almost too thick to swallow.

He was desperate. Just where she wanted him.

"Yeah, that's it," he hissed on a pained exhale. "Such a filthy girl. My dirty sunflower."

In some twisted paradox, his words unhinged a part of her that only came out behind closed doors. The part that craved debasement even more than praise. A part that needed the escape of his rough hands and harsh tones.

The threat of danger had always turned her on, the thrill of uncertainty pushing her to the edge. But somehow, Grant made her feel *safe* at the same time. Such a ridiculous notion. She never asked for security, for a man to be gentle or kind. Yet Grant cared for her wellbeing without making her feel like a burden. It felt like she could push harder. Like he'd throw himself off the cliff so they could both tumble into the abyss.

She let her eyes roll back and embraced his need as her own. Her throat burned as mascara. Hot tears ran across her face. She craved his release almost as much as he did, to take his climax and feel it roll through them both.

"Dammit, I'm close," Grant panted, his voice on the verge of cracking. Her pussy clenched as his cock swelled. "Where do you want it?"

He'd be plenty long enough to reach past her taste buds, but she'd learned not to take any chances. Nothing ruined the mood like ending on a bitter note—literally. Besides, there were better ways to savor the moment.

"My face," she mumbled around his shaft.

Her request affected him better than she hoped. He let loose another strangled groan, then ripped himself out of her mouth and spilled over her swollen lips. His arm shook as he held her under his cock, pumping with jagged strokes. A hot, sticky mess spurted onto her forehead and dripped down her cheeks, her chin, her chest...

Grant's head tipped back in ecstasy, and she sighed in their shared pleasure. It felt too good to let go. To relax and let his release coat her skin—let it stain them both with the sinful memory. He could claim to be a good, wholesome country boy all he wanted, but they both knew the truth. He wanted to be as dirty as she was.

His dimple came out as they regained their breath, and he stroked a finger along her neck. "You make one hell of a mess."

"Oh, I'm just getting started," she whispered.

He shook his head and pulled out a handkerchief from his back pocket. As expected, their mess only worsened as he smeared it around, her makeup staining the fabric in dark streaks. But Grant was diligent, and after a minute, he carefully wiped the last of it off and wadded up the stiff cloth.

"I'm trying to convince myself that this was a bad idea," he sighed, looking at the ground between them.

She caught his eyes, and their lips both tipped into a grin.

Who wanted to be good, anyway?

ELEVEN

Serena

Steam rose as suds spilled over the edge of the sink, sticking to her already-soaked shirt. Chatter bounced off the walls, and a growing pile of dishes clacked against stainless steel. Behind her, Grant invented mini-games while he and a group of guests chopped fruits and vegetables.

Such a shame she couldn't go on secret adventures with him every day. Losing herself in the trees—and uncovering Grant's devious side—had only left her craving more. Their escapade ended too soon. He offered to finish up in the barn so she could wash off for lunch, but part of her had wanted to leave traces of him on her skin, let it soak in, and keep a piece of him for herself.

He'd given her more than what she'd asked for. He brought them to a spot that meant something. Somewhere entirely different from what she knew, and left her with an impression she couldn't shake. Made her question why it had felt special to her, too.

They hadn't been alone together since yesterday, and every passing glance added to her anticipation. But sneaking off wasn't as easy as she hoped.

Hollow Oak sponsored a service project every weekend during the program, so they'd spent all morning at a local soup kitchen. She started off with the easiest task: greeting people as they came in and cleaning the dining area.

She hadn't expected to meet people from so many different walks of life in a place like this. The only volunteer work she'd done before was technically babysitting, which didn't really count. The funny thing about a soup kitchen was that everyone needed food, from struggling single parents to returning college graduates without jobs, the chronically ill to widowers, and those with full-time employment that still couldn't cover basic living costs.

The people who came in seemed close-knit, but they welcomed her and the guests with open arms. Her life had always revolved around the same rinse-and-repeat cliques and tedious gossip. Here, every person came in with a unique story —or three.

There were so many things she'd taken for granted, so many problems she hadn't imagined. It didn't take away her own struggles, but it was nice to see she wasn't the only one staggering through life. And she could tell some of the guests experienced a similar feeling.

Renae and her brother, Richard, worked together to tackle the aftermath of lunch hour. Although they'd both been reserved during workshops, today, they participated a little more than usual. It probably helped that they could focus on someone else.

Renae hummed as she grabbed a soapy plate and swung her hips to the song in her head. Richard took a quieter role, methodically washing off the silverware and placing them on a towel to be dried and put away. He'd done a great job at entertaining the kids—quite a few asked to touch his hair, intrigued by meeting someone from a different culture, but he'd been understanding and even learned to play their trading card game. Their parents appreciated the break and had thanked him before they left.

However, not everyone had caught the spirit of charity. At the end of their assembly line, Connor, a stocky teen with freckles, had turned his back while joking with one of the other boys. It wasn't hard to tell from their conversation that Connor thought a little too highly of himself, and it rubbed her the wrong way.

She wasn't surprised, though. Connor already gained a reputation for being difficult, often showing up late to workshops and, when he did, dragging his feet. He'd made it clear that he only cared about completing his make-up school work and viewed every other aspect of the program as a waste of his time. She'd tried to give gentle reminders and let everyone work at their own pace, but his blatant disregard had worn out her patience.

Just when she opened her mouth to remind him to focus, Renae beat her to it.

"Hey, you gonna do your job or not?" Renae poked Connor's back and motioned to the dishes piling up on the counter, which had leaked a small puddle through the towel and started dripping onto the floor.

Connor glanced over his shoulder mid-sentence, then turned and continued his conversation without responding. His friend shot a wary look at Serena and shifted uncomfortably.

Renae huffed. Her jaw clenched, and she reached out again.

Richard stopped her. "Don't. He's not worth it. I'll do the rest when we're finished."

"You shouldn't enable him," Renae muttered.

Connor scoffed.

Serena took a deep breath. "We agreed to work as a team, Connor. Each of us has to do our part."

Slouching, he slowly spun to face her. If an entire body movement could be an eye-roll, then that was it. "I already told you the water will ruin my watch." He raised his arm and flashed the band of metal around his wrist. "So I can't help out."

She pursed her lips. He had told her about the watch, and that's exactly why he'd been put in charge of *drying*. Or maybe he shouldn't wear delicate jewelry to a soup kitchen? Better yet, leave it at home before working on a ranch.

Then again...she'd come here with exactly that kind of stuck-up attitude, too. Karma was a pain in the ass.

As she tried to figure out an appropriate reply, Grant came over from his station in food prep and broke the tension. "Hey, man. Why don't I tag in? We're pretty much done, so think you can sweep up? After that, you're free to go back out front and relax."

"Sure." Connor shrugged and walked off.

Renae frowned, and Richard stepped over to fill in the empty space. They slipped back into their rhythm as Grant threw a towel on his shoulder and started working beside her.

"Thank you," Serena mouthed.

"No problem. You guys looked like you needed extra hands on deck." Grant hit her with one of his dimpled smiles and made her knees go weak.

It wouldn't have been a surprise if he acted differently after she'd gone down on him. Most guys did. She'd rather cut to the chase than beat around the bush, anyway.

But Grant hadn't changed. He still teased her whenever he got the chance and complimented her when she least expected it. Still watched over her when she didn't know how to handle a situation.

Still made butterflies flutter in her stomach when he got too close.

"Are we really almost done?" she asked, trying to push away a strand of her hair with the back of her hand without getting soap in her eyes.

"Let me get that for you." He brushed his fingers along her temple, smoothing the hair behind her ear. The heat from his touch left a brand on her skin. "Better?"

"Better," she breathed. Then cleared her throat. "Thanks again." Hopefully, the steam in the air would mask her blush. Since when did she get this worked up over meaningless touches?

"And yeah, we're only booked to work through the end of lunch," he added. "Should be heading back soon to give everyone a little free time before dinner and the group meeting."

Going back early sounded heavenly. The strain of their day had started to creep into the balls of her feet, and her back ached from hunching over the sink. This part of the job was neither glamorous nor entertaining. Dancing and partying all night had never left her this exhausted, but it'd also given her a hangover the next morning and memories she wasn't proud of.

For once, maybe her energy hadn't gone to waste.

She looked over at Grant. "Think us being here actually helped?"

He straightened, and his eyes softened. "Definitely. You did great today, sunflower."

She bit back a smile. That one sentence shouldn't have been the best part of her day.

But it was.

TWELVE

Grant

"MMN, FUCKKK..."

His fragmented moan echoed louder than intended, and he braced a hand against the hard tile walls. Every muscle in his body pulled taut as he forgot how to breathe.

Just one more. One more time to get this out of his system, one more to alleviate these incessant thoughts.

A sore, half-gratifying yet never-ending ache coursed through his stiff cock. It gave a pitiful pulse in his fist and leaked whatever had been leftover in his balls after jacking off two times in a row...and this morning. And last night. And every fucking day that had passed since that afternoon in the woods.

"Dammit," he grunted, reaching for the soap to wash himself all over again. His dick shrunk in defeat, worn out but nowhere near satisfied.

The cold showers weren't helping.

On the other hand—the one not shamefully covered in jizz —seeing Serena as often as he could wasn't *hurting*, either. There were even times when he forgot to put up his guard.

She'd taken his world by storm, brought with her a

beautiful whirlwind that was steadily chipping away at his self-inflicted isolation. Something between them had clicked, and though they hadn't outwardly spoken of the incident since, it had changed everything.

Sure, he'd fooled around with a few women after his ex left. A night out here and there, a quick hook-up. Nothing serious. Nothing that let him feel too deep. Those times had all been a way to stay numb. He'd been sure to keep his distance. Carefully held everyone away from the soft spot his ex had mutilated, ripped out of his chest, and stomped on before leaving him bleeding out on the floor.

Then came Serena. She'd cut him to the quick without trying.

And maybe...that wasn't a bad thing.

They both knew this would end after the program was over. Twenty-odd days. That's all they had, so he figured they might as well make the most of it. Maybe getting to know her and fooling around on the side wouldn't be the end of the world.

The Westons already teased him about what they referred to as his "crush." Even if they figured out he and Serena hooked up, they were both adults. As long as they kept their activities to themselves and got their work done, it shouldn't cause a problem. But for right now, their secret was too good to share.

He could go back to that moment in a heartbeat. The sight of her glossed lips wrapped around him, the delicate bridge of her nose, a flush in her cheeks, and those warm brown eyes framed by long lashes, her skin covered with his cum...

That image would never leave his mind. Worse yet, he didn't want it gone. He wanted it tattooed on the inside of his brain as a personal pornographic portrait.

He shut off the water and ran a towel over his hair. If he didn't stop daydreaming and get out of the shower, he was going to miss dinner. After shoving his thoughts aside and throwing on a clean t-shirt and jeans, he jogged out of the guesthouse and across the lawn.

During the program, the main ranch house became a multi-purpose facility, transforming the quiet hallways and cozy rooms he enjoyed for the rest of the year into a library, meeting house, and mess hall. This summer, they were hosting almost thirty people, including guests and staff. He'd had to bring out an extra table from storage to seat them all, and meal times always felt particularly crowded.

Except when he walked into the dining room, no one was seated around either of the oak tables. All the kids had gotten to their feet and were pressing together at one end of the room.

"You're a fool if you think people can't see right through your bullshit," a female voice he recognized as Renae's called out from the crowd. "You think you're better than me?"

"Don't pretend you're not a petty thief." That was Connor. "My pops says people like you don't even belong in this country —can't blame him."

"Well, I don't think you belong on this ranch!"

A flurry of action erupted, and excited chants of *"fight, fight"* rose through the air.

Dammit. That wasn't good.

Grant shot another glance around the room. The Westons must have been preoccupied in the kitchen, and it didn't look like any of the other staff had stayed for dinner. Where the hell was Serena? This was the kind of shit her presence would have prevented. *She had one job.*

But he didn't have time to go looking for her. If he didn't break this up, they were going to spill blood all over Mrs. Weston's carpet.

He pushed through the onlookers just in time to see Richard shove Connor off his sister. "Don't fucking touch her."

Renae stumbled to the side, and Connor snarled at Richard. "Get your filthy hands off me."

Richard retaliated and swung at Connor's face, making the two of them tumble into the wall. Several picture frames and a handful of ceramics rattled. The rest of the kids pressed in closer to get a better look.

"Hey!" Grant shouted, cutting through the commotion and catching their attention. The cheers withered into wary looks and panicked whispers. Unfortunately, Richard and Connor were already too invested in their scuffle to stop now.

"Break it up," he demanded, grabbing one by the arm and the other by the collar. It wasn't the first fight he'd dealt with, and he was both bigger and stronger than either of the boys. He shoved the two in opposite directions and planted himself between them.

"They started it," Connor grumbled.

Renae shot him a withering glare.

He'd expected something like this to happen sooner or later. It always did. Emotions ran high in the heat and new environments. The first week the guests got too worn out to start shit, but during their change in schedule over the weekend, the kids had nothing better to do. That's when shit hit the fan.

A sharp whistle pierced the air, and Mr. Weston appeared in the doorway with crossed arms. "We have zero tolerance for putting hands on each other at this ranch—there will be consequences, no matter who started it."

Deadly silence fell on the group as he glared at everyone in the room. Then he pointed at Connor, Richard, and Renae in turn. "All three of you, outside. Now."

Grant caught Mr. Weston's eyes and nodded to let him know he had things under control, then led the three out of the room. They headed toward the door as Mrs. Weston came out of the kitchen and sternly admonished that anyone else who acted up would get an entire day of mucking out the stables.

Connor stepped ahead and wrenched open the front door

before Grant could stop him, storming out and nearly slamming into Serena. The door rattled on its hinges as she rushed in with a questioning look, but before Serena could vocalize her thoughts, Grant pulled her to the side.

"Where were you?" he hissed, motioning for Richard and Renae to wait before going out.

"I got caught up in the barn." Serena tilted her head to try to see behind him. "What happened here?"

"A fight. We're figuring it out." He paused as her words sunk in. "Is everything okay outside?"

An unfamiliar emotion tightened in his chest. If he had been to dinner on time, he would have noticed she wasn't there. Serena might have been in worse trouble than the kids, and he wouldn't have known. The Westons could handle things here, but if anything happened to Serena...

"Yeah, I mean, nothing's wrong," she answered under her breath and interrupted his train of thought. "I was just talking with Lucy. She looked like she wanted company."

He let out a heavy exhale. "Next time, let me know if you're going to be late. One of us needs to be here."

She pursed her lips and nodded.

He tipped his head toward the door. "I need to calm down the boys. That is, if Connor even stuck around to talk, and someone needs to speak to Renae—I've noticed she tends to keep to herself, think you could try to figure out if there's a bigger issue?"

"I'll do my best," she offered and fell into step as the four of them went out to the porch.

Time to get to the bottom of this.

THIRTEEN

Serena

'THE ONE THING ABOUT BEING IN AN OPEN SPACE IS THAT THE silence started to speak.

A moment ago, before the fight ensued, the ranch had been filled with the quiet murmurings of evening. She'd almost wanted to stay here more than three weeks—in a world where people moved at their own pace and a dirty-talking cowboy brought her to magical places. Where she felt like she could truly be anyone she wanted.

Grant had taught the guests in equine therapy the basics of grooming for this afternoon's workshop, and she tagged along for his demonstration. He'd brought out all the tools they cleaned the day before, then explained how to use them and watched each of them practice. Lucy wasn't one of the horses cleared to work with the guests due to her injury, but Grant gave Serena permission to groom her.

It wasn't hard to tell that Lucy loved her mane being detangled, especially when she got a few extra scratches here and there. The coarse black hair shone more and more as Serena brushed, and when everyone else returned to prepare for dinner, she decided to stay a bit longer.

It felt as if time had slowed. Lingering shadows stretched across the barn without her noticing, and glimmers of a setting sun were complimented by Lucy's happy snorts. She hadn't realized when she started talking or how the events leading up to her community service began to replay in her mind.

The memories poured out to Lucy in a low murmur—how the frat parties night after night became less entertaining as the year went on, and the more people she'd been around, the lonelier she'd felt. Jace cared more about keeping her out of his business than taking her to his bed, and she started feeling like a shell of herself, sinking into alcohol and sex to ignore the emptiness.

Something she'd pretended not to notice until it was too late.

When she found herself in trouble, she'd pushed away all the friends who would have come to help. All she had now was Lucy—but that felt like a good place to start. Admitting her mistakes out loud was hard enough, even to a compassionate animal who wouldn't fault her for it.

By the time she finally realized how late it had gotten, she'd had to rush to wash up and practically ran to catch dinner. Then Connor had burst out the front door and nearly bowled her over as he stormed off to the boy's guesthouse. Next thing she knew, Grant pulled her aside to ask why she'd been late.

She should have known the moment of peace wouldn't last forever.

Serena met Renae's eyes as Grant escorted their group outside. What could have gone down to put him into such a serious mood? He had every right to be mad at her for neglecting her responsibilities, but still, he hadn't exploded like her ex would have. Instead, he'd almost looked concerned about *her* well-being, even though he was the one who had to break up a fight.

Why would he care about her that much?

As soon as the door latched closed, Grant gave her one last look, his eyes locking with hers as if to verify that everything was okay. "Sure you're good?"

She nodded. "I got this."

"Okay." He heaved out another sigh and looked over his shoulder, where Renae's brother, Richard, had shoved his hands in his pockets and started kicking the dirt. Looked like Connor hadn't cared to stick around, either. "One of the Westons and a counselor should be out soon. Then you should go grab some dinner."

"If I miss dinnertime, are you going to make me eat dried meat or something?" she teased.

Grant broke into a tired semi-smile, his dimple making a brief appearance. "Maybe." He opened his mouth and closed it. "I didn't get to see what happened in there, but I heard Renae shouting before the boys got into it. Try to get her to talk. We need everyone's side of the story."

Serena glanced over at Renae, who was busy pacing back and forth and clenching her fists as she shot ominous glares toward the boy's guesthouse. "I'll try."

Grant gave her a short nod, then walked over to Richard and said something she couldn't make out.

Serena took a few steps in the opposite direction toward Renae. It didn't look like she was going to open up without a little prompting.

"Want to tell me what happened?" she tried.

Renae looked up with a scowl. "Do you think that's gonna solve anything? Just give me a slap on the wrist. I'll promise not to do it again, and we can call it good."

Serena sighed. It would be easier to let Renae off the hook and go along with her pretense of a discussion. From the sound of her guarded tone, pushing her to open up obviously wouldn't work.

Her stomach gave a rumble of defeat.

But now wasn't the time to be selfish. If she'd felt better after talking with Lucy, maybe Renae needed someone to listen, too.

"How about we take a walk?" she suggested. The air outside felt balmy, warm from the day's heat but not enough to build up a sweat in her fresh shirt.

Renae's frown deepened. Before she could protest, Serena added, "It'll just be between us. Or, you can join the others and sit through another boring meeting."

The guests would be finishing up with dinner soon, and then they'd go to the last workshop of the day. It was a notoriously tedious hour. Everyone would be drained, but couldn't risk not participating and earning an even worse chore as a consequence.

She shrugged. "Your choice."

Renae pursed her lips. "I guess we can walk."

They fell into stride beside each other, heading toward the barn and then following the wire fence. Crickets hopped out of the way of her scuffed sneakers, and tufts of tall grass brushed against her legs.

She usually filled empty gaps in conversation with some wild story from drunken escapades or unconfirmed gossip. This time, Serena stayed quiet and let her eyes wander over the darkening pastures. Most of the horses had made their way back to the barn while small critters rustled high in the tree branches. A few clouds floated around the mountain peaks, soaked in deep blues and purples against the backdrop of a denim sky.

"It's not his fault," Renae muttered at last. Serena looked over as she let out a slow breath. "My brother hates to fight. He skips school to avoid it—that's why he's here. If he doesn't complete the program, he's gonna get held back a grade. He only stepped in tonight to defend me, so don't let him catch the blame."

Serena nodded. "I wasn't there. All I can go on is what you tell me." She paused. "I won't know what happened unless you explain it."

Renae chewed on her lip, then appeared to let go of her hesitation. "Connor called me out as soon as I sat down to eat. Like he had it all planned." She shook her head. "He accused me of stealing. Said I snuck into his room and took his watch."

"Why would he accuse you over anyone else?" Serena asked.

Renae scoffed. "Connor's hated everyone since the moment he got here. I guess he's tight about his parents calling him a failure for being sent to the program and wants to prove he's above the rest of us. It didn't take him long to figure out my brother's an easy target, but he also knows Richard didn't steal anything because they've been in a group together the whole time. So, he blamed me instead."

"And you wouldn't back down." Serena filled in the details. Her sister acted the same way. Couldn't let anyone get away with taking advantage of her or her friends. It led to a lot of issues at school, but Serena was only glad that someone else became the family's problem child for a few years. That is until she got herself into this mess.

Renae nodded. "If I don't defend myself, it looks like I'm admitting guilt. But when I do something about it, I'm labeled the bad guy anyway."

"What did you do about it tonight?" Serena asked.

"I told everyone the truth—that Connor's a stuck-up asshole who thinks he's better than us. I didn't want to keep arguing with him, so I got up to leave, but he grabbed my arm. That's when Richard got involved."

Serena hummed. "I see. You tried to walk away and Connor escalated the situation."

"Wait, you're gonna believe me?" Renae asked, looking over with wide eyes.

Serena gave a soft smile and shook her head. "It's not my place to judge. But I hope you know better than to lie. We both know how that worked out last time."

Renae snorted. "Yeah, I knew better than to reach for my iPod until you left, too, but I panicked." She let out a small breath and then sobered. "Listening to music helps me keep calm in those situations. That's why I brought it here."

"Is it like this for you at school, too?" Serena asked.

Renae nodded. "Our family just moved to a new area. It felt the same as being sent out here—we don't know anyone, and no one wants to know us. It's not like everyone is mean. I just... have a hard time trusting. There's a few nice girls in my class, but I try not to talk to them 'cause everyone I get close to always ends up in trouble because of me."

A knot twisted in Serena's gut. She knew the feeling.

"I'm not here because I volunteered, you know," she said in a hushed tone. Renae looked over, and Serena glanced down. "I got involved with a bad crowd. Instead of sending me to jail with them, I got sent here."

"Oh," Renae mumbled. "I didn't know."

"What I'm trying to say is that I know how hard it can be to find good friends." Serena put her hand out to pluck a few seeds from the nearest stalks of grass. "I knew some nice girls, too. I didn't think they could relate to me, but then I ended up dating a guy who didn't even care enough to try. I think if I could do anything over again, I'd put my feelings aside for the friends who cared rather than block them out."

Renae hummed as they kept walking. Then Serena's stomach broke the silence with a rumble louder than an earthquake.

They both broke out in a laugh. "You should probably go eat," Renae said.

"Yeah, probably." Serena let the wind blow away the grass

seeds in her hands and glanced up at the horizon. "Wanna join me? I'm sure they have enough for you to have seconds. Maybe we can sneak some dessert out of the freezer."

Renae grinned. "You don't have to ask me twice."

FOURTEEN

Serena

P*LINK.*

Awareness tugged at the fringe of her subconscious, pulling her out of sleep. Was it raining? She rolled over on the mattress and listened in the darkness. No, the room fell silent again. Maybe the wind had just picked up.

She'd been going to bed at record times lately, as soon as it was lights-out for the guests. Maybe getting in all those extra hours had finally caught up to her because now she felt wide awake. But there was no hint of light behind the curtains, so it mustn't be too early. Thank goodness. She exhaled and closed her eyes.

Plink.

How strong was that wind? She pulled the quilt up and under her chin and snuggled further into the pillows.

A couple of days had passed since the confrontation between Richard and Connor. The missing watch hadn't been found, and until it turned up or the boys worked things out, both were assigned to alternating dish duty. The solution was temporary at best, but at least they hadn't gotten into another altercation. The Westons strongly encouraged guests to use the principles taught in the program to solve their problems—*honesty, communication, and respect*—so they wouldn't step in unless it was the last option.

On the bright side, Renae had started to open up more. Sometimes, they'd hang out and listen to music on their breaks, and during meals, Serena invited Renae to sit with her and a few of the other girls. None of them were particularly fond of living at Hollow Oak, not that she could blame them, but it seemed they didn't hate the program itself.

Serena even found herself speaking up in the evening meetings to encourage the others. When she didn't skip her turn, more of the guests gradually followed suit. Everyone had more in common than they thought. Several came from a chaotic home and could relate to feeling like an outcast. Normally, she preferred to be the one who stood out—the girl others wanted to be, but it felt nice to be genuine for a change.

Plink. Plink.

Seriously, what was that?

Annoyed, she tossed off the blankets and sat up. The bedroom wasn't nearly as cold as usual—she'd learned to keep the window closed but could tell when nights got chilly. If it had been storming outside, goosebumps would have already covered her legs.

Plink. Plink-plink-plink.

The sound had come from the same spot every time: her window. Meaning it had to be one of two things—Grant, or a wild animal—and she didn't know which to hope for least. He wouldn't be that ridiculous...

Shuffling across the room, she yanked aside the curtain. Grant threw another pebble at the glass and grinned like a mischievous five-year-old.

She rolled her eyes, unlatched the lock, and opened the window. "Are you proud of yourself?"

"Course I am. Isn't this the best way to get a lady's

attention?" His dimples sank into his cheeks as he spoke. Moonlight glowed softly off his sandy hair. Even with Grant's height, only his head reached past the window frame, and it made the scene that much more comical.

Her expression faltered as she broke into a laugh. They'd both been busier than usual this week, especially since she'd felt guilty for being late to dinner and made sure it didn't happen again. Seeing him without the pressure of work sent a new spark of energy through her.

"Yeah, except I wouldn't call myself a lady," she teased, curling her fingers around the window ledge. The thin fabric of her tank top barely veiled her breasts, and she leaned over so her hair fell around his face. "Is this a midnight booty call?" she cooed in a sultry whisper. "Gonna show me more secrets in the woods?"

He bit his lip and reached up to brush his thumb over her jaw. Her skin tingled at the touch, the pad of his finger rough and hot.

"As much as I like the sound of that," he murmured. "I think what I have in mind will be better."

"Oh?" She arched her eyebrows. He'd piqued her interest. Getting dirty in the woods had been a great time, but he'd thought of something better?

Grant gave her a knowing look, and an electric current zapped through the air. "Hurry up and get out here," he whispered.

She glanced over her shoulder. "What if someone wakes up?"

"Then they'll assume you're asleep. It's only eleven-thirty. We've got more than enough time."

"Okay." She straightened. "Hold on, let me change first."

She left the curtain open and didn't bother to turn on the lights. The moon shone bright enough to let her move around freely, and she didn't care if Grant watched. A little show before the main event wouldn't hurt.

Slipping on leggings in place of her sleep shorts, she grabbed a jacket and her worn pair of shoes, then tossed them outside. It would be easier to climb through the window without them. Even if it'd been a while since she snuck out, she'd gotten plenty of practice in high school.

"Um, wait a second," she whispered after swinging one leg out the window. The ground looked a lot farther away when she had to balance on the ledge.

Grant stood half a step back, watching with silent concern. "Okay, maybe I'd like a little help," she admitted under her breath.

The corner of his lips twitched. "Thought you'd never ask." He reached up to bracket his hands on her hips, holding her steady as she bent her other leg.

"Don't drop me," she warned. He scoffed.

Gripping his shoulders, she pushed off the wall. Grant's biceps bunched underneath his white t-shirt, the muscles in his arms and abdomen taut as he hoisted her in the air. Damn, this guy was ripped. This hadn't even made him break a sweat.

Their eyes locked, and her body slid against his. Instead of letting her feet touch the ground, he stepped to the side and pinned her to the wall. She breathed out a half-moan. His weight held her in place, kindling a fire in her core.

She rocked her hips as his cock surged through his jeans. "Is it crazy that I missed you?" she whispered, teasing her nails along his neck.

He watched her through hooded eyes, their usual green transformed into a mossy black. "Maybe," he hummed, leaning in. "But I missed you, too."

His breath warmed her skin as he skimmed his nose over her cheekbone, then hovered his lips at the corner of her mouth.

A week and a half ago, they'd been in nearly the same position. Her riling him up and getting pinned in the guestroom. She thought she had the full advantage on day one, that there was nothing she couldn't turn in her favor. But now, her heart was hammering in her chest a thousand miles per minute, and she didn't know who had the upper hand. Or if it mattered.

His lips ghosted over hers. It drove her to the brink of madness.

She curled her fingers into the hair at the nape of his neck and brought his lips back where she needed them. He shuddered, grabbing her jaw with a grunt and tilting her head to fuse their mouths. His hands were rough and callous, his lips supple and imploring.

Her back arched as she pressed herself against his chest and tightened her legs around his waist. He smelled like leather and tasted like fresh rain. The warmth of his skin balanced the cool breeze of the night, and his soft cotton shirt felt too good against her bare arms. Too soft and inviting. It would be a downright shame if he ever let go.

She traced his upper lip with her tongue, light-headed and eager for more. He groaned. Then he licked her back.

She'd never been kissed like this. It wasn't just the passion of his lips or the brazen grip of his hands—his whole body moved with deliberate leisure like she was a delicacy meant to be savored. And he wanted every last piece.

They kissed until her lips were swollen and her lungs burned for air, but she couldn't stop. Grant broke away with a strained hum. "Sorry, I couldn't help myself," he mumbled.

She licked her lips. "I like when you can't help yourself."

"Dirty girl," he muttered, giving her a wary look. Then, he eased up enough to set her feet on the soft grass. His gaze flicked over the very obvious points of her nipples. "We should get going before I do it again."

She bit her lip, still stinging from their kiss. But before she could say anything to convince him for more, he put a finger to his lips and grabbed her hand. She barely had time to pick up her shoes as he tugged her around the back to where his pickup truck sat, idling with the lights off.

"Get in," he whispered, opening the passenger door. "And try not to be too conspicuous until we're out of the drive."

She nodded as giddy excitement flared on the tail of her arousal. It'd been too long since she went on an adventure. But as she hopped into the cab and they started rolling down the gravel road, one thought circled restlessly in the back of her mind.

His hand had fit perfectly around hers.

FIFTEEN

Grant

A GUY COULD GET USED TO THIS.

Once the ranch disappeared from the rearview mirror, Serena fiddled with the radio until she found a signal. Then, she kicked her feet up on the dash and started to sing along.

Unruly blonde hair fell in waves over her shoulders, as if she'd just rolled out of bed, and even when she sang out of key, the husky tone in her voice brought a smile to his lips. A faint shadow of dirt outlined her heels from running barefoot with him after their kiss—one that shouldn't have felt as good as it did.

If that single moment stretched out for the rest of his life, it still wouldn't be enough.

Her taste lingered on his tongue, and his gaze kept drifting to her long legs. Those leggings were the worst kind of tease. At this rate, his hard-on would never go down.

But he was determined to make the most of their night out, no matter how much he wanted to let her have her wicked way with him.

Serena caught him staring and slid her hand over the center console. Her chestnut eyes glittered with mischief in the darkness. Too late, he realized her intentions as she curled her fingers around the length of his cock. A wave of pleasure shot through his veins.

He pressed himself into the seat with a groan. "I can't drive if you do that."

"Then pull over," she purred, her suggestion a mesmerizing snare that complimented the radio's melody. Almost too provocative to resist.

Gritting his teeth, he took her hand and moved it to her lap, then laced their fingers so she couldn't try to reach over again.

"*Someone* needs to teach you patience," he scolded.

And by someone, he only meant himself—even though she wasn't his to claim. A small, neglected part of his heart ached at the thought.

"Besides," he added. "Tonight's on me, sunflower." He didn't have to look away from the road to appreciate her blush. Then her hand tensed slightly under his, barely noticeable, but he immediately let go.

"My bad," he mumbled. That was the second time he'd grabbed it without thinking.

"No...it's okay." She flexed her fingers before slipping her hand over his and resting his against her thigh.

Fuck, he couldn't stop himself from giving her leg a firm squeeze. She felt incredible—soft and perfectly molded to his grip. The leggings were thin enough to let her body heat radiate through, but the touch only made him want more. He itched to feel her skin.

Now, he was the one who needed patience. *Deep breaths.* Their night was far from over.

He looked out into the pitch-black road, illuminated by the moon instead of man-made lights, and immediately recognized where they were. Another ten minutes or so.

It'd been a while since he made the drive out here. Even

longer since he found himself missing the familiar landscape more than missing the people he used to come with.

The song on the radio ended, and Serena leaned forward to turn it down. "So, where are we headed?"

"A new hiding spot I think you'll appreciate." He flashed her a dimpled grin while rubbing his thumb along her inner thigh.

She hummed and shifted to give him better access. "I can't tell if you were always this smooth with the ladies or if you've just been guessing right."

"What do you mean?" He chuckled, a little too proud of her semi-compliment.

"Come on." Muted light from the dashboard reflected off her face as she rolled her eyes. "You went full-on country-Romeo tonight. Don't get me wrong, a girl likes to be wooed every now and then, but then there are times when you act... surprised. Like, you can put in all the effort to collect pebbles but hadn't planned on it leading to a kiss."

Heat rose in his cheeks. Why the hell was she making *him* blush?

"That part wasn't planned," he admitted.

After his ex, he hadn't bothered to take women on dates. Turns out that staying loyal to the same person throughout high school had put him on the radar, and once he was free game, quite a few were willing to get between his legs without all the romance. It'd been a nice change of pace to not take the initiative, although he sensed his partners' disappointment when he didn't reciprocate with as much enthusiasm. By that time, he'd lost all capacity to care. Just because his heart was broken didn't mean he'd been ready to fix it.

But with Serena, the usual rules didn't apply. Hell, he'd begun to wish that there weren't any rules at all. Maybe kissing had crossed some sort of invisible line. Maybe he was already getting too attached.

Even so, he didn't regret it for a second.

"I just went with what felt right in the moment." He cast a quick glance over to read her expression.

Serena burst out in a throaty laugh. "That's exactly what makes you so fun." Shaking her head, she returned her gaze out the window into the darkened wheat fields. Then she added in a quiet voice, "It's hard to believe you don't have a girlfriend."

His mouth went dry. That was the one rule he *did* know—not to pry into each other's lives—but it didn't feel right to ignore this topic forever.

"I've only had one, to be honest," he mumbled.

She looked over with her jaw open. "*Only* one?"

"Mhm." He tried several times to swallow the lump in his throat.

"Oh..." Her voice faded as she put two and two together.

He kept his eyes fixed on the road and channeled his focus into tracing the seam of her leggings. "Yeah."

Wow, this whole 'talking about it' thing was off to a great start. If one-word answers were the most he could muster, then he might as well not have brought it up.

"It doesn't matter anymore," he muttered. "After I found out she cheated, she moved out of town to start a new life." A life he never even knew she wanted. *With his best friend.*

"That was her in the picture with you, wasn't it? When you won the rodeo buckle," Serena said with a hushed tone. "Is that why you quit competing?"

He shook his head. "Not exactly."

Sure, there were other reasons. Or that's what he'd told himself.

"Like I said," he continued. "We went our separate ways. I love competing, but there was a point when I had to grow up. Get a job and all that. So, I moved in with the Westons for a fresh start."

Serena hummed. "I can tell you like it there, too."

"Yeah."

Back to single-word answers.

They both fell into silence. He was about to reach over and turn up the radio again, but then she took a deep breath and whispered, "I have people I wish I could forget, too."

He didn't know what to say, or if he should say anything at all. But he knew he'd do anything to not end up as one of those people.

❋

The front wheel dipped in a rut, bouncing the truck along the dark dirt road and making Serena's tits jiggle in her tank top.

Yeah, he hit the bump on purpose.

"Okay, seriously, where are you taking me?" Serena laughed as she kept a death grip on the handle above the window.

"Right...here," he replied, turning the bend and veering off into a large field. In front of them, water glimmered in the moonlight. There were no other buildings out this far. Just land and sky and fresh air.

The riverbed bottle-necked a few yards ahead due to a natural rock formation, then it opened into a wide section deep enough to swim in. The movement of the water kept the bugs at bay, and the spot was so far out of town that few people came out here. Especially this late.

He shut off the engine and turned to Serena, biting his lip. "Up for a swim?"

Her eyes lit up as she took in the night landscape. "Thought you'd never ask."

She paused, then tilted her head and batted her lashes. "But first, it's about time I spill some secrets of my own."

Fuck, she was already starting to make him weak. He took the bait. "Oh?"

"I haven't gone skinny dipping before..." She grabbed the bottom of her tank top and pulled it over her head without warning. His breath caught in his throat. "But I've always wanted to."

The incandescent light in the truck reflected off her skin, casting a warm glow on her teardrop-shaped breasts and accentuating the curve of her waist. God, she was perfect.

It took everything he had not to lean over and take a dusky nipple in his mouth, then trace his tongue along her ribs before dipping to the tease of her belly button. He'd never be able to hold out once she took off her pants. But he had to. He had to make this last because something this good wouldn't stick around forever.

By some miracle, he managed to drag his gaze back to hers. "Seems like I guessed right, then."

Her smile widened. "Seems like that's becoming a habit of yours." She gave him a smug look—she was gorgeous, and she knew it. As she should.

But if he didn't get in the water soon, he'd probably get brain damage from lack of proper blood flow. He yanked off his shirt and threw it somewhere behind him. "You're not allowed to chicken out."

"Neither are you," she scoffed, her leggings and a fuchsia thong flying off into the same place as his shirt. Hopefully, somewhere she wouldn't manage to find when they were done because if he didn't get to keep her, the least he could get was a trophy.

Not daring to distract himself with another glance or let her catch sight of his growing erection, he opened the door and shed the rest of his clothes. "What are you waiting for?" he teased.

The passenger door opened and slammed shut without a response. By the time he'd gotten fully undressed, she'd already started toward the water. A starry sky stretched over her silhouette, light hair swaying down her back and long grass dancing at her feet.

The entire world slammed to a halt.

She was more than beautiful. More than a distraction—she might even be the answer to a prayer he hadn't dared to utter.

Something expanded in his chest, twining its roots deeper and deeper until it'd be impossible to pull out. A midnight sunflower as awe-inspiring as it was sinful.

And *damn*, that ass.

He wanted a portrait of it to hang right above his headboard. No, on second thought, he'd take the real thing over a picture any day.

He walked to her in a few long strides and swooped his arms under her knees. She let out a shrill laugh as he held her against his chest.

"What are you doing—oh no, wait!" Her laughter died, and her hands scrambled to grab his shoulders. He continued to walk up the riverbank. "You are *not* about to throw me in there."

"That's exactly what I'm doing." He drew in a sharp breath, trying not to expire from the friction of his impossibly hard dick bobbing against her ass.

"Grant! Wait—no!" Her legs kicked to no avail as he stepped onto one of the large flat rocks at the top of the swimming hole.

"In you go."

SIXTEEN

Grant

Serena shrieked as she flew through air and plummeted into the deepest section of the river. Churning, dark blue water swallowed her whole. A rush of tiny bubbles swirled in her wake. She popped up with a gasp. "Shit! Fuck, it's cold!"

He snapped a mental photo and doubled over in laughter. No one went in without some form of protest, but hers was especially rewarding.

"You are so dead," she hissed. "Get in here! Let's see how well you take it." She sent a splash of water over his feet.

He smirked. "Alright, but remember you asked for it." Then he cannonballed into the river to splash her back.

A surge of adrenaline short-circuited his system as the cold mountain water enveloped him. Hell yeah, that's what he'd been missing. A string of curses flew from his mouth as he surfaced and sucked in deep lungfuls of air.

"You should have at least given me some time to prepare," Serena complained, flushed cheeks and glittering eyes betraying her excitement.

"Naw, better to get it over with," he countered. He swam toward her, but she swept out her arms and moved out of reach.

"I'm not letting you catch me again." Her eyebrows quirked in a challenge.

"Oh, yeah?" He sunk down and watched her over the shadowy ripples. "And what happens when I do catch you?"

"You'll have to find out," she whispered, then ducked under the water and disappeared.

He lunged to the left, outstretched fingers brushing her foot before she kicked away. It was too dark to see, too cold to feel anything but subtle traces of heat when she got close. After a minute of searching, he popped up for air and scouted the area. Where the hell had she gone? No way she could hold her breath this long...

Ah, that's where she went.

He whipped around to find her waiting behind him with a smug grin. In two powerful strokes, he closed the gap, but then she dove back underwater.

Too bad there was only one way to escape this far upstream.

Something smooth skimmed past his foot. He shot toward it, catching her leg with one hand and hooking his arm around her waist. He hauled her to his chest as they rose to the surface. But she refused to give in, squirming relentlessly and making his hand to slide up the inside of her thigh. His fingers were suddenly not just wet but hot, pressed into soft flesh.

Shit, was that her pussy?

Using the moment to her advantage, Serena twisted and broke free. He grunted in frustration and chased after her.

This time, she didn't get far. He edged her toward the shallow side of the river, their footfalls splashing against pebbles and sandy mud. The water pulled at his limbs and forced them to move in slow motion. He couldn't seem to run fast enough. But dammit, he'd never been more motivated in his life.

Serena glanced back and zigzagged but ended up cornering

herself. He cut her off and grabbed her from behind, wrapping both arms tight around her chest.

Fuck, she was slippery as hell. He stumbled backward into deeper water as she struggled to break his hold. Their bodies slid around each other, his blood pumping stronger and faster the more her ass pushed against his thigh.

Somehow, she managed to wiggle her way onto his back and locked her arms around his neck. He shut his eyes, much too distracted by the swell of her breasts and the tease of her hardened nipples. Her body heat was a white-hot iron on his chilled skin.

Then her lips were at his ear, and warm breath fanned over his neck. "It's payback time."

Serena used her weight and lurched at just the right angle to send them both tumbling into the water. Her grip faltered, and he spun to capture her as they found their footing.

Before she could react, he trapped both of her arms to her side and pressed his teeth to her neck. "Dunk me all you want —*now you're mine.*"

Serena let out a surprised squeal as he sucked at her fluttering pulse. Slowly, he loosened his hold, testing to see if she'd try to run again. But she didn't, finally worn out and breathing heavily against his chest.

"Mm, your mouth feels so good," she murmured with a shiver.

He was too lost in her to reply, kissing along her collarbone and licking the cool water off of her skin. Her hands drifted down his abdomen, skimming the contour of his muscles and tracing agonizing swirls lower and lower...

"Fuck," he whispered, letting out a groan as her warm hand wrapped around his balls.

Serena giggled—fucking *giggled* as she ruthlessly subjected him to the best type of torture known to mankind. His dick valiantly tried to harden despite the cold, and when their lips connected, every nerve ending in his body ignited at once.

He pressed them closer, flattened his hands down her back to knead her ass, digging in his fingers as he spread her open. She moaned into his mouth. *Yes.* Nothing could compare to this —to being tangled together in the wilderness under the veil of the night sky. Her body molded to his as water flowed around them, and the current of both made his head spin.

He walked them backward to the riverbank, then lifted her onto a smooth rock and took a dark cherry nipple into his mouth. Serena's back arched as he stretched her breast with his teeth, her legs dangling on either side of his chest.

"What are you going to do with me?" she whispered, watching him through wet, golden lashes.

Tie you up. Brand my name on your skin. Build a fortress to keep you by my side.

He rubbed his palms over her legs, around her calves, and under the soles of her feet, then lowered his nose to nuzzle the inside of her knee. "Something I've never done before."

She gasped as he left a hickey on the inside of her thigh. "You've never gone down on a girl?"

"Not yet," he confirmed. But her scent was already driving him wild. He took in a long, deep breath as he got closer to her sex.

"Afraid you won't like it?" she asked, her voice turning husky and low.

He chuckled and opened her thighs wider. His thumbs traced the curve of her exposed lips, and a choked, hungry growl rose from the back of his throat. He could stare at this all day. Pretty and pink. Shiny and slick. Her skin there was smooth, but a small layer of fuzz had begun to peek through.

He liked it. He liked it far too much.

"Not at all," he replied. "In fact, I know I'm going to love it."

Because it was her. Because tonight she was so happy and carefree, and nothing had ever felt this perfect before.

Serena bit her lip and tipped her hips forward. He'd already begun to dip inside, exploring his prize. They were both soaked from their swim, but as he swiped the pad of his thumb through her folds, he knew she'd need more. He stretched her pussy wide with two fingers and then spit on her clit, rubbing it in slow circles until she glistened and moaned.

"That's so hot," she whispered, still looking at him with moonlit eyes.

"That's just the beginning." He grinned. "Remember no one is out here to hear you scream."

Then he lowered his head and gave her clit what it wanted. It pulsed as he tugged it between his lips. Serena cried out, threading her fingers in his hair. She tasted even better than he imagined—wild and sweet and *damn*, now that he had her once, how could he ever go without?

"You're gonna have to tell me what you like," he mumbled into her thighs, which had clamped around him mercilessly—suffocation by pussy wouldn't be the worst way to die, but he had to make her come first.

"Just stop talking." She shoved his head between her legs, grinding herself against his mouth. It forced his jaw open wider as he flicked his tongue against her in short, fast strokes, experimenting with different angles until she tensed beneath him.

Her grip tightened on his hair, nails digging into his scalp. He groaned. Fuck, why did that feel so good?

"Look at me," she panted, clutching onto a fistful of his hair.

Reluctantly, he pulled back enough to raise his head. Their eyes locked, Her breasts rose and fell with shallow breaths. Her nipples were tight rosebuds, begging to be sucked just like her pussy. He'd already gotten her this worked up. What would it be like when she came? Would she call out his name? Would she beg him to give her more?

He licked his lips. One way to find out.

"Not bad for your first time," she breathed while studying his face, which must have been dazed and more than a little sticky. "Do you want to know how to really please a woman?"

"I want to know how to please you."

She let out a soft exhale, half laugh, half sigh. "Then you'll have to multitask."

He wasn't naive enough to not know what she meant—and he'd fingered enough women to know their bodies were all unique. Some liked it fast and hard; others preferred it slow and deep. Each had a specific angle. That one place that would shatter them every time.

He nestled a finger inside her, searching for the special spot. "Like this?"

"Yeah," she panted, all but breathless. "Curl a little more...*ah, there*." Her hands slipped from his hair, and he sealed his mouth over her clit. She clung to the soft grass above the water as he slowed his strokes, wanting to draw out her moans and make her ride his face until they both expired.

"You like being here more than you admit," he mumbled as he licked.

"What?" she whispered, disoriented.

"Being out in the country. You enjoy it more than you thought you would." He used one hand to hold her open while tracing her clit with the tip of his tongue.

"*Ah,*" she gasped. "Why are we having this conversation now?"

"Because I know you'll be honest." Plus, the way her voice fractured as she tried not to come was the sexiest thing he'd ever heard. He twisted his finger deeper and picked up the pace. "Tell me you don't like being eaten out on a backroads riverbank."

"Fine. Yes, I like it." Her response came out as a series of moans more than actual words. "I like the open air. I like trying new things. I like being here with you."

He smiled as her legs began to shake. "Do you think you could fall in love?"

Shit. He hadn't meant to phrase it like that. With that word. Instead of letting her reply, he slipped another finger inside and picked up the pace, thrusting against the rough patch in her swollen walls.

"Fuck, Grant. I can't..." She squirmed as her thighs wrested with his head.

"Go on," he rasped. "Give it to me."

Her muscles pulled taut, and the sound of her cry swept across the quiet landscape. Her pussy tightened in rhythmic contractions. He didn't stop—*couldn't* stop—her taste sweeter and smoother as he lapped up her orgasm. He held her still until she unraveled completely, slowing just enough to let them both indulge in the moment.

"Okay, okay, I really can't take anymore." Serena gently pried him off and breathed out an exhausted sigh.

He avoided her eyes by hoisting himself onto the rock beside her, only now noticing his toes had gone numb. They'd probably been out longer than they should've. He cleared his throat. "Let's get dried off. Probably shouldn't be out here for too long."

She didn't protest as he scooped her up and started walking back to the truck, eyes fixated on the sky.

Good. Hopefully, she'd forget about what he said.

SEVENTEEN

Grant

"I never knew you could see the Milky Way so clearly," Serena mumbled, boneless in his arms and covered in goosebumps.

He glanced up. Sure enough, a strip of sparkling stars hung overhead. The sky never looked the same way twice here. Sometimes it was dark and stormy, other times it was bright and close enough to touch, like right now. But it was always different.

Some people assumed that if humans weren't around to build and destroy, things wouldn't change. But change was nature's way. Even good things, beautiful and magnificent things, weren't meant to be the same forever.

"It looks better when the moon isn't out," he replied simply.

Serena hummed. "You're used to all of this, then?"

"I've seen it before, yeah." He looked down and smiled at the sight—her face soft in the silver light, wet hair plastered across her shoulders, nipples puckered from the cold. "But I'm not used to it. I don't think it will ever get old."

Especially not nights like this or all the other nights they could share beneath an ever-changing sky. Before their month ran out, that was.

"You might be onto something." Serena laughed, her eyes warm and softer than usual. "But don't think that means you're off the hook."

He tensed and looked ahead, stepping through the grass to swing open the passenger door. Of course, they couldn't skip over him saying words like 'love.' Especially not when it had slipped out at the worst possible time.

Serena's hand grazed his chin and guided him to look at her. "I want my turn to play with you, too," she whispered. "Who knows when we'll get a chance to sneak out again."

He relaxed with a light-hearted chuckle. Did that mean she'd taken his words as a joke? Or maybe she'd misheard. In any case, if she wasn't going to mention it, then he wouldn't, either.

"I should have known that's what you wanted, my dirty girl," he murmured. "I won't say no. But how about we get warm first?"

She nodded, and he pulled out the bag of towels he'd packed under the seat. After wrapping her up and laying an extra one behind her, he got into the driver's side and turned on the heater.

"You came prepared," Serena commented as she fluffed her hair with a towel. "I didn't see these on the drive over here."

He leaned into the seat with a deep breath. "It's a habit, I guess." Even if it'd been a while since he took anyone on a proper date, he must've fallen back into the motions without noticing. Taking care of the little things had become second nature—he'd never planned on being single, of only having to think for himself.

He ran a hand over his head and pushed away a few strands of damp hair. "Am I doing too much?"

She held his gaze, flashed a mischievous smile, and leaned over the center console. "All of you is too much."

The world faded as her lips brushed his, and he closed his eyes. He had no reason to enjoy this so much. To crave even one more moment with her.

She ran her tongue along his bottom lip, and he brought his hand to the back of her neck to deepen kiss, sweeping his tongue in tandem with hers. Making out in the car felt different from kissing outside. More intimate. Like they were sharing a secret, and if he kept it, then things might end differently this time around.

Her hands dropped to his lap, tugging at the towel around his waist. *Fuck, yes.* His cock immediately jumped toward her as if in answer to an unspoken command.

"Especially this part of you," she hummed with a pleased tone, her words swallowed in their lazy kiss. "But I don't mind."

He nipped at her lips. "Are you sure about that?" Her kiss felt as starved as his, and he knew just how well she could take him. He didn't have to hold anything back. "Because I don't think you'd be satisfied with anything less."

She moaned as he twisted her hair into a rope and wound it around his wrist. Then he guided her from his mouth to his awaiting cock. Any other words they might have said were lost as her lips wrapped around him, her tongue hot and throat tight.

Even though she struggled with his size, she didn't resist when he forced her to take it all. His dick was hard to the point of pain, desperate for relief, but it'd never felt better as she swallowed around him.

"That's it." His voice came out broken and gritty as if he was begging for it—because he was. "Fuck, I missed this."

They were both out of breath when he finally let her up for air, but they didn't have time for breaks. He pressed her down again, keeping her hair locked around his wrist and allowing her to set the pace. Her saliva ran over his balls, her hands splayed on his thighs as the tips of her nails make little crescent marks in his skin. It was heaven and hell all at once, perfection yet one step short of completion.

His gaze caught on her bare back. He ran a hand along her spine, slipping his fingers between her ass cheeks. "Dammit," he rasped, agonizing over the fact that his dick couldn't be two places at once. "Wet for me again, sunflower?"

Serena replied with a moan that reverberated through his cock, and he had to bite his tongue to keep from coming on the spot.

"Mm, yeah. Your pussy knows what it needs." He played with her clit until her arousal coated his fingers, then pumped in and out of her as she bobbed up and down, filling her from both ends.

It didn't take long for her to start trembling, all the tricks he picked up earlier bringing her to the edge in a matter of minutes. And as much as he loved the thought of dragging this out more, he wasn't going to last much longer.

"You're too fucking sexy," he praised. "Such a dirty girl, hungry for my cock and my fingers at the same time. One orgasm just isn't enough, is it? Go on, give me one more."

She shuddered as her pussy latched onto his fingers, and his dick throbbed inside her mouth with jealous rage. That was another thing he hadn't done—given into the temptation of fully being inside a woman. The mere thought of filling not just anyone, but *her*, of how perfect her pussy would feel wrapped around his dick, her heat trapping him as she took her pleasure, was enough to drop-kick him straight over the finish line.

"Serena," he rasped, her name the only word that registered through the haze in his mind. "I'm—*fuck*—I'm coming."

His grip loosened, and she slipped her hand around his dick as the last strand holding him together snapped. A blinding void consumed his vision. Liquid heat shot through his veins. He groaned as he came in her hands, completely emptying his mind as thoroughly as his balls.

The air grew heavy with their labored breaths, and his heartbeat raced away as fatigue won over. Lord knew if he had the time and energy, he'd let them go all night. As it was, he didn't know if he'd be able to walk straight in the morning.

Serena raised her head, face flushed and satiated. He stroked her cheek and wiped away the drool from her chin. "Napkins...in the glovebox," he grunted.

She helped him clean up, and then they both dressed and headed back to the ranch. He could drive together like this for hours, his hand on her thigh, his thoughts filling with nothing but the sound of her voice.

As they rolled into the drive, Serena turned off the radio and he dimmed the headlights. He parked in the same spot, then they wordlessly crept along the back wall of the guesthouse. Just before reaching Serena's window, something cracked under his boot. He froze as she looked over at him. Lifting his foot, he caught the glint of metal and glass covered in dirt.

"Is that a watch?" she mouthed.

"Yeah," he whispered and kneeled to pick it up. The face had splintered in multiple places, and a deep scratch marred the band. They must have been thinking the same thing—this belonged to Connor, but how did it end up out here and with this kind of damage?

"I'll show it to the Westons in the morning," he concluded.

Serena shook her head. "How are you going to explain finding it outside the girls' guesthouse at whatever time it is now? Let me take it."

She held out her hand. He sighed before giving it up. "I don't like where this is going."

"Me either." Serena glanced up at a window on the second floor. "But we'll deal with it."

He nodded, and they crossed the short distance to her window. With a little effort and a lot of finesse to not make any noise, he hoisted her up, and she crawled back into her room.

"Night," he whispered. A sense of melancholy tugged inside his chest.

"Night." She bit her lip. "My answer is maybe, by the way."

Maybe? But he hadn't asked anything...

Oh, that.

"You didn't have to ans—"

She pressed a finger to his lips, then closed the window and drew the curtains shut.

He stood outside for another minute as his mind struggled to piece it all together. When he asked the question, he hadn't been clear, nor did he himself know what he'd really intended to say—so did she mean *maybe* to falling in love with the countryside...or with him?

EIGHTEEN

Serena

"You look exhausted." Renae sat beside her as they gathered for lunch.

Richard joined on the opposite end of the table, and she was glad to see several others automatically fill in the empty spaces. Slowly but surely, everyone at the ranch had begun to feel like a mini-community.

At least, everyone but Connor and his 'boys club,' who made it their mission to drag their feet and ignore the leaders who tried to encourage them—but luckily, they were the minority.

"That's 'cause I am." Serena stopped mid-bite and replayed her words. Had country slang already slipped into her speech? Almost two weeks of living at Hollow Oak, and nothing had gone as she expected. She groaned and scooped up a bite of Mrs. Weston's taco salad.

Renae laughed while picking at her own food. "Same. I can't wait to go home." She sighed. "I miss my dad's cooking. And pizza."

"Your dad cooks? Mine just buys us takeout when it's his turn." A few of the girls pivoted closer to Renae, and they broke off into their own conversation about homesickness and family meals.

Not long ago, Serena would have been the first to complain about being stuck in this dusty no-man's land. But now...

She lifted her eyes to the large windows that stretched to the ceiling. Thick, wooden beams framed a view of golden fields where the sun shone relentlessly, the air dry enough today to scorch her lungs. It reminded her of how cool and refreshing the river had felt last night. Of how she'd gotten used to watching clouds move across the sky or looking toward the mountains to see what the weather would be like in an hour.

Of thinking that her perspective about life might not be as complete as she first thought—or maybe the life she'd chased after for so long wasn't what she wanted anymore.

From the view outside, she caught a glimpse of Lucy happily grazing in a small pasture. Her recovery was going well, according to Grant and the vet who visited this morning. Lucy had finally been allowed to go out on her own for a few hours each day and, despite the heat, meandered as far away from her stall as possible. Serena didn't blame her. Spending the morning in the stuffy tack room had put sweat stains on her shirt, and she was more than grateful for a break in some air conditioning.

She tuned back into the conversation just as one of the girls complained, "I hate sharing bathrooms. The hot water runs out in two minutes."

"Tell me about it," Renae chimed in. "I have no time to get ready in the mornings, and my hands are a wreck."

They took turns placing their hands on the table, showing new calluses and chipped nails. Serena glanced at her own fingers, scowling at how awful they looked. Odd that she hadn't noticed until now. "Oh yeah, I'd give anything to go to a salon." Serena inwardly cringed at such a shallow problem, but she *did* like looking nice. "Can't believe I'll be holed up in a barn for my birthday."

"Wait, it's your birthday?" one of the girls asked.

Serena nodded. "This Saturday."

"I heard we have to put up two miles of fencing this weekend," Renae grumbled. "So maybe you won't be in a barn?"

"*Great*," Serena emphasized. She'd forgotten to check the schedule to see what project they had this weekend. "Sweating my tits off and getting a sunburn sounds like a much better birthday party."

"Well, we can't have that...but remember to mind your language." Mrs. Weston popped into view and gave her a stern look. The group scooched over to make room at the table.

Most of the guests had been cautious around the Westons at first, but they were only strict when it came to keeping everyone focused. Both shared bits of their life story during workshops, including the less fortunate years and had earned almost everyone's respect after admitting their mistakes—and explaining what it had cost them.

"Sorry. I'll find a way to make it through," Serena added. It really wasn't that serious, anyway.

"Name your favorite dessert," Mrs. Weston replied. "I'll make something special Saturday night."

"For real?" Serena perked up.

Mrs. Weston chuckled. "All work and no play makes Jack a dull boy. We're still going to put up that fence, though."

A collective sigh of disappointment arose from the group.

"Ice cream sundaes sound good," Serena suggested. "Everyone could pick a topping they like." It would make a perfect treat after a hot day.

That cheered up the crowd, and they began flooding Mrs. Weston with requests. She nodded at each one in turn, seemingly able to remember them all at once.

Everyone might grumble when they got the chance, but the kids deserved a reward for working hard. They showed a lot of improvement, not just in attitude but also in their workshops, and this would give them something to look forward to instead of missing home.

Mrs. Weston leaned over and held her hand up in a stage whisper. "Don't tell him I said this, but this'll officially make you older than Grant, so you get bragging rights, too."

Wait...how would Mrs. Weston know? Oh—she had filled out a medical form along with a safety waiver of some sort before going to the ranch. Mrs. Weston must have seen her birth year. But somehow, she hadn't pictured her and Grant being so similar. "We're the same age?"

"Mhm," Mrs. Weston hummed. "Until Saturday, that is. Grant will catch up to you in October."

Something about the barely-there smile on her face felt off. Like she'd given out secret information. But by October, the program would be over. They'd be back to their normal lives, and anything between her and Grant...they both knew it wasn't meant to be a permanent thing.

Serena set down her fork and pushed away her plate, no longer hungry. "Too bad he won't have his party with the rest of us."

"Indeed, it is," Mrs. Weston agreed, and the conversation drifted in a different direction.

Ten minutes before lunch ended, the harsh screech of a chair filled the room. Connor stood and glowered at their table as he stalked into the kitchen. Serena frowned. He and Richard were still on alternating dish duty. Neither seemed happy about it, but Richard hadn't complained or used it as an excuse to be late. They weren't any closer to being on talking terms, but from the tension in the air, things would come to a head sooner or later.

As the rest of the group finished and started gathering for

the afternoon workshop, Serena motioned to Renae to stay behind. They hadn't gotten the chance to speak at breakfast, but she didn't want to delay this any longer. "Wait a sec."

Renae shared a look at Richard, then he nodded and left with the others. "What's up?"

Serena reached into her pocket and pulled out the broken watch to show Renae under the table. "I found this outside the guesthouse last night. It was by your window."

Renae's eyebrows furrowed. "I swear I didn't take it."

"I know." Serena put the watch away before someone else saw. "I think Connor wanted to frame you. If he's anything like the guys I used to hang out with, then the fact that nothing's happened will bother him until he gets his way."

"He needs to back the fuck off." Renae glared over toward the boys. "If my brother won't do anything about it, then I will."

Serena reached out and touched her arm. "Hey, hold on."

"Sorry." Renae paused and took a breath. "It just gets under my skin."

"You have a right to be mad—I feel the same way, but that's what he's counting on." An old-fashioned conversation with fists might be what Connor actually needed, although she couldn't admit that here and didn't want Renae getting hurt in the crossfire. "I could show this to the Westons, but I wanted to ask what you wanted to do first. It might work against you."

Renae considered before responding. "Hiding it from them might also work against me. Go ahead and tell them. If you're right about Connor, then all we have to do is prepare for him to try something stupid." She took a breath and regained her composure. "Actually, some of the girls brought it up, and we talked about what happened the other night. My roommate knows I didn't do it, and several of them sensed something off about Connor. I think they'd help keep an eye out if I asked."

Serena nodded. "That sounds like a good plan."

Renae gathered her plate, visibly less stressed than she'd

been last week. "Turns out having friends is kinda nice," she added. "We all have our own issues, but you know, that's what makes helping each other easier."

Serena grinned, proud to see Renae embracing her new friends. "I'm glad you found a way to work together. We'll figure this thing out, I promise."

Renae nodded and went off to join the others. Serena stayed behind and pretended to nibble on her food. This drama might feel inconsequential, but she'd seen how fast things could escalate. Seen how someone could hide their darkest side until it came down to the line, and she was tired of watching good people get hurt.

Her eyes locked with Grant's from across the room. She hadn't come here wanting to find friends, much less anything—or anyone—else. She certainly hadn't expected to find someone like him. A person who had every right to cast her aside but hadn't. Someone who cared about her without needing a reason to.

He'd said her name when he came in the car. Not a nickname, not a curse, not the name of the girl who broke his heart.

She'd wanted to hear him say it again every night since.

But regardless of their age, his experience with love far outweighed her own. Every other person she'd fucked with had been an exchange, simply for the benefit of pleasure or an ego boost. There'd been no use complicating it with emotions. Besides, no one had given her a reason to fall for them, and she hadn't cared to look for one.

Grant was completely different. She didn't need a reason to fall for him—she just had.

And unlike anyone else, he was the first person she'd regret having to walk away from.

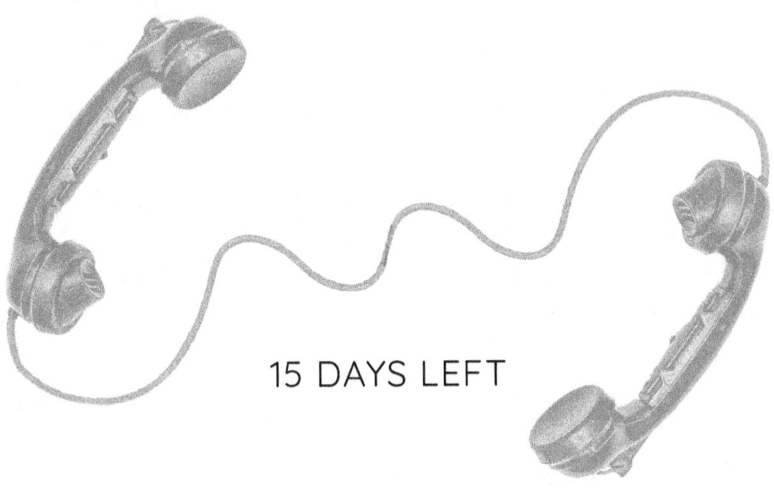

15 DAYS LEFT

Lexi:

"Happy freaking birthday!"

Serena:

"Shh! You're gonna get me in trouble making the phone ring this late. But thank you."

"You really think I'd let someone else be the first to wish you happy birthday?"

"Never in a million years."

"So...what's the update with bootylicious in the boots?"

"You're having too much fun with those nicknames."

"Why, yes I am. Don't hold out—give me all the details."

"I can confirm, cowboys are hot."

"I have eyes, ya know. Don't I at least get the PG-13 option?"

"If you insist...he's a ten. And I mean in inches."

"Whew. Okay, yeah. I don't wanna know the rest. I guess you're doing all right, then."

"Yeah, I'm good."

"I sense a *but* coming."

"The only butt here is one covered in Wranglers."

"Omg. Seriously, what's the hesitation for?"

"Grant's a really good guy."

"...and you caught feelings."

"It's hard not to."

"Then why fight it?"

"Cause he lives in a different world. I wasn't even supposed to be here."

"You know that's just an excuse."

"I haven't told him about everything yet."

"Do you want to?"

"I'm not sure."

NINETEEN

Grant

THE SCENT OF FRESH COFFEE WAFTED THROUGH CRISP MORNING air as dew drops sparkled on the grass. A few clouds stretched across a sky painted in blended hues of indigo, pink, and orange. This time of day, outside was cool enough to counter the burn in his lungs, his muscles warm and mind quiet.

He jogged up the stairs of the front porch and laced his hands behind his head, taking slow breaths in through his nose and out through his mouth. Every day before breakfast, he took guests on an early run around the front pastures. It was a task he genuinely enjoyed—got the blood pumping and energy flowing for the rest of the way. Plus, mornings were the one time no one cared to complain. Even Connor acted somewhat more pleasant, though he made it a point to run ahead of the group.

But it hadn't taken long for Serena to become as adamantly opposed to morning cardio as she was to the cowbell, and soon, she'd managed to find a way around it. Mrs. Weston found an old CD player for meditational music and some blankets to use for stretches and palates instead of jogging. Quite a few of the guests appreciated having a second option, including Richard and a handful of the guys.

The general mood on the ranch had steadily improved with Serena's suggestions. Mrs. Weston kept hinting that he should convince her to come back next year. As if he needed more reasons to want to keep her around.

He paced in a small circle, nodding to guests as they went inside for food and watching Serena's group finish up in the first rays of dawn. She turned her face to the sun, hair a bright silhouette of golden light. The tank top and leggings she wore molded to her body, and it wasn't hard to remember the way she looked without them.

Memories of cold water and warm skin flooded his mind. The way his heart raced when they kissed. How his thoughts calmed whenever they spoke.

His breath caught—and it had nothing to do with the run.

The scene was exactly the kind of thing he'd wanted for himself when he pictured growing old. A beautiful woman on a beautiful stretch of land, surrounded by peace and the potential to live any way they wanted. Someone whose company he could enjoy no matter what they were doing. Even when their bodies ran out of youthful energy, she'd still have her bright spirit and inquisitive nature.

He shook his head and looked away, not wanting to get caught staring too long. Serena had made it clear that life in the country wasn't a part of *her* dreams. And even if he could make her stay worthwhile, he had no right to ask for more. He'd seen what happened when people felt an obligation to a place or a person who didn't share their vision. Even if they claimed to be in love.

Voices broke through his thoughts as Serena's group got up and folded the blankets, then strolled into the main house to join the others for breakfast. Saturdays at Hollow Oak were as much of a work day as any other. Animals still needed to be fed, chores wouldn't do themselves, and staying active outside felt better than being cooped up indoors.

Today wasn't any Saturday, though. It was Serena's birthday.

She walked up beside him and propped a hip on the porch railing, amusement flashing in her brown eyes. "I'm gonna start a petition. Cowboys should wear gray sweatpants more often."

He chuckled and tried to brush off the rise of satisfaction from her words. Yeah, he'd have to change out of these sweatpants. Not unless everyone wanted to see how *happy* she made him. "Noted. And city girls should come out more often to see country sunrises."

"You were watching me." Her eyebrows lifted, but the corner of her eyes crinkled. She liked the attention. Good thing he liked giving it to her.

He grinned. "It's hard not to, sunflower."

She gave a satisfied hum and turned to look out toward the barn. "I was just enjoying a calm moment before being forced into hard labor for the rest of the day."

He snorted. After breakfast, the guests would load up a bus and head to McLauren's property to fix up a stretch of cable fencing. The winter storms had done a number on their farm, and on top of that, Bill had been diagnosed with cancer last year. His wife was worried she wouldn't be able to keep things maintained by herself and had considered selling some of the land. Not to mention the medical expenses.

Today would mean the world to them. And the guests were going to love her hand-squeezed lemonade. He was kinda jealous to be missing out.

"I have good news," he announced. "Grab something to eat, and then you're coming with me."

Serena turned, trying to look skeptical, but her enthusiasm was impossible to miss. "Where are we going?"

His grin widened. "Nothing too exciting." Their last escapade had far surpassed his expectations; unfortunately, they wouldn't get to be alone today. "Gotta run into town for a few things. The Westons wanted to visit with the McLaurens, so they asked if we could take care of it."

He shuffled his feet and ran a hand along the back of his neck. A few nights ago, he'd had no second thoughts about stripping down together, but when it came to doing something sweet, he wasn't sure how straightforward to be.

Because if it were up to him, he'd take her out on a proper date, bring her home with a bouquet of flowers, and pretend she was the only woman in the world.

"Thought you might wanna come along." He shrugged. "Pick out a birthday present or somethin'."

She raised an eyebrow and bit back a smile. "You better not be joking."

He pursed his lips. "That depends on whether you can bring me a coffee without switching the salt for the sugar."

Serena gave him a playful shove, and went into the house. She reappeared with a steaming mug in each hand and had her head turned, saying something over her shoulder with a guilty grin.

He tipped his head in a silent question.

Serena rolled her eyes. "Renae thinks you're taking me on a date. I told her it's not like that."

"Oh, really now?" he teased. He knew it wasn't like that. But it could be.

She handed over his coffee and set hers on the railing. Anyone looking would notice they were a little too close, a little too comfortable existing within each other's space. Probably too happy for people who had immediately gotten off on the wrong foot.

"When you take me on a date, it's not gonna count as part of my community service," Serena muttered.

His smile felt like it split his face in two. *When*. Not *if*. He could work with that.

"Sounds like a plan."

Serena blew on her coffee, took a sip, and then set it down. A moment of silence passed before she spoke. "You still haven't asked about what I did to end up here."

He rubbed his thumb against the ceramic mug. They'd chosen to share a few intimate moments, but he'd be arrogant to assume he was entitled to more. If she wanted to share anything else with him, that would be her choice, too. Honesty shouldn't depend on whether someone asked the right questions.

"You can tell me whenever you want me to know."

She chewed her lip. "What if it's not just what I did? What if it's who I was?"

"Sunflower." He set down his cup and took her face in his hands. "I don't give a damn about who you were. As long as you figure out who you want to be, I'll help you get there."

She nodded with a small smile. Before he did something rash, like kiss her without caring about the consequences or who saw, he dropped his hands and picked up his coffee.

"I don't know who I want to be yet," Serena whispered low enough so only he could hear. "But I'm starting to enjoy who I am with you."

His heartbeat must have been loud enough to echo across the whole valley. It certainly must have been loud enough to say what he couldn't. That he hoped she liked him enough to stay.

TWENTY

Serena

The sundress she packed had been left tucked in a corner of the suitcase, wrinkled from neglect. She'd only taken it to demonstrate how unfit she'd be for any kind of excessive work —but it turned out the job wasn't bad, after all. And she didn't need fancy clothes to impress Grant.

At least today the dress would come in handy, and a change of pace felt nice. As Renae and the rest of the guests pulled out on a bus headed to the McLauren's farm, she and Grant drove in the opposite direction, armed with a shopping list from Mrs. Weston and a credit card.

Once they got off dusty dirt roads—back to pavement and civilization—she rolled down the window and let warm wind blow through her hair, tapping her fingers on the ledge to the beat of the radio. Driving like this had kinda become their thing. Just vibes and good times. And she loved it.

Country fields speckled with silos and farmhouses slowly merged into smaller plots of townhomes, with rusted cars parked out front and dogs barking from spacious backyards. Several had been well-kept, the vintage architecture a refreshing change from the sleek functionality she grew up around. Other properties weren't so lucky, their roofs either missing shingles or covered with tarps, the siding patched in mismatched paint, and porches so slanted she worried they'd fall off just from her looking too long.

Until now, her stay at the ranch had felt secluded, cut off from the rest of the world. She'd almost forgotten that the town had other inhabitants—not all had abundance to share like the Westons, either. What were their stories? And where did Grant fit into all of it?

They passed by the local grocery store, a couple of bars, and an antique shop that was probably as old as the merchandise inside. Then they pulled into an empty parking spot on Main Street. A bright turquoise storefront caught her attention, and she sat forward for a better look. Small flowers decorated the display window, and cursive writing on the sign read *Mirage Salon*. It instantly pulled her in.

The radio went silent as Grant turned off the engine. "So, did I guess right?" He looked over with a sheepish grin. "Would this place have something suitable for my birthday girl?"

She pursed her lips to hide a growing smile. "Oh, but I thought you're opposed to all things that aren't practical. What did you say again about my 'uptown style'?"

Grant broke out in a hearty laugh. "I said if you were going to tempt me, then you wouldn't get your way that easily." His green eyes shone under the shadow of his hat, and he lowered his voice. "Not that I didn't want to see you try."

Inside the truck, his well-built frame and broad shoulders dominated the space. Heat simmered under her skin. Holding his gaze, she leaned over the center console. "Who's trying to tempt who?"

Slowly, he traced his thumb over her cheek and brushed the hair from her face, deliberately dropping his eyes to her mouth. Then he brought his lips to the shell of her ear. His low, throaty hum sent a shiver down her spine. "If I wanted to tempt you, sunflower...would you be able to resist?"

Most certainly not.

The salon's door opened with a clatter of bells, and she jumped back, her heartbeat racing a little too fast.

That had been close. What were they thinking? In a place this small, it wouldn't take much to start the rumor mill. They had two more weeks together, and after that, she'd be gone. The less people who had something to gossip about, the better off for him when she left. They had to be more careful.

A frown pulled at the corners of Grant's mouth, but it disappeared, and he cleared his throat. "We only have a few hours, so we should probably get going."

She agreed and reached for her purse. "Hold on, I left my window down."

"It'll be fine. Better to let the breeze in, anyway." Grant opened his door and squinted up at the sky. "Doesn't look like rain anytime soon."

She shook her head. "Good to know, weatherman."

He gave her a knowing look, his dimple appearing with a lopsided grin. They both knew she'd picked up his habit of relying on her senses more than the weather app. Of relying more on her intuition in general—even though something definitely felt off at the moment. She pushed it aside as they walked together to the salon.

Grant stepped ahead and held open the door. "Ladies first."

"Why thank you," she replied in her most 18th-century maiden voice.

Who knew going out with a man could be this enjoyable? Jace had only sent her off with a wad of cash and expected her to come back with both their errands done. His version of a date had been exclusive to the bedroom. Even on that front, Grant was far more creative.

The salon itself looked gorgeous. Clean glass accents

complimented pearly white walls and natural wood flooring. Several spa stations lined the right side, while a small desk and waiting area occupied a nook on the left. Plants and hanging vines filled the gaps, basking in the ample sunlight and showing off small pastel blooms. It felt like stepping into an oasis. A place like this in the city would always be busy, but they were the only ones here.

"Grant, long time no see," a woman greeted from the front desk as the chime announced their presence. Her flaxen red hair had been styled in a loose Dutch braid, and long bangs framed a youthful, freckled face.

The way she smiled at them was a little *too* friendly. Not that it mattered—Grant was a single man. Casually fluffing her hair, Serena put on her most charming smile. No, it didn't matter because she'd make sure to be the better option for him, anyway.

"Hey Melissa," Grant replied. "Can't say I'd have any reason to stop by more often."

"For the hundredth time, call me Missy." The woman's hazel eyes turned to Serena, and they faced off in a smiling duel. "You brought me a new customer! To whom do I owe the pleasure?"

"Serena," she cut in, keeping her voice light enough to sound polite. "I'm working with Grant at the summer program."

"Ah, I see." Missy's eyes flickered between them, obviously reevaluating the situation.

"I am in desperate need of a refresh." Serena flashed her nails and approached the counter, where several color samples and binders of hairstyles were propped on display. "Grant really should have brought me here sooner."

"Melissa and I went to high school together," Grant explained, stepping up beside her. "She left to get her cosmetology license and came back here with a husband to boot."

Wait. She was married?

Missy laughed. "Well, there's a little more to the story than that. Getting hitched wasn't part of the plan. But life doesn't always work out how we expect..." Her gaze flicked away from Grant as she trailed off, then she splayed her hands on the counter. "What can I do for you today? Mani, pedi—both? Don't be shy to ask for whatever you need."

Serena hummed as if trying to decide, but all her attention was on Grant. It really wasn't her place to intrude, yet the unknown history between them had worked its way under her skin like a relentless itch. And she had to scratch it.

She picked up a palette of reds and pinks, then tipped her head toward him. "When was the last time you got your nails done?"

"Woah—you're gonna drag me into this?" he joked, stepping away.

Without thinking, she hooked a finger in his belt to pull him back. "Everyone knows it's no fun to do these things alone."

"Is that so?" he murmured.

She shrugged, feigning ignorance as he narrowed his eyes.

Missy nodded in approval. "I promised not to tell a soul, but my husband gets his feet done once a month. Completely worth it, if you ask me."

It was proving hard to dislike Missy when she had such a kind attitude.

Grant wiped a hand over his face. "Trust me, neither of you want to go anywhere near my feet."

Missy raised her eyebrows. "I've seen it all. Just remember to tip me extra when you realize the calluses are gone."

Serena gave him her best puppy-dog eyes. He groaned.

"Fine. You two win. But don't blame me when the boots come off."

Missy clapped her hands. "Excellent. I'll get things set up. Why don't you two find a spot and get comfy? Serena, take whatever color you want while I grab some things from the back." Missy motioned to the case of nail polish and left them alone.

Grant shot Serena a warning glare. "I don't know what's gotten into you, but you should be careful. If you give me a boner, I intend to use it."

She bit her lip with a gasp. "How bold of you."

"Try me." Her eyes widened, and he smirked.

Resisting the temptation to do just that, she led him to one of the salon chairs and they sat down as Missy came out with a rolling cart of supplies. "Alrighty! I got everything ready to go, plus deodorizing spray for your boots." Grant scoffed as Missy shook the can. She laid out towels on their footrests, then set two basins of warm water that smelled like lavender and sage next to the chairs. "We'll do a quick soak first, so get settled in."

Serena hung her purse on the arm of the chair and removed her sandals. The warm water felt heavenly on her worn feet. "Grant mentioned you went to high school together?"

"Mhm," Missy hummed. "I'd been best friends with Payton since elementary school. Kinda shocked us all when everything went down and she left for good." That must be Grant's ex. Serena glanced over at him. Missy didn't miss a beat. "Oh, he didn't tell you..."

"He mentioned her," she added, not wanting to throw him under the bus. "I didn't ask for details."

Grant sighed and tentatively put his feet in the water. "I do have a life outside of wallowing in self-pity."

Missy tsked as she blasted Grant's shoes with spray. "And

I'm not blind. You've always worn your heart on your sleeve. Not to mention even Payton wouldn't have been able to get you in one of these chairs. I can tell you two are more than coworkers."

Grant looked at Serena with a silent inquiry.

"It's...complicated," she said.

Grant leaned back in the chair. "Maybe it'd be better for a mutual party to tell the story."

"That's a tall order, but I can try." Missy pulled over a stool and soaked a cotton ball in nail polish remover. "Let's get this old paint off, first."

Serena let Missy take her hands as she continued. "Like I said, I thought Payton and I were close. She knew every guy I'd ever had a crush on, but I had no idea what she'd been up to." Missy's face fell, and memories danced around her eyes. "I got the call from her mom at six in the morning. Grant was already at the hospital when I arrived."

"She had me as her emergency contact," he added, voice flat. "They said she'd been in a car accident—that was all I knew at the time."

Missy shook her head. "Kev was in the next room over. They were both pretty bruised up, lucky to be alive. Later, we all found out they'd been drinking and decided to take a night drive. Went too fast around a curve and caught a loose patch of gravel. Ended up flipping the car."

Serena's heart plummeted. "That sounds terrifying."

"I'm sure it was." Missy finished with her fingers, then motioned for Grant to lift his feet. "We all had a lot of questions. Our friend group was kinda close. When it came out why they'd been together—what had been going on behind closed doors—" She pursed her lips and went silent for a few seconds, focusing on her work.

"Some people said they saw it coming," she continued.

"That Payton wasn't the type to settle down with a good guy. It made me sick. She and Grant were the dream." Missy's eyebrows pinched together. "Kev left to get therapy in the city, and Payton followed. I lost contact with her after that."

Serena looked over at Grant, who was staring out the front window at the street. That was a hell of a lot worse than he'd implied. "I'm so sorry," she whispered.

He blinked and turned toward her. "It's over. Nothin' to be sorry about."

Missy finished and wiped off his feet with a light hum. "There. Feel better?"

He wiggled his toes. "Actually, yeah."

She grinned. "You're welcome."

Grant took out his phone and checked the time. "As much as I've enjoyed crashing your gal session, there's some things I need to pick up before we go to the store. Mind if I head out and come back when you're done?"

"We should be finished in an hour," Missy offered.

"It'd be awful if you happened to leave me here overnight," Serena teased half-heartedly, still processing what she'd heard.

Grant scoffed and bent to pull his socks and boots back on. As he got up and passed the counter, he opened his wallet and tossed several bills behind the desk.

"Hey, I brought my purse. I can pay," Serena called.

He chuckled. "When will you figure out I'm the kind of guy who likes to take care of my woman?"

Emotion tightened in her stomach as he tipped his hat to them and walked out of the salon. Shock. Gratitude. Guilt.

This whole time, she hadn't known Grant at all.

She'd been pretending they could act like a couple when no one was watching and then go back to strangers whenever it was convenient. But that's the very thing his ex did behind his back to ruin their relationship. On top of that, she'd normalized taking far too many chances with alcohol—driving with people who were less than sober and ignoring the safeguards. Putting herself at risk without a second thought. Choosing to party with people who only cared about taking off her clothes.

If Grant knew *her* past, he'd realize the truth: that, in the end, she was exactly what he'd been trying to get away from.

TWENTY-ONE

Grant

Bringing Serena into town had struck a chord in both of them—but judging from the expression on her face when he left the salon, he wasn't sure it had been the same one.

He hoped she'd find some part of the place he called home as charming as he did. There really wasn't much to brag about; their small town had little to offer in the shopping department, but Serena had surprised him in more than one way before. Even if the city offered more amenities, it was also crowded and impersonal. In this part of the country, real entertainment came from the land and the people who lived on it.

She and Missy seemed to hit it off well. Although, he hadn't expected to fall down the rabbit hole of Payton's accident. Not that he'd been trying to hide it. Just that he didn't think it mattered anymore. He didn't *want* it to matter anymore. Serena brought the sun back into his life, and he'd be damned if he let her slip away because of what she learned.

After he left to buy personal supplies, he checked on her secret present, then picked out a nice card and hid it in the truck. When her nails were finished, they went to the grocery store and filled two carts with food for this week's meals and her special birthday sundaes.

Even a mundane task like walking through the freezer aisle with her had been entertaining. She wasn't a particularly efficient shopper, picking things out with her eyes rather than relying on the list. They kept having to backtrack for items they missed, but it hadn't felt like a chore. Doing just about anything with her had turned into his favorite pastime. Not to mention how much he enjoyed seeing her prance around in a sundress, the definition of beauty itself.

However, it bothered him that she acted more distant than usual. Her smile faded back into one of social courtesy, and she'd passed up far too many opportunities to tease him. He missed her husky laugh and the mischievous glimmer in her eyes. Had he said too much earlier? Or not enough?

Unfortunately, they hadn't had the chance to address it. When they returned to Hollow Oak, there was another problem to tackle first—Mrs. Weston tasked them with preparing dinner, and he thought spaghetti with frozen meatballs would be simple enough—but Serena was a disaster in the kitchen.

"Should I remove the plastic before I put these in the oven?" She held up a stack of frozen dough for dinner rolls across the center island.

It was a miracle she'd survived this long without basic cooking instincts. "Pretty sure there's instructions on the box," he replied. Giving her the answer would be easier, but it was better if she learned for herself.

"I swear I looked for those...oh, found 'em," Serena hummed. A quick glance showed her nibbling on her lip as she read. She might be helpless, but she was still cute as hell. "Yep, gotta remove the plastic. First, I need to preheat the oven, then bake for twenty minutes."

"I already set the oven. It should be ready," he said.

Thank heavens the main house had air conditioning, or else it'd be hot enough inside to rival the sun. The ranch's kitchen underwent renovations a few years back and got upgraded with two ovens, a commercial stove, and a chest freezer to accommodate the summer guests. Plus, plenty of counter space to work, which was good because they were making a seriously huge amount of food. Two giant pots of spaghetti were already boiling on the stove as he worked on dumping cans of tomato sauce into aluminum trays of meatballs.

Serena popped three pans of rolls in the top oven as he carried over the meatballs. "Can you open the bottom one for me?"

"You got it!"

He smiled at her enthusiasm. Compared to when she started the job, her ease at learning new things had grown exponentially.

She stepped aside and helped him put the last of the meal in to bake, then he glanced at the clock and let out a sigh of relief. "Should be done just in time."

Serena slumped against the center island and tipped her head back with an exaggerated sigh. "I thought I was getting out of work today, but I'm *still* sweating."

He leaned beside her and chuckled. The room fell silent as they took a moment to relax.

"Hey, has something been bothering you?" he asked after a pause. "You seem...off."

She looked away and tapped her nails on the countertop. "It's nothing."

Bullshit.

He pivoted to face her, bringing his hands to her sides and locking her against the counter. "Look at me."

A hint of apprehension crossed her face before she could hide it, then she licked her lips and looked up at him through her lashes. "Everyone will be back soon. Do you think we have time to—"

"I always have time for you," he interrupted.

If he had to work a little to get her talking, then so be it—and he wouldn't pass up an opportunity to enjoy her. Serena's pulse fluttered as he ran his nose along her neck and breathed in her scent. Fuck, she was always so responsive. He almost liked her more after a day outside than freshly showered.

She sucked in a shaky breath. "Grant...are you sure you're okay with this? We aren't—" She groaned as he sampled the salt on her skin. "This isn't an official thing between us."

She placed a hand on his chest without pushing him away. "I don't want to hurt you."

He pulled back enough to search her warm, brown eyes. The flush in her cheeks. A slight pout of her lip. Watching their connection fade twisted his gut like a hot knife. The feeling he'd come to associate with finding out the truth.

"I knew what I was getting into before we started," he said. "If this is just a fling—if that's what you want to believe, I'll accept it." He might as well have been bleeding out on the kitchen floor from saying those words. But he meant it.

"I'm not sure we can—that we should—be anything more." Her gaze flicked down.

He swallowed thickly. "What do you mean?"

"I've always been the girl who did whatever I wanted, whenever I wanted. I'm not used to anything else." She hesitated, then the rest spilled out all at once. "I ended up here because I was drunk in the backseat of a car with a guy who gave me favors for sex. I'm not going to pretend that's not who I was a few months ago. Or that I wasn't any better than your ex."

He watched her struggle to look into his eyes, then finally give in. They glistened with a pain he wished didn't cut him so deeply.

It was clear that no one had gotten this close to her before.

No one had earned her honesty, not the kind that stripped away her pride.

He also knew no one came here without a past. Bits and pieces of her life came out in the group meetings, but nothing this personal. Nothing that had the power to come back and hurt her.

"First of all, you're not Payton. You didn't promise yourself to anyone else, and I'm not expecting you to promise yourself to me." He slid the hand she'd placed on his chest up and around his neck, bringing their bodies flush. "But we should be clear with each other. Is that what this is—an exchange?" She shivered as he leaned in and kissed along her jaw to the hollow below her ear. "Using each other for our own benefit?"

He couldn't deny she'd been little more than a distraction at first. Something new and pretty to play with. But behind her shiny facade was a woman who had the power to do anything —to be anything she wanted. She only had to decide who that person was.

"No, it's..." She sighed and parted her lips, turning to indulge in a broken kiss.

Their hips rocked in sync, and blood rushed to his groin. It was damn near impossible to think when her tits were so soft and full, perfect for his hands. When her thighs were hot and smooth against the rough denim of his jeans. If this was the most of her he got, he'd still feel like the luckiest man in the world.

She squirmed when he gripped the ticklish curve of her waist, following it to her ass and lifting her on the counter. Empty cans and plastic wrap clattered to the floor. Neither of them cared.

"It's you," she panted, finally gasping for air. "You're the first person I think about in the morning. The first person I've wanted near me all the time, even if it doesn't lead to anything else. This whole place is a world I never knew existed, and you make me want to be a part of it. I don't know what to call that, but that's what this is to me."

He nipped at her skin and practically growled in satisfaction. She wanted him. Not just for a night. Not just for some ambiguous date in the future. She wanted him the same way he wanted her, which was a far more intense revelation than he imagined.

She dropped her head to his chest. "What if I want it...for more than right now?" Her words were a whisper as if merely saying them would be too big of a risk. "What if I mess it all up?"

He held his breath, overwhelmed by emotion and the straining need of his restricted cock. Her sundress had ridden up to offer a tease of her panties, and it was all he could do not to pull them to the side and reveal her pretty pearl underneath. To show her exactly how good they were together. That nothing else mattered. But some things were more important than fucking—even if he couldn't list more than one at the moment.

Exhaling, he threaded his fingers through her hair and held her to his chest. Against his heart, where she belonged. "You're right. You can't forget your past and pretend it didn't happen." He hooked a finger under her chin and lifted her face. "Otherwise, how would you ever learn? But don't condemn your future, either."

She smiled softly. "It's so easy to believe that when you're here." Then doubt sobered her expression. "What about when I go home? How is this going to work?"

"Just stay." He tugged her into him again and pressed his cheek to hers. "Stay here. Stay with me."

She shook her head at the same time his dick throbbed pleadingly against her thigh. "You make it sound so simple. I have to finish school, and I'd hardly be helpful around here, anyway."

"You really don't know how much you've done for me, do you?" he mumbled as the knife of truth twisted in his chest.

She brushed her lips over his and rubbed her thigh along his dick. "Is it more than this?"

A groan tore from the back of his throat. He shifted to grind his erection into her soft center. He could tell she was wet and ready for him, the dampness carrying her sweet, musky scent and wrapping around him like a velvet glove. The sting of their undefined fate only sharpened his hunger, turned his lust into greed.

"Yes. So much more than this." He flattened a palm between her shoulder blades and rocked her over his cock, putting extra pressure on her clit. "But you should know—if I have to play dirty to get you, sunflower, I will. I'll do whatever it takes." He locked their eyes. "Nothing can stop me from having you."

Losing wasn't an option. Not this time.

She opened her mouth, but the crunch of gravel jolted them back to reality and the roar of a bus turning into the drive ended their privacy. Immediately, he stepped back and let her straighten her clothes.

It didn't help that she looked like she'd been about to come.

However, her uncanny way of turning the tables on him kicked in, and that glint he loved so much sparkled in her dilated eyes. "You're always so sure of yourself, cowboy. Making this work might not be as easy as you think." She trailed a hand down his leg and casually whispered in his ear, "But I'd like to see you try."

TWENTY-TWO

Serena

FLUFFY CLOUDS FLOATED BY PEAKS OF SILVER-BLUE MOUNTAINS like giant balls of cotton candy—a blissful illusion compared to reality. Those same clouds did nothing to alleviate the sweltering heat or the taste of dust that had settled on her tongue. Forget a tan; she'd be burned to a crisp by the time they got back.

A subtle buzz of conversation overlaid the clink of shovels on rocky soil, and the metallic ring of a hammer and nails echoed through the open field. Part two of replacing the fence at the McLauren's was underway, and despite the working conditions, their group had progressed well. Only a 50-foot stretch or so stood between them and the finish line.

Surprisingly, most of the guests seemed eager to complete the job rather than annoyed that they had to return a second day. Guess they'd deemed it a worthwhile cause—or simply unavoidable. If nothing else, the work had worn out the group enough to discourage more drama.

She wiped a bead of sweat rolling down her face with a gloved hand and shifted her weight. "Whew, you did this for six hours yesterday?"

Renae snorted. "Yeah, while you were partying it up on the town, the rest of us were out here working our asses off."

Serena stretched her arms before picking up a U-shaped nail and positioning it over a cord of barbed wire. "Oh, really? I thought you enjoyed last night's dinner and ice cream." She glanced to the side with raised brows.

Renae rolled her eyes. "Yeah, sure. Thanks for being born on such a convenient date. Here"— she reached over and adjusted the nail— "if you hold it like this, it'll be easier."

In a single day, Renae had become an expert at fencing. All Serena learned was that a hammer was her arch nemesis. She'd been lucky enough not to ruin her new nails, even though she'd chosen clear polish so they'd be easy to patch up. As much as she loathed manual labor, her mini vacation to the salon had been just that—a break from work, not the end of it.

Ahead of them, Grant helped a separate team pull out the old, rotten posts and cut apart tangled wires. His shirt had become plastered to his skin and soaked in sweat, the muscles in his back and abdomen flexing as he lifted a broken log and tossed it into the bed of his truck. It was one hell of a distraction.

The cowboy hat cast a shadow over his face, but the lines of his dimpled smile showed as he joked with the others. Somehow, he found a way to make the most grueling tasks feel like just another day and one to be grateful for, too.

What a contrast to Jace, who had only made life more difficult. Even her hidden fears didn't seem so threatening with Grant around. She focused on pounding the nail into the new post. Despite her best intention not to be changed by the program, she cared—about him. About the ranch. About bettering herself and her life. Choosing things that wouldn't just benefit her in the moment but would lead to happiness in the years ahead.

Grant was definitely one of those things.

The way he'd always been open with her—so freely vulnerable and passionate—threatened to split her heart in two. But she couldn't stay like he'd asked. That felt too much like running away from her problems, and he deserved to be more than an escape plan.

Last night, she'd found a birthday card slipped under her door with his handwriting inside. It hadn't been a poetic message or confession of love, just a note to meet him in the loft after lunch. He hadn't needed to write his declaration for her to remember it: *If I have to play dirty to get you, sunflower, I will.*

And Grant playing dirty was a far more electrifying proposition than she'd prepared for.

❋

The bus jolted and bounced along the road as they rode back to Hollow Oak. Their bellies were full of sub sandwiches and hearts warm after a grateful farewell from the McLaurens. Grant looked deep in conversation with Richard across the aisle, while behind her, Renae chattered with her friends.

"Look, I got a tan!"

"I hate to break it to you, but that's a sunburn," Renae chuckled.

"Aw, come on." A fit of laughter followed from the others.

"Hey, Renae, I hope it's not rude to ask—I heard darker skin doesn't burn, but is that really true?"

"I wish I got a free pass. Just because I have more melanin than you doesn't make me immune to the sun."

"Ah, that makes sense. I call dibs on the shower, by the way."

"Not if I get there first."

Serena shook her head at their antics and turned around. "You can always use the hose outside."

Renae scoffed. "You're lucky you have a bathroom all to yourself."

"It comes in handy." Serena hummed. "Actually, I might visit Lucy first. I get dirty after walking her anyway. One of you can use my shower if that would help."

Renae's face lit up. "For real? You love that horse, don't you?"

Serena shrugged one shoulder. "Yeah, I guess I do." There were a lot of things she'd begun to love a lot about this place. "I can tell she's starting to feel better. One day, I want to see her compete again."

"That would be cool," her friend chimed in. "We aren't allowed to have pets at home 'cause grandma gets sick, but I like the horses here. They're so friendly."

The bus braked with a huff, and the girls looked out the window as the ranch's sign passed overhead. Then they started fussing about who would get to use Serena's shower as it slowed to a stop.

Before the doors opened, Mr. Weston stood to announce that, per the usual Sunday schedule, they had free time until dinner, and a small cheer erupted on the bus.

He cleared his throat. "I hope you've all experienced the importance of working as a team. What we accomplished in one weekend would have been impossible for any of you to do alone—or for the McLaurens. Good work. I expect to hear your reflections on that in tonight's group discussion."

He helped Mrs. Weston off the bus, and the rest of the guests followed. Serena waited for the crowd to file out and then rose to her feet, stepping off and veering left instead of straight toward her room. She *should* shower, but it'd be the best time to talk with Grant while everyone else was occupied.

Inside the barn, heat soaked through her sweat-dampened tank top, and the now familiar scent of dry hay filled the air. Lucy greeted her with an expectant whinny. They'd gotten into the rhythm of a quick treat after lunch, followed by a walk around the outdoor arena while Grant set up his afternoon lesson. Lucy had officially been allowed to go out on her own, but the vet wanted her to maintain twenty minutes of hand-walking every day.

"How's it going, girl?" Serena gave Lucy a few scratches under the straps of her halter, then took a treat from the bin and extended it in her hand. "Sorry, don't have time for our stroll today. You can blame Grant."

Lucy crunched on her treat and stared into Serena's eyes. Normally, the horse would get impatient if she didn't see the lead rope, but today, she stayed calm. Could horses understand even if words weren't spoken aloud? It certainly felt that way.

"Don't give me that look," Serena chided. "You love him, too."

Lucy nudged her hand, and as Serena reached out to give her more scratches, her words registered. Did she love Grant? What would that mean?

She sighed. "Look at me, getting my new nails all dirty just for you." Lucy closed her eyes as Serena hit her sweet spot. "Bet you'd like a spa day, too, huh? I could paint your hooves."

A snort sounded from the doorway, and Serena spun to see Grant striding through the barn. She froze. "How long have you been there?"

"Only long enough to hear about you wanting to paint a horse's hooves." His dimple flashed as he came to give Lucy a few scratches of his own. The horse looked to be in seventh heaven, absorbing both of their attention at once. "Don't think she'd care much for that, but if you brushed out her hair and braided it with ribbons, she'd happily trot around and collect admirers."

"Kinda sounds fun, actually," Serena replied.

"That's mostly done for English riding competitions, while Lucy here does western. But she would look good with a plaited mane." Grant entered the stall and reached over to unhook the half-door leading to the pasture. Sweat and sun had curled the tips of his hair around the edge of the hat, his shirt streaked with dried mud.

Lucy pivoted and happily pranced outside. "I haven't seen her limp at all recently," Serena noted. "Will she be able to compete next year?"

Grant hummed. "She should if her recovery keeps going well. Vet said he wants me to test her trotting this week."

"Then, for her next competition, I'll do her hair."

He laughed. "Sure thing, sunflower. She'll be extra enthusiastic if you're waiting with treats at the end."

His warm gaze turned on her—those same green eyes that had carefully watched over Lucy and then watched over her the same way for the past two weeks. The same quiet intelligence that always seemed to see more than he let on.

She took a deep breath. "You wanted to talk?"

He nodded up toward the loft. She'd only been up there once to store extra blankets. It'd be a cozy fit with the two of them, but no one would interrupt up there.

"We should be in the clear until dinner," he added.

"Then lead the way."

TWENTY-THREE

Grant

BARE FLOORBOARDS LET OUT A SOFT GROAN AS HE STEPPED OFF the ladder onto the loft. Hay lined the shallow walls, and an A-frame roof angled to a peak above their heads. Long, white linen curtains hung to one side of a large window that overlooked the pastures. A beam of light reflected off flecks of dust and radiated a warm glow into the intimate space.

If the well in the woods had been his escape, then this was his hidden sanctuary. If visiting the creek under the veil of night had been sneaking out, standing here in the luminance of day was coming home.

Except his definition of home had shifted once again. This time, not from a shattered illusion to the sting of reality, but from the only path he'd known to the spark of life that had rekindled since Serena showed up at Hollow Oak.

He turned just in time to see her pause on the ladder, the sun highlighting new freckles over her cheekbones and rich brown eyes focused below his waist. She flicked her gaze up to his and flashed a not-so-guilty smile.

She'd been staring at his ass.

Fuck, her unspoken thoughts left him just as helpless as his own. He shook his head with a brief sigh. "We haven't even started yet."

"Started what?" She playfully sank her teeth in her bottom lip, full and curved into a delicious tease.

Mercifully, she'd worn full-length pants for their work in the fields instead of her usual—and his favorite—shorts, but due to the heat, she'd stripped down to a thin tank top that might as well have been lingerie for what it did to his brain chemistry. Not to mention how his blood flow had already begun to revert south, an inevitable, if not underhanded, effect of her presence. How dare she be so casually provocative, so recklessly sinful, when he could barely manage to compose himself?

Serena finished climbing and stepped toward him. The earthen aroma of hay and her natural scent mixed with floral notes of lingering perfume, plunging him into a dizzy spiral. She looked up at him through her lashes. Warmth crept into his face, mirroring the flush in hers. "Gonna convince me to run away with you?"

The question hung in the air, and she reached to trace a hand up his thigh, dipping under the hem of his shirt. The fabric was still damp with sweat, torn from barbed wire, and streaked with stains. It didn't deter her; getting dirty never had, in the end.

But her movements felt different than usual. Thoughtful, almost introspective. As if she knew they came to talk, not touch—yet couldn't stop herself.

He shivered as her fingers slid over his skin. "Is it working?"

The truth was he had no plan. No elaborate scheme to get his way. Just a persistent throb in the center of his ribcage and an endless reel of future regrets playing through his mind.

All he had was his own honesty to lay bare next to hers, and hope they could make something of it. That whatever happened, they got to experience it together.

Her gaze flipped down in an unexpected sign of uncertainty. He lowered his head and brushed his lips over hers, preventing retreat. A barely perceptible sigh escaped from her hesitation, and he inhaled it for his own consumption. His hands sought out the heavy teardrops of her breasts, the curve of her hips, the swell of her ass...

"Grant, we've been working all morning. I'm—"

"Fucking *edible*," he finished, sealing their kiss.

Whatever protest she'd been about to utter crumbled as her mouth parted and he stroked his tongue along hers. He kissed her like she was his oxygen, like if he didn't get enough, then this burning in his chest would consume him entirely.

She kissed him back like she wanted him to burn.

His dick hardened into an impudent rod against the zipper of his jeans, apathetic to the voice of reason that whispered certain conversations should come first. Concepts of *first and last, now and later,* didn't apply when all he could focus on was pebbled nipples and how sweet she tasted after she came. The sound of his name when her voice grew thick with pleasure.

Serena must have also felt an urgency for more—to tear apart the last barriers between them—because she rucked up his shirt, and he finished the job, yanking it over his head. In the frenzy, his hat fell to the floor with a thud and pierced the barn's silence.

They froze. A shudder passed through them, and he broke the kiss.

"I shouldn't have started—" she whispered, then cut herself off and bent to pick up the hat. Her fingers circled the rim as she stretched on her toes to put it back on his head with a blush. "I like when you wear it."

"I like that you like it," he replied.

Tension sparked between them.

"It's hard not to get lost when you look at me like that," she breathed.

"Like what?"

Serena gave a slight shake of her head, and her lips quirked up. "Like you'd do anything if I asked."

It was his turn to bite his lip, still tingling and even less satisfied than before. He took a breath to ground himself. There was no time for a preamble, so he blurted the conclusion he'd come to after mulling it over all night. "I was wrong to ask you to stay here."

She opened her mouth to reply, and he silenced her with another kiss. Dammit, her lips were too warm, too soft. His hands stroked her jaw and guided the angle of their kiss. Every touch between them set off a biological earthquake that wrecked his system. And all he wanted was more.

"Hear me out," he whispered, keeping his thumb on her chin. A rasp slipped into his voice as he tried to focus on words—*logic*—instead of what was right in front of him. "I know you have your own life. I want you to keep reaching for your goals. You should finish school...and maybe I should, too."

She pulled back, hands splayed on his chest. A delicate wrinkle pinched the skin between her eyebrows. "What do you mean?"

"It's too late to register for fall semester, but I can go in the spring. I've been meaning to look into it for a while. Plus, it wouldn't be hard to drive here on the weekends if they need me." He pushed a stray hair behind her ear. "Then I can be a regular boyfriend, take you on dates where you dress up all pretty just how you like."

She scoffed despite the glimmer of a smile in her eyes. "You don't need to be *regular* to be my boyfriend." Then, her expression softened. "But I also don't want to be the reason you leave the place you love most. Don't sacrifice your goals for mine."

"I'm not," he insisted. "You thought you'd be miserable stuck out here, hate working with a guy like me." She let out a husky laugh, warm breath tickling his neck. He pressed his lips to her forehead. "Maybe you can help me enjoy the city in the same way."

She leaned into him with a soft sigh. "The city can be fun. I could show you my favorite restaurants and where college kids go not to be seen—but it's nothing compared to what I've experienced here." Her body melted against his. "To the magic of being out in the open, being free. I feel like a new person, and I want to keep that. I want to keep discovering new things with you by my side."

"Then we'll find a way to have both." He nuzzled into her hair. "As much as I enjoy looking up and seeing the Milky Way, I'd rather bury my face in your silky skin. Instead of hearing the crickets sing, I'd rather hear a symphony of your laughter and the melody of your moans. I want us to teach each other what it means to live no matter where we are."

At that, she raked her nails down his side and hooked her fingers in his belt. The sting of her desire fused with the image of long, red scratches on his skin, and he sucked in a desperate breath that offered no relief.

"It sounds too good to be true," she whispered. "We need to think it through. No rushed decisions."

"Alright." He knew his mind wouldn't change. Once he made it up, there was never any going back. But it was reasonable enough to let them form a proper plan. Especially when there were other things he'd rather be doing with their stolen hour.

"In that case, I'll let you think *long*"— he lifted her thigh and angled his hips into the place where neither of them wanted to wait— "and *hard* about it."

Serena tipped her head with a low, wispy exhale that felt like a direct caress around the crown of his cock, which was leaking precum and far beyond any capacity to be ignored. Her nails scratched over his flat nipples, leaving four bright red lines across his abdomen. The urgency from earlier twisted deeper, ensnared every atom in his being, and tied them to hers.

"Let me give you this, at least," he panted into her neck. "Something I haven't given anyone else."

TWENTY-FOUR

Grant

HE'D BROUGHT THEM HERE TO AMEND HIS FAULTS, NOT TO TUMBLE head-first into offering himself on a platter. But that's where they ended up—and nothing had ever felt this significant.

Nothing before Serena had felt truly complete. Like he'd been waiting for a future that never came. Now, he had something better. He'd found a woman who not only fell in love with his world but wanted to show him hers. A person who taught him to embrace the freedom that'd been right in front of him the whole time.

And he wasn't going to let it pass him by.

Serena hooked her leg around his hip and rolled against him, the heat of her pussy bleeding through their jeans and sending a hot coil of pleasure along his shaft. "You've never done this...had sex?" Her voice came out incredulous, cut with a dark, covetous undercurrent.

He looked up from her neck to see her eyes flutter open. "No. Not like this."

Not in the full sense of penetrating a woman—nor in the sense of how it physically pained him to be outside of her. Like he might suffocate just from abstaining.

Not like me and you.

He rocked his hips again, letting the jagged friction steal his breath and watching her lips part in a silence gasp. The dark pink of her tongue darted out between her teeth, and he vividly recalled how it felt to be buried in her throat. The way she had swallowed and stroked him, how he hadn't been able to stop thinking about it ever since. How he knew being in her pussy would feel a million times more euphoric.

"You're asking me to take your virginity," Serena clarified on the tail end of a moan. She didn't phrase it as a question. It was a statement. A declaration.

"Yes."

"Will it mean something?"

They had both agreed *they* meant something, that the cavity in his chest had been hollowed out explicitly for her, but this was more pointed. Would his first time matter? Did he want it to?

He paused. "Yes."

She groaned and dropped her head to his shoulder. "I just said we needed to wait, and that makes this all the more selfish, but..." Her voice lowered to a fractured whisper. "I want it. Please."

He'd asked for this, could hardly function without the thought of stripping himself bare right here, right now—but *her* begging for it? Hearing *her* voice break?

He practically disintegrated at her feet.

"Fuck."

With one hand planted on her hip and the other working open his zipper, he spun them and bent her over the nearest hay bale. His balls already felt tight and heavy, his cock all but ravenous. This wouldn't be sweet—it wouldn't be candles and romance and lovemaking. It was flesh on flesh, a carnal feast that he'd starved himself of for far too long.

"It's yours," he panted. "All of it is fucking yours. Every inch, every drop." He groaned at the thought. "Damn, it's going to be so much."

Just before he shoved his clothes down his hips—boxers and all—Serena's hand circled his wrist. His dick throbbed incessantly beneath their palms.

"It's not just this moment that I want." Bent at the waist, she had turned to look at him over her shoulder and wore the most erotic expression he'd ever seen. Sun-bleached hair lay in a golden waterfall down her back, her clothes rumpled to show off the tan skin at her hips. Lips parted and plump, eyes fixed on his.

"It's not just here, not just now," she whispered. "Not just once. I know we can't be anything official until after I go home, but I can't stand the thought of leaving without knowing we'll be more." She took a breath. "What I'm trying to say is this means something to me, too."

He leaned down and pressed his body into hers, capturing her in a heady kiss. "I know."

Her skin proved to be too tempting, her torso trapped under his chest and thighs flush with his. He smoothed a hand up to cup her breast. The flicker of her heartbeat raced against his fingertips. "You try to act like nothing affects you under the surface, but I see the truth. You want me as deep inside your flesh and bone as much as I'm about to be in that tight, hot pussy."

At that, she deepened the kiss and curled her hand around his cock, forcing a strangled moan from his lips.

He bit into her shoulder to muffle the noise. "I can't wait any longer."

He fumbled for the condom in his back pocket as Serena shoved down her jeans, leaving only the red string of her underwear between them.

"You came prepared," she noted.

"Had it on me since we went to the river," he admitted. "Got the extra-large one, so it won't break." Sure, they hadn't been the most meticulous when it came to protection, but he wasn't ignorant, either. Even if she was on birth control, he didn't want to increase the risk to their health or wellbeing.

"So, you were thinking about it the whole time," she murmured, still looking back at him. Except now, her lips were stained to match the flush in her cheeks, her hair messy and tossed over one shoulder. She arched her back and pushed her hips in the air, making her ass even more round and large against his bare thighs. "Did you dream about it? About being inside me?"

"Yes," he admitted, voice ragged and broken. "I dreamed about it. Woke up in wet sheets and then fantasized about it again in the shower. I think about you too damn much, sunflower. All the time. I can't stop. *Oh, shit—*"

His brain short-circuited as he pushed aside her underwear and spread her open, saw the place he was about to fill, how wet and pink and swollen she was. Where he'd have to thrust to make her take him in. Her clit shined with arousal, needy and ripe between a short layer of fuzz that had grown in the past few weeks.

"I've never had those kinds of dreams before." Serena blazed on, filling his ears with her seductive voice and dirty secrets. "I started dreaming about you being on top of me—about me being on top of you. Wanting you so deep that when I came, I forgot how to breathe. Wondering if I left my curtains open at night, if I could catch you looking in and give you a show."

He grit his teeth. Until this point, they'd been careful not to leave any noticeable marks, nothing that would cause unneeded speculation. But he couldn't stop from digging his hands into her ass so hard that he'd be surprised if the whorls of his fingerprints didn't show in a bruise tomorrow. She didn't even flinch.

"Be careful what you ask for, sunflower. I wasn't lying when I said if you got me hard, I would put it to good use. I'll take you any way you want. As many times as you need. Anytime. Anywhere." He hissed as he stretched the condom over his erection, rolling right up to the root. "And I'm going to come too soon if you keep making me talk like this."

Serena smiled, her eyes sparkling as he pinned her with a glare. Of course. She'd been saying all those things on purpose, watching him. Testing him.

Well, now it was his turn.

"Hold yourself open for me. I need to see all of you," he demanded. The jeans had bound her at the knee so that her thighs were forced to press together, but he needed her exposed. Completely.

She reached back with one hand, new nails smooth and polished, and grabbed the plump place where her thighs met her ass. Where the bruise of his claim had been marked in red. Her pussy was so slick that the tips of her fingers struggled to find a good grip.

"Use both hands."

"Grant," she groaned, but did as she was told.

"That's it," he hummed. "Such a dirty girl. Showing yourself off. Dripping because you need me so bad."

Without being able to hold herself up, her face rested flush with the hay, her eyes trained on him. He watched for any sign of discomfort, but all she did was shift to give him a better angle.

For good measure—and because he wanted to see it—he let a thick wad of spit fall to her tailbone. A tremor traveled up her back as it ran over the soft pucker of her ass and slid into her core. He sucked in a deep breath. Then guided the tip of himself along her slit, dipping to rub her clit.

Her heat immediately enveloped him. He'd only gotten in

the head of his cock, just the first inch, but even heaven couldn't compare to this. Silk and honey and ecstasy.

He glanced up to see her lips part as he rubbed himself over her clit, rocking back and forth until her legs began to shake, meeting him thrust for thrust. His hands skated along her thighs, ventured up to play with her sweet asshole, and over her back, pressing her down. Soft moans spilled into the air.

This alone would be enough to push him over the edge. Enough to make him fight for any shred of self-control.

But he was nowhere close to finished.

"I want to feel you come on my cock," he panted. "Tell me when you're almost there."

Serena had dutifully kept herself spread, but her eyes fell closed, and small wrinkles of concentration scrunched her forehead. "I want you inside," she whispered. "I'm close already."

"Don't move," he instructed, then grabbed her hips and plunged all the way in—all at once.

His string of curses almost drowned out her mewls. "Ah," she moaned. "Fuck, I forgot how damn big you are."

He grinned as a fever shivered up his spine. "Told you it'd be a lot. You can handle it, dirty girl. I'll make it fit."

Her hands dropped, but he didn't care, taking advantage of the extra space to reach around and play with her clit. His first thrusts were slow but deep, all the way out and all the way back in with a swivel of his hips. Exploring every angle and drinking in her reactions. Each stroke felt like a puncture wound to his chest, bursting his lungs and drenching him in a stream of hot desire.

But even better was how Serena began to quiver around him, her pussy clenching tighter and clit throbbing against his finger. Her channel grew slick and wet, and this was too much, too good. He couldn't stop, but he was going to burst any minute now—

"I'm coming," she gasped. "Shit, I'm coming."

She writhed under him as if struggling to get closer and farther at the same time. He shut his eyes and let out a wounded hiss. Not now. *Dammit, last just a little longer.*

When he opened his eyes, he roared and pounded into her like a man reduced to nothing but feral instinct. Hard enough to make her bounce with every thrust, fast enough that her moans broke with the vicious moments. Her tits and ass jiggled as he forged on, and this was it—this was the beginning of the end because he'd die if he stopped now.

A second orgasm rippled through her, not as intense as the first and more drawn out as if her body was coaxing his own to come. And he was nothing but beholden to her will.

He didn't have time to give warning. Didn't have time to process it before his dick jumped once, twice, then erupted in heavy spurts. The orgasm flared all the way up to the back of his skull as cum filled the condom, emptying from a place deep inside his balls. All he could do was gasp through it and pull Serena close to bury his face into the nape of her neck.

She twisted to nuzzle his cheek. Then he was drowning in her kiss, holding her face while his dick went limp inside her still pulsing cunt. He could barely form a coherent thought, pleasure and exhaustion creeping into his limbs.

"We have to do this again," he panted. "Didn't get enough of you."

She let out a breathless laugh. "I agree. Although, it's enough to make me sore tomorrow."

"Good," he huffed. "I think I'm gonna be sore, too."

TWENTY-FIVE

Serena

SHE WAS DEFINITELY SORE. SO SORE THAT SHE'D HAD TO SHIFT positions all day while trying not to look conspicuous. But it was a good kind of sore. The kind that made her crave more.

It'd been months since she'd had any action, and even then, nothing could come close to what she felt yesterday. Grant certainly hadn't held back. Not that he'd ever been one to do things half-hearted—that's exactly what made him so addicting.

Luckily, the morning had been quiet, and chores went by without issue. Unluckily, Mr. Weston enlisted Grant for some sort of special lessons, and they'd barely seen each other outside of breakfast and lunch. Finding time to sneak off together had been difficult enough before she'd acknowledged her feelings, much less when it came to communicating them. How could she begin to explain emotions that only seemed real in fiction?

Even when they got a moment alone, it felt too short. Like borrowed time that hadn't really been theirs to begin with. Worse, pretending to be just coworkers had been increasingly harder to maintain. Grant could light a fire under her skin from a mere glance, and she had to be careful not to stare back too long. It felt like he somehow turned her transparent, that every palpitation of her heart would be broadcast to the whole world.

If Grant did move out to be closer to her, they wouldn't have to rely on stolen moments. But his being on campus came with another set of problems. Her ex wasn't the kind of guy who could let go and move on. Even though Jace had been the one to break things off—and last she'd heard, he got beat up in a gang fight—but entitlement had been his fatal flaw. At one point, he'd accused her own friends of setting him up and convinced her to turn on them.

She wouldn't put it past him to try and scare Grant off. If Jace had the audacity to show up at her door, she'd slam it in his ugly face. But was Grant ready to handle that? Could he stand up to a guy who wielded knives and guns like playthings?

"We're both fools for trying to make this work," she muttered under her breath to Lucy, who wasn't paying attention. The horse's ears swiveled as they finished their last lap around the area, much more interested in the guests gathering at the barn than being a therapist. "At least we want to be fools together," Serena sighed to herself. "All right, let's go see what everyone's up to today."

On the ranch, it was easy to forget about future problems. A refreshing breeze had blown in off the mountains, and for once, the temperature outside matched the cool blue of the open sky. Flaxen grass swayed over fields of wildflowers, and the air felt heavy and moist with the promise of rain. Good weather had put everyone in a better mood. Or maybe it was the fact that the program was officially halfway over. By now, most guests had more or less adjusted, and the countdown to returning home had begun.

She waved at Renae, who was preoccupied with chatting with the other girls, then led Lucy over to the fence where Grant and Mrs. Weston were hitching up the horses used in lessons. Grant tipped his hat in greeting, his dimple betraying a slightly too-enthusiastic smile.

The shadow cast from his jawline made him look downright sinful, matched with a fresh white t-shirt that stretched taut over his chest and the usual pair of crisp jeans. Dust coated his boots from whatever he'd been doing this morning. She smiled and bit her lip, silently cursing how her heart flipped without so much as speaking a word to each other.

"Good afternoon, ladies!" Mrs. Weston called as she tested the knot on the lead rope for a gentle horse named Appa—a rusty brown mare with a spotted rear, named after her breed and fondness of apples. "How we feeling today?"

"Lucy's walking great," Serena replied. "She gets more energetic every day, although I think she feels left out from missing the lessons."

"Maybe we can fix that," Mrs. Weston mused and turned to Grant, who was being nudged by Lucy for scratches. "It'll be a good day to see where she's at. Would you like to use her to demonstrate?"

His smile widened. "Yeah. Sounds perfect to me." Then his attention shifted to Serena, green eyes flashing under the brim of his hat. "I'll need you, too, if you'd like to volunteer."

"Sounds more like voluntold," she muttered, wary of his excitement. That couldn't mean anything good. He winked in response. Her traitorous heart skipped again.

"I'm sure Lucy will appreciate it," Mrs. Weston chuckled. "But you only answered half of my question. How are you, dear?"

Serena shrugged, hoping her giddiness hadn't been too obvious around Grant. "As good as any other day."

Mrs. Weston nodded as if verifying an unspoken inquiry. "I'm glad you decided to stick with us. It might not be what you expected, but I hope that's not a bad thing. We certainly appreciate your contributions."

"It's not a bad thing at all. I'm just glad I could be useful." Serena laughed. At some point, the ranch had even begun to feel like home. "I wouldn't have imagined this place in my wildest dreams, but it's grown on me. By the way, what happened to the watch I found outside my window? Did Connor say anything?"

"Ah, yes," Mrs. Weston hummed. "I think we'll all find that out soon enough."

Serena raised an eyebrow at Grant, hoping for a decryption, but he only shrugged, equally confused. It looked like they weren't getting a proper answer until later.

"Better get started with the lesson, then," Mrs. Weston continued. "I'll be here to help, but the reins are all yours."

Grant took the cue with a nod, then walked to the front of the group and clapped his hands. "Okay, break's over. Listen up." He paused as the guests settled down. "First, let's make sure you remember what we went over last week. I expect you can grab the proper gear from the barn and saddle the horses up on your own. I'll be watching to give corrections as needed."

So far, workshops for equine therapy had covered basic grooming and handling, including how to tack up a horse. Most of the lessons were held outside to avoid the stuffiness of the barn, but actual riding lessons weren't part of the—

"After that, today we get to learn how to ride," he finished.

Her jaw dropped. What? Anxiety iced over her veins as the guests scurried into the barn, abuzz with anticipation.

"Hey," she hissed under her breath when Grant came back. "I didn't prepare for this. I have no idea what to do on a horse. I'm gonna be a terrible example!"

"That's why I wanted you," he countered, much too pleased with the prospect of using her as a test subject. His damn smile and that confidence in his eyes warmed her chest, melting her worry as fast as it had come. "You can show them what not to do, and I'll give you instructions as we go."

"In other words, you think I'm gonna mess up," she huffed.

"Like I said—you're perfect, sunflower. Don't sweat it." He put his hands on her shoulders, fingertips brushing under the hem of her shirt for a second too long. With a nudge from Lucy, he moved to scratch her cheek. "You'll be nice, won't you?"

Lucy snorted in response, tossing her head with a nod of approval.

Well, if they believed in her so much, maybe she'd be all right. Serena rolled her eyes. "I can't catch a break with you two."

Grant chuckled and added in a low murmur, "I hope you're not still sore."

Her blush must have given her away—or maybe it was the glare she shot back in reply. Either way, it only made Grant laugh harder. The husky rumble from his chest both eased her nerves and spiked her pulse.

"Oh, I'm gonna have a fun day," he declared.

Shit, she was so fucked.

TWENTY-SIX

Grant

Sunlight danced between patches of dappled shade, a gentle breeze whisked away the heat, and a rosy blush graced the face of the most beautiful woman in the world—life didn't get better than this. Perfection might be too elusive to capture for good, but for one precious second, it shimmered and glinted like a glass trinket in the afternoon light.

"Here ya go." After helping the guests gather their equipment from the barn, he'd collected Lucy's gear and now hung it over the fence, handing Serena a helmet. Her eyes lingered at his shoulders and chest for a beat too long, and he restrained himself from pulling her in for a kiss...which would probably lead to more. "Remember how to put it on her?"

Her eyes finally found his. "I think I can manage."

Behind her confident demeanor, he sensed a hint of doubt. Asking for help wasn't Serena's strong suit, but instead of backing out, she seemed more comfortable trusting him, which was a compliment that made him all but glow with pride.

"I'm here if you need me," he assured. Unable to resist, he plucked a strand of hair behind her ear and wrapped it around his finger. Goosebumps rose over her chest as she broke into a smile.

"You better go do your job, Mr. Instructor," she whispered. "Or else you're gonna get distracted."

"Hm, we wouldn't want that," he hummed mournfully. "If you insist. I'll be right back."

Making rounds among the guests, he offered reminders as they began brushing and putting on the tack. There were about a dozen participants and fewer horses, so they'd been divided into groups of two or three per horse. It ended up better that way, allowing them to work together and catch each other's mistakes.

Not everyone in the program enrolled in equine therapy. Some guests, like Connor and Richard, opted for the alternate course. Although, it seemed like his sister's enthusiasm had sparked an interest in Richard, who started asking questions about life on the ranch in their free time. They'd also had a few deeper discussions, including how Richard struggled with the bullies in his new school. So, Mr. Weston roped them into self-defense lessons—the old man may be more than both their ages combined, but he could put them on the ground every time. Even Grant had picked up a thing or two.

"Did we do this right?" Renae asked, waving him over.

He checked Appa's pad and saddle, then followed the reins to...a halter. "Everything is good, except it looks like you forgot the bridle."

"I told you we were missing something," her partner muttered.

"But isn't that basically the same as this?" Renae asked, pointing to the halter straps around the horse's nose.

He shook his head and picked up the bridle, which had fallen into the grass on the other side of the fence. "A halter is used to lead a horse from the ground or when you need to secure them with a rope like we've done here. A bridle is used when riding to communicate with the horse, using a bit—" He showed them the thin metal bar that would fit inside the horse's mouth.

The second girl scrunched her nose. "It looks uncomfortable."

"There are some bridles made without one and some made out of plastic or rubber, but if bits are used correctly, they shouldn't hurt a horse," he explained. "Riding is a partnership. You want the horse to understand what you ask it to, and in return, it trusts that you understand how to treat it well." Both girls nodded. "Let's see you put it on," he prompted.

Appa had gotten lazy in her later years and stood still as the girls unbuckled the halter and pushed it back to her neck. She'd also been well-trained, and when they put the bit up to her lips, she opened without complaint and moved her jaw until the bridle slipped into place.

"There," he approved with a nod. "Now clip on the reins, and you're all set. Also, double-check the girth around her belly and make sure it's positioned comfortably behind her front legs; she likes to puff out her stomach." He gave Appa a knowing look and patted her shoulders before moving to the next group.

Working with horses had been second nature as far back as he could remember. He'd been put on top of a horse before he'd learned to walk and got involved with the 4-H program along with his two brothers, though he was the only one who'd taken to competing in the rodeo.

While his family didn't operate a ranch, they owned a variety of animals and often offered riding lessons to the locals. To their credit, his parents had been very laid back when it came to raising kids. As long as he'd had a passion, his family supported him—within their means, of course. That's why they knew something was wrong when he sold his horse.

However, there were some wounds that empathy couldn't

fix. Moving to the ranch had helped take his mind off the confusion and aftermath of the accident and subsequent breakup. Gave him a place to reevaluate his expectations and goals in life. Helping someone else was the only thing that kept him motivated—without merely numbing the pain.

Most days, the only ones he really helped were the animals, but there were other times, like today, that he could do a little more. Seeing the kids build relationships with the horses and tune into their self-awareness made it seem like his soft heart—which lately had felt like a crippling weakness—could be turned into a strength.

He took the time to visit his parent's place on the weekends, but Hollow Oak was his safe haven in more ways than one. The thought of venturing out of his hometown had always been daunting. Yet, seeing Serena embrace the unknown had quietly implanted a desire to broaden his own horizons.

Going to college might not be so bad, after all. Maybe it'd be like getting in the saddle again for the first time.

"You ready for this?" he asked Serena as Mrs. Weston finished checking her saddle and then headed off to help the last group.

She pursed her lips and made a show of putting on her helmet. "If you think so."

"I know so." He grinned. "I've been waiting to get you in the saddle for a while, sunflower."

She snorted. "Just any ol' saddle, or yours?"

They both knew the answer to that. He winked. "First time is the most thrilling. I'm kinda jealous."

When Serena opened her mouth to reply, he grabbed her waist and hoisted her into the air. His shoulders were about level with Lucy's back, making it easy to toss her in the saddle. He glimpsed a bruise near the hem of her shorts as her leg lifted, and his breath caught. Instead of letting go, he curled his hands around her hips and skimmed down to her calves.

As expected, Serena's shriek of surprise got everyone's attention. He collected himself before turning to address the group, who were all watching with wide eyes. "Mrs. Weston will be bringing around a stool and helping you mount. Do not try to climb on the horse by yourself. I only skipped that step to show you how to sit once you get in the saddle."

Glancing up, he checked that Serena had found her balance. Her eyes were bright, and she had one fist wrapped fast around the saddle horn, but he recognized the flush of exhilaration coloring her skin. Her subtle shifting would seem like getting used to the new position for everyone else, but he knew she was feeling where he'd been inside of her yesterday.

Fuck, now he was thinking about how she'd looked when she came. How her pretty pink lips had parted, and the low sound of her moan had been followed by the tight grip of her pussy...

Serena raised her eyebrows, waiting for instructions. He cleared his throat.

"Start by putting your feet into the stirrups." He angled his body to show the others and gripped Serena's ankle to position it. "You want to balance on the ball of your feet like this. Your partner can help adjust them to the right length."

He moved his hand up Serena's leg and demonstrated how her knees would be able to absorb and follow the horse's movement, then continued to her hips and explained the alignment of her body with the saddle.

Lucy shifted impatiently, causing Serena to lose balance and tense under his hands. He rubbed his palm over her thigh to steady her. "I got you," he assured, then turned to address the guests. "As you can see, when the horse moves, you want to move with it, using your seat in the saddle and the stirrups."

He glanced at Serena. A flame jumped between them that had nothing to do with riding horses. He looked back to the others.

"Today, I want you to focus on finding your center of gravity, which will be in your hips. Your partner will lead you and the horse around the area. Then, you can switch roles. All these horses have been trained to respond to vocal commands like 'walk,' 'slow,' and 'stop.' You can also gently nudge them with your heel to move and pull back a little on the reins to slow or stop. You don't need to use unnecessary force. Questions?"

When no one spoke up, Mrs. Weston began to bring around the plastic stairs and helped them mount. He turned back to Serena and Lucy.

"How's the view from up there?"

Serena grinned. "I'm starting to understand your love of horses a lot more."

"If you wanted to sweet talk me, mission accomplished."

She groaned. "When do we get to the good part? A girl's got places to go."

"Think you can manage to go a lap on your own?" He watched Lucy to see if her injury was flaring up, but she looked just as eager as her rider.

Serena chewed her lip. "Yeah. I wanna give it a try."

"Go on." He tipped his head. "Holler if you need me."

Serena nudged Lucy forward, and the pair started off along the fence. He might have predicted they'd get along, but at this rate, Serena would be wearing her own pair of boots and a cowgirl hat before he knew it.

He liked that. A lot.

TWENTY-SEVEN

Serena

She thought Grant had been closed off at first, secretive about his work on the ranch and his history with the rodeo— but now she knew the truth. Some things couldn't be explained. They had to be experienced.

Riding on Lucy's back was like nothing she anticipated. Even at a steady walk, she felt every shift of the horse's muscles rolling underneath her, each hoof lifting and falling, the sway of Lucy's gait rocking her in the saddle. The ground moved beneath them almost as if they floated above it.

She'd felt the peace of a sunrise and the calm of watching a river reflect the stars, but the awe from seeing the world on a horse outmatched both.

Lucy's strength—and an equal amount of patience— astounded her. At one point, when the adrenaline had begun to fade, she sat a little straighter and braved a look around. Lucy's ears perked up and quickened her pace.

"Woah, there," Serena cautioned, one fist clutching the reins as the other flew to the saddle horn. "Keep it slow. Don't think I'm ready for more yet."

Lucy tossed her head, compromising with something of a

prance as she completed their circuit. It was almost like the horse was having as much fun as she was.

By the time she got back around to Grant and Mrs. Weston, her cheeks had begun to hurt from smiling so much. She'd also discovered several muscles she didn't know she had.

"You're still in one piece." Grant stepped forward as Lucy came to a stop. "Although, I hope you know it wasn't a race."

Looking behind her, she saw the others trailing almost halfway across the ring like a row of little ducklings. "That wasn't me. Lucy definitely has a competitive streak."

He shook his head with a dimpled smile. "Mhm. Something tells me you'll let her get away with it before long. Or is riding horses too country for a city girl such as yourself?"

She laughed at his jab. "I might want to do it again. But right now, I think this city girl needs a break."

"You're welcome to visit after the program ends and take lessons," Mrs. Weston suggested as Grant brought over the stepping stool. "I'm sure you could convince Grant it's worth his time. And as Lucy improves, she'll need to be ridden more regularly."

"Her owner will be busy competing until the season is over," Grant added. "I don't think they'd mind if you asked."

Something dense and heavy weighed on her heart. Eventually, Lucy would go home, too. Wanting Grant hadn't been enough. She'd grown attached to everyone here.

"I'm not sure how much I can fit in before school, but I'll look into it," she replied.

Grant helped her down, then swung in the saddle with practiced ease. His posture exuded nothing but confidence, a true sight to behold as he tipped his hat and gave her a smoldering look. "Gonna check things out for myself."

She stepped back to the fence line with Mrs. Weston, unable to take her eyes off him as he rode over to the others. There was a rhythm to his movements, all muscle and power, knowledgeable enough to guide Lucy with invisible commands. A rugged man in full control.

He was meant for this, she realized. Meant to use his body, mind, and spirit all at once. To live for his passion.

"He needs to compete again," she thought aloud.

"He will," Mrs. Weston replied. "Just needs the right push."

"Think I could be there to see it?"

Mrs. Weston laughed. "Oh, of that, I have no doubt."

❋

She left her curtains open that night. When a dark shadow moved across the window, she'd excitedly slipped out and followed Grant to the well, their path lit by the Milky Way and a crescent moon.

He'd made her ride him with his back against a tree, their bodies hidden under the oak leaves and sighs silenced by the breeze. Despite her soreness—or precisely *because* of it—he forced her to slow down just before she came. Again and again. The pain had made it better, everything inside burning and clenching until neither could take it anymore.

She'd come so hard it felt like her bones split, like the air scorched her lungs, and she'd never breathe the same again, but she kept kissing him through it all. Kissing and praying that his soft lips and strong arms wouldn't leave. He'd swelled and spilled into the condom as they kissed, then he laid in the grass and let her ride his face until the sky finally broke open and rain chased them indoors.

In the morning, she physically couldn't get out of bed. Her body ached so much it felt like she'd been run over by a truck —a very sexy truck whose whispered declarations still echoed in her ears. She'd gotten up the strength to emerge after morning exercise, only to be greeted by a very chipper Grant.

How he could do this day after day and have so much energy was a mystery.

She hadn't seen him again and, at lunch, found herself looking forward to their next riding lessons just to be in the same place together. Renae and her friends were excited about the lessons, too, debating who would get a turn to ride first. Richard sat on the other side of his sister, increasingly more curious as the conversation continued. He hadn't signed up for equine therapy but seemed like he'd taken an interest in it.

Mr. Weston caught her attention as he came in from the kitchen and walked across the dining room toward Connor. The poor kid didn't notice until Mr. Weston was right on top of him, then abruptly sat up straight.

In his hand, Mr. Weston held out a watch nearly identical to the one she and Grant had found outside the guesthouse—except it wasn't broken. Not a speck of dirt or a single splinter marred the glass face, which had been shattered by Grant's boot. Or maybe it'd been broken before they stumbled onto it.

"Found this in the kitchen the other day. Is it the one you lost?" Mr. Weston asked.

Connor looked at the watch and then back at Mr. Weston. His eyebrows pinched together as he searched for words. "See? It was left there after Richard did the dishes. I told you he must've stolen it!"

By now, Renae and the others paused their conversation to listen in. Mr. Weston crooked an eyebrow. "You've been equally assigned to dishes, which is why I figured you were the one who left it there. Besides, I thought you said Renae stole it. Why would they steal something only to leave it lying around?"

Connor's face turned red. "How would I know? I wouldn't do that kind of thing."

Mr. Weston shook his head. "I assumed you'd appreciate having it back, but seems like you care more about telling me who took it."

"No, I just—I want it back," Connor stammered.

"You sure this is yours?" Mr. Weston reiterated.

"Yes, it's mine." Connor snatched the watch and put it on his wrist.

"Then I suggest you take better care of it next time," Mr. Weston added. He held Connor's eyes for another second before walking out of the room.

Low whispers followed his absence. Connor glared down at his wrist and snapped at his friends. "Shut up. I'll prove they were the ones who took it."

Serena held her breath. Apparently, Connor hadn't learned from the last time he tried to start something. But now everyone would be watching. Grant's eyes followed the action from across the room; muscles tensed like he was gearing up to intervene. Renae balled her fists as Connor sauntered over to Richard.

But Richard didn't shrink. There was a new resolve in his posture as he calmly pushed away his food.

"You think you're so smart, playing me as some kind of a fool," Connor accused.

"—and a liar," Renae interjected.

"It's okay," Richard said quietly and rose to his feet. Connor's eyes widened as if noticing for the first time that Richard was taller. He squared his shoulders and turned to Connor. "I'm not scared of you."

Connor stepped back with a laugh. "Of course you aren't. *I'm* the one who should be scared—*I'm* the victim!"

When no one spoke, and Richard didn't move to attack, Connor scoffed. "You can't hide forever." Then he retreated to his table and began muttering with the others.

Serena rolled her eyes. What a coward.

Richard sat and continued eating in peace, all the while with half the room staring at him. Renae leaned in after a few conversations started to pick up. "Where'd that come from?"

He shrugged. "Grant and Mr. Weston showed me a few tricks. I knew I could pin him if I had to. Did you know he was a wrestler—Mr. Weston, I mean? Anyway, he told me a fight can be over before it even begins. Guess it works."

Serena smiled and looked over at Grant. He was smiling, too.

TWENTY-EIGHT

Serena

MORE RIDING LESSONS MEANT MORE SORE MUSCLES, AND FOR THE third day in a row, she collapsed into bed like a rag doll. The soft mattress enveloped her heavy limbs, sheets smooth on her skin as she breathed in the faint scent of fabric softener.

Evening storms had become more frequent over the week, but tonight, the sky was clear, the darkness complete. All the guests were asleep, and the house had fallen silent save for the chirp of crickets outside and an occasional creak from old wooden beams.

A girl could get used to this. No chaos of wasted frat boys and no stressing about tests she hadn't studied for. The comfort of knowing she'd wake in a place that felt like home—with people she cared for as much as family.

Rolling over, she snuggled into the quilt. Even if she had the energy to sneak out again, going every night would eventually lead to them being caught. Better to play it safe and keep things spontaneous.

But her mind still drifted to Grant. And her heart.

At some point, she'd started to believe him—that the future could be whatever they wanted. That *she* could be whatever she wanted. Neither of those things would feel right without him by her side. It was true she fell in love with the country, but she'd also fallen in love with him. A man who had become her adventure as well as her safe place. Someone who showed her how to love and live to the fullest with every breath.

It was time she returned the favor. Not that he needed to discover his dreams—Grant may have lost sight of his passions, but they'd never lost sight of him. He had a natural connection with horses and people, and she knew his drive could take him to the next level. It wasn't necessarily about winning a rodeo buckle or becoming a star, although she knew he would, it was about being true to himself.

There was only one Grant Hartford, and the world wasn't ready to see him shine. Her lips curved into a smile against the pillow, imagining being there to congratulate him on a well-deserved victory.

As she began to drift off, a distant crash tore through the veil of sleep. She tensed. It hadn't been quite deep or loud enough to be thunder, more like a cascade of falling ice—or shattered glass. Flashbacks of broken bottles and slurred shouts resurfaced from her memories. Fear coiled her muscles, and she instinctively curled to protect herself. Stilling her breath, she waited. Listened.

Had she imagined it?

Cautiously, she climbed out of bed and padded over to peek through the curtains. No one had their lights on, and a layer of dense clouds blacked out the sky, making it nearly impossible to see. Not even the moon cast its waning glow.

The sound echoed again. She startled, this time aware enough to pinpoint that it had come from the opposite direction of her window, near the front of the ranch.

Her gut twisted into knots. Something wasn't right.

She slipped on a pair of pants and hurried out to the

common area, leaving the lights off to conceal her presence. With deaf fingers, she pried open the front door and stepped onto the porch. Cold air drifted inside as goosebumps rose along her arms. The hairs on the back of her neck stood on end. A sea of darkness waited as her eyes adjusted much too slowly.

Subtle movement from the main house caught her attention, and she gasped as another window burst into tiny, glittering fragments. The entire front wall of the ranch house had been smashed in, its beautiful glass exterior left in jagged pieces on the ground, the inside exposed and ruined. Her hands began to shake. Who would do this?

Then she saw him.

A hooded figure hunched over under the last broken window in the far corner. It didn't look like whoever it was wanted to break in. A burglar wouldn't have been this obvious or taken as long to grab what they came for, and there weren't any vehicles to get away with.

No, this was worse. *He* was worse.

Chilling dread choked her windpipe, closed in around her like an inky phantom from the past. Would Jace have come looking for her? Did he want some sort of twisted revenge for getting him in trouble with the cops?

She glanced around wildly, searching for his bike tucked into the shadows, but it'd be impossible to find if he wanted to hide it. Her knees buckled, and she fell to a crouch on the ground, heart hammering in her chest.

Deep breaths. Slow down.

She had to be sure. Forcing herself to think rationally, she crept onto the lawn for a better look and used the landscaping along the gravel drive for cover. Cold dirt coated the soles of her feet, and grass tickled her ankles, but all she could feel was the blood rushing through her veins.

Whoever it was, she wouldn't let them get away with this.

Maybe she could distract them before they caused more damage.

The perpetrator finished whatever they'd paused for, and she saw their face as they turned. A fleeting sense of relief transformed into shock. Not Jace—it was Connor. But what would doing this prove? Why hadn't someone else stopped him? The Westons must have been alerted to the disturbance by now.

And where was Grant when she needed him?

Connor tossed aside a crowbar, glass crunching under his feet, and went to search in a cluster of bushes along the side of the house. It didn't take him long to find what he wanted. He'd probably hidden it there sometime during the day.

She froze.

He carried what looked like a gas canister—and headed straight for the barn.

Toward the horses.

Her body moved without a second thought, racing through the yard as she screamed. "Stop! Connor, what are you doing?"

He spun and stared at her, a flash of surprise crossing his eyes before it turned to vehement anger. The night shadows blurred his features, and instead of his face, she saw Jace's. Instead of Connor's voice, she heard one from nearly forgotten nightmares. "Fucking bitch, you shouldn't have come out here."

She grit her teeth. It didn't matter what he had to say.

Using the momentum from her sprint, she grabbed the canister and tried to yank it away. Connor didn't let go, cursing and spitting as they grappled. Fighting in the dark felt like fighting blind. The seal on the lid loosened, and a trickle of liquid seeped into her pants, soaking the cotton. A pungent, sweet odor filled her lungs.

Something thudded in the distance.

Connor outmatched her in raw strength, but she had enough experience to hold her own and refused to give in. With a burst of adrenaline, she shoved him back and twisted against his wrist until the canister flew from both their hands.

More liquid splashed onto her arms, dripping to her feet and sliding between her toes. She prepared for Connor's next attack, but he hadn't raised his fist.

"Always talking with those losers—like you're one of them," he panted. "I've hated this place since the moment I got here."

"Connor. Stop," she repeated. Pleaded.

"You can't cover this up. I left proof. Everyone will blame them, not me." His eyes narrowed in concentration as he reached into his back pocket.

"I saw you do it," she countered. "Don't make this worse." He'd been sent here as an opportunity to turn his life around, but he was throwing that all away.

"That's why I have to," he mumbled, fumbling with something in his hands. "I have to. He told me I had to."

She realized too late what he meant. Saw the match only as he swiped it across the surface of the small box in his palm.

Then flames lit up the night.

TWENTY-NINE

Grant

HE'D JUST SWITCHED OFF THE LIGHTS WHEN HIS CELL BUZZED from on top of the dresser. For a moment, he stood frozen, staring at the blue glow that illuminated the room. Late-night phone calls made him nervous.

These days, only a select group of people could get a hold of him. A few texts to family here and there. He used to stay up all night on video with Payton, but after the breakup, scrolling on social media made him sick. It was a waste of time, anyway.

Although, he had gone online to check the local rodeo standings earlier today. A few folks he knew were having great runs, including Lucy's owner, who entered with a different horse and was on track to win state barrel racing championships. Maybe Serena would enjoy going to a rodeo with him. She'd already hinted at wanting to watch him ride— he wouldn't admit it, but it felt great to show off a little. And she was so easily impressed.

Holding his breath, he walked across the bedroom to pick up the phone. Mr. Weston's contact ID appeared on the screen.

"Yeah," he answered.

"Security cameras picked up movement on the front porch,"

Mr. Weston's gruff voice came through on the other end of the line. "Connor's out there."

Grant cursed. "I checked everyone's room less than an hour ago. They all had their lights off. I didn't even see him leave. Is anyone else with him?"

"No, can't see anyone else. But after he took the wrong watch the other day, I have a feeling he's up to no good. And here I was, hoping he'd come clean."

"What do you want me to do?" Grant asked.

"Hang tight. Keep an eye from a window if you can. I wanna see what he's planning or catch him in the act if he tries anything."

"Right." Grant glanced outside his window to check on the ladies' guesthouse. Everything looked quiet over there. Even Serena's lights were off. "I'll stay here and watch from inside. Call if things change."

"Yup." Mr. Weston hung up, and Grant tucked the phone into his pocket. Good thing he hadn't changed out of work clothes for the night.

Exiting his bedroom, he passed the landline in the common area and debated on contacting Serena. She'd been overly exhausted between riding lessons and their *personal* lessons this week, and he felt guilty for wearing her out. More on account of affecting her work—not about making her show off every inch of herself and learning every possible way to bring her to orgasm. He'd willingly do that every night for the rest of their lives.

No, better not to wake her. He could handle Connor if things went sideways.

He quietly walked to the porch window and pressed himself against the wall, peering across the yard toward the main house. The night was pitch black, but sure enough, he caught sight of a figure walking through the lawn.

What was that troublemaker up to now? As disheartening

as it was to admit, sometimes the program wasn't enough. Sometimes, people didn't listen until they faced hard consequences. Ones they couldn't take back.

Connor held a long object in his hands, twirling it as he paced back and forth. He stopped for a moment, then pulled back and swung at the first tall window.

Grant clenched his fists, forcing himself to look where he knew the security camera had recorded everything. He also knew where the gun was stashed inside the ranch's entryway and how to use it. If anyone else had pulled this stunt, they'd have been shot.

It became harder and harder to breathe as Connor destroyed one window after another. Hadn't this been enough? Those would cost more than a month's salary to fix. The Westons could manage it, but their money shouldn't be wasted on that when he relied on it to save up for college.

The phone buzzed from his pocket. He took it out and read the message from the lock screen.

FRANK WESTON:

Called the cops. Stay inside. Don't want you getting hurt.

While he appreciated the concern, he didn't care to let the ranch take damage either. Fuck Connor and his crowbar. He was about one second away from wrestling the kid to the ground.

He forced out a tense exhale. His responsibility was to keep the others safe. Someone might wake up with all this noise, and it'd be better if he stayed here to stop them from complicating the situation. In the corner of his line of sight, he checked that the ladies' guesthouse remained dark and sleepy, then sent a silent prayer that the sheriff would get here sooner rather than later. Response times were slower since the ranch was outside of town, but it should only take fifteen minutes with lights and sirens.

In the meantime, Connor had ended his assault and crouched in the far corner. Grant watched him closely, trying to figure out his next move, then Connor slipped around the side of the house and out of sight.

Shit.

He unlocked his phone to notify the Westons. Before he finished, Connor reappeared on the path to the barn—and a shout pierced the silence. Grant's eyes tore open as he looked up to see Serena running across the yard, already halfway to Connor. What the hell was she thinking?

The phone dropped from his hands, and he fumbled to get outside. Dammit it all. The door banged against the siding as he raced after her. But she'd been fast and had a head start. Serena got to Connor before he could catch up, and they began fighting over something.

The scent of gas fumes polluted the air. Fuck, this was bad. He couldn't make out what they were saying over the thud of his footfalls and the rush of adrenaline through his veins. A container flew sideways across the lawn. He only needed a few more seconds...

The flicker of a match illuminated Connor's face.

"Get down and roll," he yelled as flames licked across Connor's hand. Grant shoved Serena backward into the dirt and rammed into Connor. Both of them tumbled to the ground, smothering the fire, but the match fell before it went out.

The crackle of flames whooshed, jumping across the lawn following a trail of leaking gas. A loud boom rang in his ears, and a wave of heat exploded behind them. Bright light soared into the sky.

God, no. Please let her be okay.

They'd gotten far enough away to avoid being caught in the blast, but he'd lost sight of Serena.

His thoughts jumbled, and panic bled into every frantic beat of his heart. Blinking, he searched for her through the haze while shielding Connor beneath him. His ears rang as he inhaled thickening smoke. The fire had blazed a trail through the yard, and he had to squint to see into the harsh flare. Flames danced across his vision, flickering in and out.

Then hissing filled his ears. White powder covered the embers sparking near them. Mr. Weston aimed a fire extinguisher in a wide perimeter around the blaze. Luckily, the fire had started far enough away from the buildings that it hadn't spread too far.

He caught sight of Mrs. Weston as she covered Serena with a fire blanket. A feeble exhale escaped his lips. He needed to get to her, needed to make sure she was all right. But shit, he couldn't leave Connor alone.

"Fucking idiot," he cursed, digging his knee into Connor's back and eliciting a groan. "Almost got us all killed."

"It's not my fault," Connor mumbled.

Grant pushed his face further into the dirt. "Yeah, then whose is it?"

"Pops said he'd be proud. He told me—" Connor stopped and cut himself off.

Sirens wailed from the road, and then people swarmed around the yard—cops rushing in and barking over their radio, the Westons trying to keep guests inside who had woken and were wandering out, neighbors who heard the noise and drove over to help.

An officer finally came and took Connor, then Grant rushed over to Serena. She'd been moved away from the fire, sitting on a patch of grass with her knees up. The blanket fell off one shoulder as she stared at the commotion through glazed eyes.

"Sunflower," he breathed, forgetting to be cautious as he clutched her to his chest.

"I tried to stop him," she whispered.

"You did. The police have Connor. He won't do anything else." He smoothed back her hair, panicking again at the unmistakable scent of gasoline and singed fabric. "Are you hurt? Were you burned?"

Still staring at what was left of the fire, she shook her head. "I don't know. They told me to wait for the medics."

"Are you in pain?" He lifted his arms from where he held her. "Tell me. Tell me where. I'm sorry, I shouldn't have grabbed you."

Finally, she looked at him. Her eyes were dilated, her breaths shallow. "Grant. I knew you'd come."

"I'm here." He ran his thumb along her cheek, warming her chilled skin.

She shivered. "You're not mad?"

"Fuck, no. Why would I be mad?" He started to hug her again but stopped himself.

She gave a soft smile and leaned into his arms. "I'm okay, it doesn't hurt."

He tucked her against him and pulled the blanket back over her shoulder. "Everything is going to be okay."

They stayed like that for a while, him listening to her heartbeat as she sunk further into his embrace. Eventually the shock began to thaw.

"When I looked at him, I saw my ex," Serena whispered. "And when you came...it was like that night all over again. Him blaming me. Taking the bottle and smashing it on the ground. Leaving me without caring to look back." She turned to nuzzle into his chest. "I thought you'd hate me, too."

"No, sunflower." He rocked her back and forth. "I'd never hate you. I'd never leave you. You were brave and strong. You did good." He'd been about to say something else, something important, but a fire truck rambled down the driveway followed by EMT responders.

Now wasn't the time.

The medics ran to them first—the two people closest to the explosion—and although he didn't want to let anyone near her, they each went through a basic wellness check. Turned out he had a light burn on his arm, while Serena had more severe ones on her feet and legs. She'd managed to keep herself relatively unharmed by smothering the flames that had ignited on her clothes.

"Doesn't look like either of you have third-degree burns, which is more than luck—it's a miracle," the EMT was saying, then turned to Serena. "Take over-the-counter medication when the pain kicks in. The burns should heal with proper care, but I'd go to a hospital if they blister or get worse."

She nodded, and they were both handed some gauze and ointment, then the medical team went to Connor and the others.

"I'm gonna go help clean up," she said, moving to follow.

He grabbed her shoulder and pivoted the well-intended step so she faced him. "No, you're not."

"Have you seen the damage? I need to help." She motioned to the crisp lawn covered in white power and broken glass, then the gaping windows and smoke-filled interior.

Good to see her energy had come back, at least.

His lips curved in a tired smile and he pressed a kiss to her forehead. "You're going to shower and get some rest. We'll do what we can tonight and you can help in the morning."

She hesitated, tipping her head to meet his eyes. "I'm okay, really. Don't worry."

"You're soaked in gas and need to clean those wounds. Or do I need to get my rope and tie you to the bedpost myself?" He arched an eyebrow.

She broke out in a laugh. "Bossy cowboy. Fine."

"Such a stubborn woman," he muttered. Did they all lack a sense of self-preservation?

As he watched her walk off, an unfamiliar feeling welled in

his chest. It wasn't like the last time he'd rushed in, only to be pushed away. She trusted him to take care of her. Wanted him to hold her instead of hiding the truth.

They'd both been the ones left behind in the past, but things could be different this time. From now on, no matter what happened, they were going to get through it together.

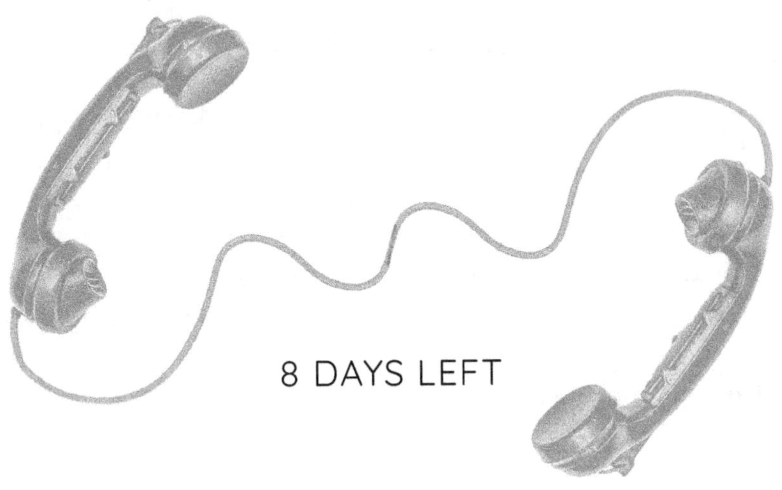

8 DAYS LEFT

Serena:
"Don't panic."

Lexi:
"Uh-oh. What happened? And why do you sound like Mom on one of her bad days?"

"One of the guests tried to set the ranch on fire tonight."

"Oh *shit*. Are you okay?"

"Yeah, that's why I called. I got a few burns from trying to stop him, but I'm okay. Don't want anyone at home panicking if it gets on the news."

"Thank goodness. And what the hell, who would do that?"

"Not everyone wants to be a good person."

"Yeah, I guess. Is Grant okay?"

"So you *do* know his name."

"He's gonna be my future brother-in-law, right?"

"Woah...slow down. He wasn't hurt, by the way. Although, I'm not denying anything."

"Hold up. You're *not* denying it?"

"...I gotta get some sleep."

"Wait wait wait—"

"Goodnight, Lexi."

"We're still on for the girl's date when you come home?"

"Of course, I'll let you pick the place."

"And I'll let you spill the tea."

"Ha-ha. Sounds like you need to get some sleep, too."

"At least pretend like you miss me."

"Love ya, Lex."

"Love ya too, sis."

THIRTY

Grant

As it does, the sun rose the next day.

Then it fell, as it does.

The second hand on Mrs. Weston's antique clock ticked faithfully in its usual cadence. As if nothing unusual had happened at all. Muted voices filtered through the walls, swirling into white noise that tangled inside his head like distorted fog.

Everyone else had gathered in a meeting room for their first regular activity of the day. He'd stayed behind after dinner for a moment of quiet and just...hadn't been able to get up.

The numbness returned.

A draft wound through the dining room, like the air was holding onto the memory of last night. Plastic nailed over the broken windows kept out the elements, but it did nothing to regulate the temperature. Or maybe he was just cold.

When the panic faded, and emergency responders left the scene, he'd gotten a few hours of restless sleep before getting back to work. Their weekend project turned into fixing up the ranch. All the guests were more than willing to help with repair efforts. By the end of the day, a company had already been scheduled to replace the windows, the floor was swept and vacuumed and swept again, and a few pieces of damaged furniture were assessed or repaired to their best ability. Even Sheriff Gaines came over to lend a hand and while he was at it, collected their statements and the security footage.

The police found a strip of torn fabric from the sleeve of Richard's shirt on one of the windows—clearly placed by Connor, who claimed he'd gone outside because he saw Renae "lurking" around the barn. The only ones who pretended to believe his lies were his parents, who had also covered up his history of attempted arson to keep him eligible for the program.

Turned out his record had been hiding a few important details. His school counselors filed a concern about his mental health and, paired with multiple reports of bullying, made the school threaten expulsion if things didn't change. Hollow Oak had been Connor's last-ditch effort to stay in their good graces. Fortunately, neither the Westons nor Serena decided to press charges, and pending further investigation of the phone record with his parents, Connor would likely be placed in the custody of a more intensive care facility.

As the chaos died down, the whole group seemed more at ease with Connor gone. He should've shared their relief. However, instead of peace, the quiet invited his thoughts to wander—made him acknowledge the ones he'd been trying to ignore. Feelings he thought he'd buried.

Doubt. Fear. Helplessness.

That's why he sat alone at the table, nursing a glass of whiskey the Westons wouldn't notice went missing. He used to sneak out for drinks with his friends and thought nothing of it, but when their group had gone their separate ways, the liquor was the only one that stayed. The only one who had cared to listen. Laughter and late nights became loneliness and early mornings. Drinking wasn't a habit he planned on, but it kept coming back.

The ceiling's reflection shimmered in the amber liquid as he rocked the rim over the wooden table, and a hollow sound filled the empty room. He took another sip and focused on the burn that coated his tongue and the burn in his chest.

Involving himself with Serena had been a risk worth taking. A risk he'd choose again and again, even if things didn't work out the same way. Falling in love was a good thing—but then, why did it fill him with dread, like he'd been caught in a whirlpool? One that intended to drag him back to the night of the accident, of the months where he'd broken a little more each day.

He knew some things were better off gone. He didn't want Payton back and no longer wished for the same effortless happy ending. He'd been naive to think good things came easy. No, it wasn't that he missed what he could've had. It was that he didn't want to lose what he'd found.

What if he hadn't gotten to Serena in time? What if he hadn't been able to protect her—what if he couldn't in the future? What if there came a time when she didn't *want* his protection?

Could he even live with the possibility?

All were questions he didn't want answers to. The only thing he *did* know was that Serena shouldn't see him like this. He sank lower at the thought, and because fate could be just as cruel as it was kind, that's precisely when hinges creaked down the hall. A few moments later, she stepped into the entryway.

Perhaps it was the gloom in his head, or how the plastic diffused the last light of dusk, but she appeared exceptionally angelic. A cream and pink-patterned jacket fluttered over her tank top and stopped short of her hips, which slanted as she leaned against the wall with crossed her arms. The same exhaustion he felt reflected in her eyes. Even so, the corner of her mouth curved as he glanced over.

"You don't usually miss the meetings," she noted.

He gave her a crooked, half-hearted smile. "Don't usually drink, either."

He watched as she took in his hunched posture, the way his hand had gone limp around an almost empty glass. He tipped it toward her. "I'll share."

She eyed the liquor and licked her lips, then sighed. "I shouldn't. Plus, I didn't come for whiskey."

"Suit yourself." He took another swig, leaned back in the chair, and closed his eyes. Gentle footsteps padded behind him. Soft hands wrapped over his shoulders, then slid down his chest and under his shirt. He breathed into her touch, heart beating against her fingertips.

"Your warmth is so much nicer," he mumbled. The effects of his drink were nowhere near as comforting.

She laughed. "Good to know."

"I didn't want you to see me like this," he admitted. "But I'm glad you're here."

She rested her chin on top of his head. The ends of her hair tickled his neck. "I'm not proud of how you saw me last night, either."

"Don't worry." He placed his hand over hers. "It's impossible for you to be anything but beautiful."

She laughed again, and the husky melody splintered through his defenses. "I thought I was ready," he admitted. "Thought I'd gotten past all the pain, that I could handle the possibility of losing someone." He swallowed and opened his eyes. "But...not when it's you."

She shifted into his line of sight and squeezed his palm. It might as well have been the shock of a defibrillator for how it coursed through his veins. "If it helps, I wouldn't want to lose you, either."

He wound a strand of her hair around his finger and smiled for real, even though loving her still hurt. So much. But that was better than not feeling anything else. "That does help, more than you know."

She brought her hand to his face and poked his dimple. "If I've learned one thing from being here, it's that life is a cycle of hurting and healing. Sometimes it sucks. Sometimes it doesn't. Sometimes you find someone who helps it all make sense. At the end of the day, going through that is so much more worthwhile when we have each other."

"Sunflower," he breathed, then stood and captured her face in his hands. Committed to memory the sweep of long lashes above intoxicating, deep brown eyes. The way her smile stole his last breath—how she gave him a reason to draw another. "Always pointing me to the light."

"That's because you are my light," she whispered, then pulled him close and skimmed her lips over his jaw, trailing soft kisses to the corner of his mouth. Their noses brushed and she paused to take an unsteady breath.

Impatiently, he fisted her hair and bit her bottom lip, eliciting a moan as he dragged it between his teeth. "Don't promise yourself to me if you're not ready for it."

She scoffed. "Don't be so certain you can handle me."

"Oh, I can handle you just fine." Tightening his grip on her hair, he ran a hand down the front seam of her shorts and dipped to the place where she'd grown hot and needy.

Her hips rocked, but just as she found a rhythm, he dropped his hand to the glass of whiskey. She all but growled, tracking his movements with a lustful gaze. He chuckled at her grievance as his dick echoed her protest.

"I can tell when you want something, you know," he murmured.

Her mouth parted, his teeth marks red on her lips. "Yeah? What is it that I want?"

"The same thing I do." Lifting the glass, he used his knuckle to brush a strand of hair behind her ear. Then, he emptied the rest of the whiskey in his mouth.

His thumb stroked her jaw, and she leaned in to accept his offering. He groaned when their lips met, tasting her as she swallowed the liquor and licked into his mouth for more.

Fuck, he'd never drink by himself again. Not when he could have this. Her whiskey kisses obliterated the numbness, brought all his heartache and worry to the surface, then burned it away like kindling caught in a firestorm.

He sucked on her tongue and popped open the button on her jeans. She rolled her clit into his pal, and quivered, legs shaking as he walked her backward. His fingers curled into her pussy.

"I'm already close," she panted.

He pushed her against the wall. "Good. Watching you come gets me hard as fuck."

Muffling her moans with his hand, he quickened his pace and worked her clit the way he knew she liked. Her fingers dug into his biceps and only made him push harder, deeper. She came with a sob as he rocked into her relentlessly, soaking up the shivering heat of her arousal. The sweet scent that made his mouth water.

"Need more," he rasped.

"We don't have time," she whispered.

He was too far gone to care. "One taste. Please, sunflower. Let me just have one taste."

She tipped her head back with a defeated whine, and he covered her neck in open-mouth kisses, traveling across her chest. Her nipples were pebbled and ripe, so red and delicious—

The creak of hinges shattered their silence.

He never moved so fast in his entire life. After a fleeting wide-eyed glance, Serena stumbled toward the bathroom as he flew to the kitchen, tossing a couple of already clean pots in the sink and turning the pipe all the way on. Hopefully, the sound of running water would indicate he'd been doing dishes and not trying to hide the world's largest boner.

Shit, that had been too close.

Even worse, the next time he got his hands on her, he might not be able to stop.

THIRTY-ONE

Serena

"RIGHT HERE?"

"A little farther down. Yes, that's it. Right there."

"Okay. I'm putting it in."

She took the level and helped hold the shelf as Grant drilled in the last screws. The way that man handled a power tool made her wonder what other toys he'd be good with. She bit her lip, not caring if he noticed her staring at his furrowed brows or drooling over the flex of his shoulder and forearms.

Yeah, Grant would be great at using all sorts of tools.

When he finished securing the bracket, she stepped back and assessed their handiwork. Weeks of sorting, cleaning, and building finally paid off. The tack room had transformed from a chaotic dust bowl into a marvel of organization.

Benches built out of cinder blocks and upcycled planks lined the room, with space underneath for crates and pairs of work boots. One wall had been dedicated to saddles displayed on custom-built racks, each with a hook for their matching bridle and girth. She'd even gotten creative and added a unique charm for each horse to keep the sets together. Saddle pads hung from clips on a small clothing rack in the corner. Vertical plastic pockets held various wrappings, brushes, and sprays next to the door. Along another wall, more hooks and wire baskets hung from pegboard for extra riding equipment and supplies.

All in all, she still didn't know how to use half the things in here, but at least everything had a place and wasn't left in tangled piles like before. The Westons gave her a generous budget to work with, and she'd usually go all-out, but Grant suggested a few cheaper alternatives, and it turned out great—with cash to spare. Enough to ease the repair cost from Connor's rampage.

Grant finished arranging the leftover items on the shelf, then stepped beside her. He let out a deep breath and wiped a bead of sweat from his forehead. "We're done?"

"We're done," she confirmed, then pivoted on her heel and flashed a wide smile. "Thanks for all the help. Having a cowboy around sure comes in handy."

"I was just following instructions." He chuckled at her enthusiasm. "This looks amazing, sunflower. It's about time this place got an upgrade."

She should be used to his compliments by now, but a blush heated her cheeks. "The work you did really pulled it all together. I might even be a little impressed."

He smirked, a dangerous combination of full lips and dimples framed by a chiseled jaw. The plain white t-shirt and dark denim jeans only added to his country charm. "Dreaming of the day I build you a walk-in closet?"

"Ha." She rolled her eyes, then gave him a questioning glance. "Are you serious?"

"Why not?" He shrugged. "I'd build us a whole house if you wanted."

Us. That damn blush got hotter.

"Or..." He hummed in thought. "There might be other things I can build." When she gave him a questioning glance, he put both hands on her hips and turned her around. "Bend over for me, hands on the wall."

His simple touch was enough to burn through her clothes. "Um, like right here?" She laughed but bent as instructed and stretched her palms across the wood. Brazen of him to get naughty out in the open, but she'd take every opportunity they had left.

And though she'd never admit it, the rough command in his voice got her riled up. She wanted to see how far she could push before he pushed back—and how he'd do it.

"Just for a minute," he clarified.

"Uh-huh." She rolled her hips and wiggled her ass, sure that he could see plenty through the gap of her shorts. "Take all the time you need."

He snorted.

The soles of his boots creaked as he moved across the room, but she couldn't figure out his plan. Why walk away *after* she'd gotten in position?

"I've always wanted to try this," he murmured. Just as she was about to turn around, a swish cut through the air, followed by a sharp sting on her ass.

"Ouch!" Her hands flew up, and she jumped, casting a wide-eyed look over her shoulder. "What was that for?"

He bit back a smile while holding his chosen instrument of pain—a riding crop—ready for another strike. "Not feeling it?"

"Oh, I'm feeling it." She rubbed her backside. "It makes me want to fight you."

Grant laughed and shook his head, moving to set down the riding crop.

"—But I'd also want you to win," she mumbled.

He paused. "That can be arranged."

She held his gaze, raising her eyebrows in a challenge. Light slanted through his irises, illuminating bright splinters of green that broke off into ominous shadows. He took a step closer, brandishing the riding crop in his palm. Lord have mercy—she'd created a monster.

He tsked. "You weren't supposed to move."

"And you're supposed to turn me on," she shot back. As if she hadn't already been turned on from watching him work. As if the fading throb on her skin hadn't made her blood rush, almost hoping for more.

Another tsk. "Patience, sunflower."

He pursed his lips, and with a playful huff, she turned around. This time, she prepared for the smack, but instead, it came as a teasing tap right between her legs.

"Oh," she exclaimed, curling her toes as her clit pulsed. How had his aim been so good?

Before she could get another word out, the swish sounded again, and a stripe of pain seared through her jeans. Her thighs squeezed together on instinct, but she sucked in a breath and widened her stance, wanting to keep her legs spread and give him easy access.

Which proved to be a mistake.

Anxiety sharpened her senses as she listened for the swish, but he made her wait. When it came, the crop cracked directly on her clit. Hard.

"Ow, okay. That one hurt." Tears welled in her eyes, and she crumbled, bracing her hands on her thighs.

"Sorry, sorry." Grant rushed to her side and smoothed his palms over her back. "I accidentally put too much strength into that one."

"Too strong for your own good," she joked, even though her voice rasped as she tried to breathe through the pain.

"I'll probably need to practice," he admitted.

She attempted to stand straight, then immediately decided it'd be best to sit on the bench. "Maybe start with learning to hold back."

"How do you know I wasn't?" he teased.

She groaned, and he pulled her onto his lap, cautious not to brush against the red burn marks that lingered on her calves. One of his hands settled over her thigh as the other cradled the back of her neck.

"I could kiss it better," he murmured.

He'd already brought his lips to hers, and she replied by sealing the kiss and letting herself melt into the distraction. The pain lingered, but it almost felt pleasant while wrapped in his arms. Like he could soothe any ache.

"Would you ever let me tie you up one day?" she wondered aloud. "See how many times I could make you come—milk out every last drop?"

"Fuck," he cursed and bit her lip. "I admit, that sounds interesting." The imprint of his semi-hard cock pressed into her ass, an eager volunteer. She ground against it, and his lips parted in a silent moan.

His pupils darkened as he rubbed a thumb over the bite marks he'd left on her skin. "Would you ever be sweet for me? Let me take complete control for a night?"

She captured his finger between her teeth and bit down, giving him marks of her own. He didn't so much as flinch. "Maybe. For one night."

"What's the catch?" His eyebrows shot up.

She grinned. He knew her too well. "You'd have to become rodeo champion first."

He slanted his head. "How'd you know what it's called?"

"I've been looking into it," she admitted. "When I first asked, it seemed like you didn't want to tell me, so I learned on my own."

He leaned over and pecked a kiss on her nose. "Too curious for your own good. Well then, now I have lots of things to practice."

Her heart flipped. Had he agreed to compete again that easily? All based on her silly little challenge?

A bang echoed from the main area of the barn, and they both startled. Grant pressed a finger over his lips, then quietly slipped her onto the bench and stepped outside. She heard him sigh before he reappeared in the doorway. "Must be almost lunchtime. Lucy's eager for her daily treat and to get outside."

"Guess that means we gotta get back to work." She slumped with an exaggerated frown as he walked over to her.

He dropped his head and mirrored her deflation. "Yeah, guess so." Then he placed a hand on her knee. "Are you sure you're okay?"

She nodded. "You sure know how to distract a girl."

"Oh, this isn't over," he warned.

"No, it's definitely not," she agreed.

THIRTY-TWO

Grant

THE OVERNIGHT CAMPING TRIP WAS BY FAR HIS FAVORITE PART OF the program. Preparing for it beforehand—not so much.

It felt like he'd run a marathon the past few days between coordinating with previous guests who were invited to join as extra assistants, a stable that let them lease more horses for the week, and getting supplies out from storage. Tents, sleeping pads, firewood, distilled water, and cooking gear, as well as food for themselves and the horses, had to be packed or transported to the campsite beforehand. Even with everyone pitching in, he'd barely gotten a spare moment to think.

But as soon as they started down the trail and he sat back in the saddle, taking a lungful of fresh mountain air, everything became worth it.

Evergreen trees and speckles of wildflowers lined the wide dirt lane, curious animals watching their trek from the woodland. The trail into the foothills started along the fence line behind the barn, crossed through an open field, and veered into the woods with a gentle slope.

They'd taken off after lunch and had been going for a good two hours already, stopping for a moment to enjoy a scenic view of the mountains, then turning around to look at Hollow Oak sprawling across the valley below. A view he'd seen many times but would never tire of.

A wide, bright blue sky mirrored the craggy peaks they rode toward, and a crisp breeze accompanied the pleasant heat of the sun on his back. A few darker clouds hovered to the north, but by the time rain fell, the group should be dry and sleeping soundly inside their tents.

He'd ridden these trails so often that he knew them like the back of his hand, either from camping with friends or taking a weekend off to explore alone. Since the program had such a big group and inexperienced riders, they wouldn't get too far in, but regardless of scope, this path inspired him every time. Nothing quite matched being surrounded by nature and taking only what their horses could carry.

Leading the group along the trail, the Westons rode side by side. He couldn't hear their words from this far back, but Mrs. Weston made an exaggerated gesture with her hands, and a few of the guests behind her laughed. She turned with a stage whisper and pressed a finger to her lips. He forgot how social she could be when she wasn't working behind the scenes. Last year, she'd stayed back with a few guests who opted out of the trip, but this time around, everyone had been onboard—including Serena, which he had hoped for but hadn't fully expected.

On the other hand, Mr. Weston wore what might've appeared like a bored expression. But every now and then, he'd contribute a nod or chuckle, and in response to Mrs. Weston's antics, he turned with a remark of his own that earned him a kick in the leg. The girls behind them burst out in a fit of laughter as Mrs. Weston shook her head. The man was a better listener than some gave him credit for, and it wasn't hard to tell how much he adored his wife.

Forty-four years. A damn long time to be married to the

same person and still be having that much fun. Even though he'd seen them bicker, the Westons also shared countless moments like this.

Finding his own person to share those moments with had once felt like a too-distant fantasy. A hopeless aspiration. Now, he'd gotten lucky enough for someone else to consider him *their person*.

The fact that he'd been able to single out Serena's laugh so many times on the trip indicated how comfortable she'd grown in his world. Lucy was cleared to go, too, and so far, the pair had been busy socializing with the other guests and making sure no one felt left behind. Not many people could brighten the mood the way his sunflower did.

Another benefit of the trip was he had no chores. They had no classes or workshops—meaning no distractions.

He'd always preferred to act rather than think. To *do* instead of waiting until he got overwhelmed with worry or regret. But Serena asked him to think through their next moves, so he let his mind wander. Went over the type of life he planned to pursue and thought about how, and if, college could contribute. Not every path he'd pictured for himself had been tied to the ranch.

He tried to imagine a life without her, and that's how he knew any sacrifice would be worth it. God willing, maybe they could still learn and laugh together fifty years from now. It didn't really matter where.

Two pairs of riders ahead, Serena weaved in line with Renae and Richard, then turned and motioned for him to join. He raised a hand and pointed at himself. She rolled her eyes and gestured again.

Grinning from ear to ear, he nudged his horse and caught up with them. "I started to think y'all forgot about me back here. Wouldn't even have noticed if I got eaten by a mountain lion."

"Better you than one of us," Renae teased.

"Are there really mountain lions?" Serena asked, her eyes wide.

He laughed. "None that would attack a group of people and horses this big."

"I'm still not sure I won't fall off." Richard hadn't stopped holding onto the saddle horn since they left, but he looked much more comfortable than when he first mounted.

"You're doing great," Grant replied. "The only thing that would make Appa bolt is if you threw an apple past her nose. Even then, the fastest she'd get to is a trot."

"Oh, I think I have one of those in my pocket!" Renae pulled out a shiny green apple and held it in the air.

Serena tried to stifle her laugh as Richard glared at his sister. "Don't even try it. I will bring you down with me."

"You know what? I could use a snack." Serena held out her hand to Renae and turned to Richard. "There, I took care of the threat."

"Personally, I'd prefer falling off a horse to more self-defense lessons with Mr. Weston," Grant admitted, chuckling.

Richard groaned. "I only managed to get the upper hand with him that one time."

"Hell yeah, but that's not a small feat. You were on fire the other day," Grant said.

Richard grinned. "It's been fun learning with you. Actually...I wanted to know if you could teach me some of the stuff you went over in your equine lessons? I didn't mind the alternate classes, but I want to know more about horses, too."

"Of course." Grant glanced at Serena, who was preoccupied with munching on her apple, and tried not to get distracted as she licked the juice from her lips. "That's why you called me over? You helped with the lessons, I'm sure you could've explained the basics."

She shrugged. "Maybe I prefer listening to a professional cowboy."

"Or you weren't paying enough attention." He raised his eyebrows. She sighed. "Well then, let's start from the beginning..."

❀

When their group made it to the small clearing where they'd stay overnight, the Westons and several returning guests had already begun to show the others how to set up camp. Grant dismounted next to Serena, then helped her, Renae, and Richard off their mounts.

"I'd say it's time for an afternoon nap." Renae stretched her arms above her head, and a *pop* came from her spine. She peeked out the corner of her eye to see if Grant would take the bait.

He pursed his lips. "Your horse is the one who did all the work. Now it's your turn to make dinner."

"Ugh," Renae huffed.

"Thank you for being nice to Richard." Serena patted Appa on the neck and held out an apple core in her palm. "Here, I saved this just for you."

Appa immediately took interest and picked it up with her lips. Such a polite horse. Lucy snorted, kicking her hoof on the ground and nudging Serena's shoulder.

"I brought treats for you, too. Don't get jealous," she scolded.

"You spoil them," Grant chastised, walking up beside her.

"What can I say? A girl's gotta look out for her own." Serena flipped her hair and gave what she probably meant as a cute eye roll. It made him want to throw her over his shoulder. *He'd* be the only one she needed to look after her.

Renae agreed with an enthusiastic nod, and Richard

shrugged as if to say he hadn't figured out how to deal with women, either.

Grant shook his head with a defeated sigh. Their little exchange helped shake him out of his mind and enjoy the present. And he'd be a hypocrite not to admit he wanted to spoil Serena as much as she spoiled Lucy and Appa.

"Come on, I'll show you how to tie the horses up. Then you need to take off the saddles and give 'em a good brush." He led them to the lean-to barn at the edge of the woods, built to hold supplies and provide a roof for the animals. Hay had been hauled up in an ATV the day before, and a hand pump pulled fresh water from an underground spring into troughs along the side.

The campsite sat at the junction between two hills, a smaller one with a stream and a larger one that buffered the wind. A central area had been cleared and flattened for the firepit, with another graded just slightly downwards to drain potential rainfall. Several more sites like this were scattered up the trail for multi-day trips, with the land split between the Westons and a few other families that had lived here for generations. As far as he was concerned, a better place didn't exist to spend a night or ten outdoors.

Their group split as everyone got to work. While the guests who enrolled in equine therapy tended to the horses, the rest got busy prepping food and setting up tents. He walked through and helped make the horses happy, then went to check on Serena. He couldn't help hovering when it came to her first camping trip.

He found her circling a flat tent like a wolf assessing its target. "I think it goes like this?" She laid two poles in an X across the top. "No, that's not right. Like this, then?"

The girls assigned to share with her watched in equal confusion as she rearranged the poles in parallel lines. None of them looked confident.

"You had it right the first time."

Serena glanced over her shoulder, and her expression brightened as their eyes connected. Damn, he couldn't help but feel invincible when she looked at him like that. Like he'd move mountains if she needed—which he would. Even if he didn't know how, he'd find a way.

"And the cowboy comes to save the day," she greeted.

He had to remind himself not to snake a hand around her waist and pull her in for a kiss. "Or maybe I'm here to say you were right all along."

She laughed. "In theory, but I admit I'm lacking when it comes to execution. Let's see how an expert does it."

He obliged and showed them how to raise the poles, then hammered the stakes down a few more times for good measure. As the girls began to set up their sleeping pads inside, he brought out his hand shovel and started digging a small trench along the outside.

Serena crouched next to him and watched as he worked. "What's that for?"

"Redirects the rain so you don't wake up soaked."

"Ah, clever." Picking up one of the rocks he'd wedged against a stake, she continued digging in the opposite direction from where he'd started. "I bet it feels like we're holding you back, having to slow down and teach us everything. I'm sure you'd fly through this camping by yourself."

"Not at all," he replied. "And I don't think of it that way. Have you noticed how the returning guests know their way around? They were all beginners at some point, too. I'd be the one holding you back if I didn't share what I know."

She paused to stare at him. "Where did you come from?"

He tipped his head. "What?"

"Never mind." She chuckled, then winced. "Oh no, I don't think I can get back up."

"What's wrong?" He reached out and steadied her as she wobbled.

"The pants. I put gauze over my burns, but they rub when I move." She pressed a hand on the back of her calf.

His brows furrowed. Jeans would be best for riding, but in hindsight, they probably irritated her injuries. "You're supposed to let your skin get fresh air. I brought extra burn ointment. You need to use it and change your bandages if they're bothering you."

"That would be great, but I only brought these and leggings." She motioned to the small pack she'd set against a tree.

"You can wear my sweatpants," he offered.

She pouted. "Don't you want them?"

The girls inside the tent would easily be able to hear their conversation, but her thoughts came across loud and clear. Now, he wished they were camping alone. Then she wouldn't need to wear pants at all.

He narrowed his eyes. "I'm not asking. And now that you mention it, I might be better off without them."

She burst out in a fit of laughter. "Whatever you say."

THIRTY-THREE

Grant

Logs crackled and snapped as copper light flickered through the dark hues of dusk, illuminating Serena's legs in a warm glow. She'd kept well out of reach from the embers, but being near open flames didn't bother her as much as he thought it would. Her strength and resilience continued to amaze him.

With his back against the old stump she sat on, he stretched toward the warmth of the fire and let her feet rest in his lap while he tended to her burns. They made it seem like she'd been too exhausted to do it herself, but in reality, he needed an excuse to keep his hands on her.

What he really wanted was to pull her down and rediscover how she felt beneath him. Lick over her skin like the flames and give in to every dirty thought that crossed his mind. Ever since they'd been interrupted—twice now—it felt like the clock had begun spinning twice as fast. Even if he knew he'd see her after the program ended, he had one thing left to say. But it never felt like the right time.

She wiggled her toes, and he realized he'd stopped rubbing in the ointment. He looked up to see her lips quirk in a smile.

"Are my thoughts too loud?" he asked.

"No such thing." She smirked, then shifted her foot to nudge his groin.

He jumped and wrapped his hand over her ankle, setting it firmly on the ground. A quick glance confirmed no one had caught her in the act. Thank heavens. Everyone seemed to be preoccupied with their own conversations, enjoying a well-earned break as their dinner cooked in the fire.

"Don't be so bold when you know I can't do anything about it," he muttered under his breath, discreetly adjusting his pants.

Serena bit her lip. "Or maybe I'm giving you more reasons to follow through with all those threats."

"Then you better be ready when I do," he replied.

Even barefoot and in baggy clothing, he couldn't keep his eyes off her. A messy braid fell over one shoulder, the gold strands shimmering along the curve of her neck. He knew if he pulled her jacket back, the cold air would tighten her nipples into pretty peaks under her shirt. His sweatpants were a size too big, and their tight cinch accentuated her small waist, drawing his eyes to the flare of her hips.

Leaning on her hands, she looked so naturally breathtaking that he could've mistaken her for some type of woodland royalty. Or the personification of a succubus straight out of his most guarded fantasies.

"I'm glad you seem to be enjoying yourself," he noted instead of letting his thoughts drift too far.

"I am." She sighed and gazed off into the fire. "I do miss my creature comforts, but I find the company makes up for what nature lacks."

He snorted. "So you'd go camping with me again?"

She hummed. "Only if you promise to take me to new places. It feels like going on an adventure, like learning to live again."

"I'll take you on as many adventures as you want, sunflower," he murmured.

She smiled down at him, and this was it; he had to say it. He had to tell her. Who cared if everyone else heard because he meant it—

"Timer's up!" Mrs. Weston called across the camp. "If you put your food in with the last batch, it should be done now."

Serena perked up as he bit his tongue. "Does that mean dinner's ready?"

"Yep, let me grab both of ours." He stood and pushed his emotions aside.

Their experience wouldn't be complete without his favorite meal: foil packets stuffed with meat, potatoes, and fresh vegetables seasoned perfectly in salt and butter. When the group finished eating, there were no leftovers in sight. Clean-up was as easy as throwing away the plates, and roasting sticks and marshmallows were passed around as the flames diminished to white-hot coals.

The forest grew dark, clouds hiding the stars with a black veil. A chilly breeze carried the scent of fresh rain, and everyone huddled closer to the fire. Yawns bounced from one person to the next in a comical domino effect.

Mr. Weston stood, waiting while he gathered the group's attention. "As you know, we're done with official workshops and meetings. Tomorrow night, you'll all be packing to go home and return to your lives—hopefully with a few new ideas and perspectives." He cleared his throat.

"I want to congratulate you all for making it to the end and offer my personal thanks. I've seen you get up and rise to the occasion every day this month. None of you volunteered for this" —his gaze moved over Serena— "but you did volunteer your efforts, and that hasn't gone unnoticed. In my opinion, it says far more about you than it does about the program.

Despite our best intentions, it's your choice in the end to benefit from what we offer."

Grant thought about Connor. Seemed like he'd been more of a victim of his circumstances than anything else—but just like Serena, and just like himself, that didn't have to become their destiny. Even if leaving the ranch felt daunting, exploring a world different from his own could be exactly what he needed.

"Per tradition," Mr. Weston continued, "we invite each of you to share a highlight or thought about what you learned during your time here, but don't feel obligated to do so. You're free to pass or say something simple. Not all of us are good at making speeches." He grimaced.

Mrs. Weston chuckled and stood beside him. "I'll take that as my cue." She gave him a pat on the arm. "Actions are often better than words, anyway."

"This summer has been more eventful than I would have liked," she sighed. "I worry about each of you. We've done this program for many years without anyone getting hurt, and I feel responsible for not being more cautious."

Grant shifted as guilt twisted his gut. Serena nudged his shoulder, and he met her eyes. She didn't blame him, nor would she want anyone to be burdened by her injuries. His fingers curled, itching to grab her hand, but he kept still. She seemed to understand and brushed her leg against his arm.

"Despite that, I am proud we were able to get through these difficulties together. One event can either tear us down or build us up, and you all reminded me how important it is to keep improving. I hope to have helped all of you, but know that you taught me something, too," Mrs. Weston finished.

The spotlight passed to a returning guest, who shared some of the challenges they faced since being home. The rest continued in a similar fashion. Several guests chose to pass, while others spoke about skills they learned or what they hoped to change.

Halfway around the circle, Renae stood for her turn. Grant noticed the boys who had sided with Connor avoiding eye contact. Perhaps their guilt served a purpose.

"Honestly, my first few days here were hard," Renae started. "I'm used to not fitting in. Then a few of you became my friends—wanted to know me for me, and that mattered a lot." She shared a smile with Serena, then a couple of the girls sitting next to her. "So, I appreciate everyone who gave me a chance. I hope we can keep in touch when we go home, and maybe I can keep learning about horses, too." She finished with a nod and sat down.

Richard fidgeted with his hands next to her, speaking while seated. "Uh, I'm not great at talking or being the center of attention..."

He paused, looked at Grant, then took a deep breath and stood. "I learned we aren't all good at the same things, but we can all do something. Even if it takes time to find our strengths, or see our weaknesses in a new way. I'm glad you didn't let me give up. Going forward, I want to help others learn the same thing."

Grant tipped his hat in approval. They'd talked privately about Richard coming back for riding lessons next year, and he'd love to teach the kid more. The Westons even agreed to sponsor him if needed. Grant hadn't thought about training someone else to take his position, but now that his plans were changing, he knew Richard could be a great addition to the program if he wanted the job.

The wind picked up and blew smoke in a different direction, making them shuffle around the fire as the last few guests spoke. Then Serena rose to her feet and brushed off her hands. Everyone listened a little more intently.

"In a lot of ways, I wasn't prepared to be here. I almost didn't come at all." She chewed her lip. "But I found someone willing to teach me even when I was too prideful to ask." Heat crept across his face as she spared him a quick glance. Whispers passed through the group. "I found a new home, and I'm excited to see where that leads. Thanks for letting me be a part of the program with you all."

He couldn't have been more proud. This wasn't the same woman who bickered with him over suitcases and shied away from farm animals. She'd grown into a woman who wasn't afraid to rewrite her life and, more importantly, someone who showed him how to do the same.

Everyone's eyes turned to him. Shit, he hadn't thought about this part.

He stood and looped his thumbs in his jeans. It took a moment before he knew where to start. "I think I needed this summer as much as any of you. I—" His breath caught, and his chest felt like it was about to burst. "I love Hollow Oak. I love working on the ranch, but I forgot that the best part of loving something can be sharing it with someone else."

He looked over at Serena and squared his jaw. "Keep working hard. Keep searching for good things, and when you find them, don't let go."

THIRTY-FOUR

Serena

LIGHTNING FLASHED ACROSS THE SKY—A WHITE-PURPLE STREAK in the clouds that made a silhouette of the trees before it frayed into ribbons. The flare illuminated their cozy campfire just as Grant finished speaking, and the group went still. A simultaneous *oh shit* realization passed through their faces.

"Change of plans. Time to go inside your tents," Mr. Weston announced. The heavy emotions from a moment before vanished in the face of nature's whim, and everyone broke out into a frenzy, rushing to take cover.

The storm came all at once, from nothing to a downpour. Thunder crashed through the trees with a deep, powerful resonance as if the sky itself was splitting in two. Rivulets of rain forged new pathways in the gravel, and now that trench Grant made around her tent seemed like a godsend.

She'd hoped to get a moment alone with him after what he'd said. To thank him and figure out how to express what had been weighing on her heart—what she only had one day left to say.

Instead, Grant anchored an arm around her back and steered her straight to her tent, where the other girls were scrambling inside and fumbling with the flap. "Don't try to go out in the storm," he instructed. "Keep dry and stay away from the edges of the tent. You should be fine. It'll pass."

Watching him switch into automatic protector mode reinforced everything she felt, but she only got in a brief "thank you" and a nod goodnight. A void tugged at the center of her chest that festered as he walked off to help the others.

Soon, she'd be the one walking away. Back to her family and a campus where people knew who she used to be, not who she'd decided to become. Shaping her old life into a new one wouldn't be an overnight fix, and potentially a lonely one at that. But she'd spent enough time alone on the ranch not to mind forging her own way, and it wasn't the thought of being alone that bothered her. It was being without *him*.

Just like when she'd found Grant slouched over the dining room table. The haunted look in his eyes reminded her all too well of how she'd felt on her way here. Fighting doubts she didn't want to acknowledge and hiding from her fear of failing. She'd carried plenty of regrets herself—knew how old pains could transform into new ones while you weren't looking. Things like that, the feelings that went so deep you couldn't see where they started or ended, were hard to explain and even harder to share.

But somehow, she understood his struggle without needing words. Wanted to help him through it as much as he helped her. Even though she claimed it'd just been sex between them, all their discussions opened her eyes to what he'd been through, too. And sparked a hope that she might have a bigger purpose in his life.

Despite the complexity of it all, Grant made the solution seem simple. Like she'd given him an answer even though all she'd ever had were questions of her own. Like she *was* his answer.

Then he became her answer that morning in the tack room,

when life felt simple, and no problem was too big to solve if he was with her. When he'd talked about competing, and building houses, and doing things to each other she wouldn't dare tell another soul. She'd actually pictured herself with him—cheering him on from the stands, cooking dinner together in their house, letting him bind her after she'd bound and toyed with him.

It seemed too good to be true, yet that's just how being with Grant was. Too good. Too perfect to leave to fate.

But time had become her enemy.

Raindrops pelted the tent in never-ending waves, and the wind beat mercilessly against one side. Thunder collided overhead. The walls looked like they were caving in, but the poles held strong. Grant had made sure their tent would be secure. The other three girls barricaded themselves in sleeping bags and foam pads, chattering about the storm.

"That was intense! Did you see it?"

"Yeah, scared the shit out of me. I've never seen lightning like that."

"I know! What about you? Hey—hey, are you awake? Guys, I think she fell asleep already."

Another flash of lightning revealed a girl-shaped lump curled into a ball next to Renae. She could've gone quiet due to sleep or from anxiety, but either way, talking about the weather wouldn't help.

"Let her sleep. It's probably better to rest while we wait out the storm," Serena said with a yawn. Grant's sweatpants had gotten wet at the bottom, but they were too comfy to take off and smelled like him, so she rolled up the hem and crawled into her sleeping bag. "And by the way, I'm proud of you guys. Not just for opening up tonight but for surviving the whole month. I know how tempting it was to give up."

"Thanks. I really liked what you said, too—" A yawn

interrupted the girl's sentence. "Didn't realize how tired I was until I laid down."

Renae chuckled and flopped around in her sleeping bag, settling on her side facing Serena. Soft, even breaths filled the tent. "I meant it. Thank you for being my friend," she whispered.

Serena smiled, although the dark made it impossible to see. "You're welcome. That goes both ways—being able to help you gave me the chance to connect with everyone else."

"Yeah, Grant was a super helpful teacher and all, but it's also good to have someone you can relate to, you know?" Renae sighed. "You two are so cute. I hope I get to fall in love someday."

A hot blush took the chill out of her face. Guess they hadn't done such a good job hiding it, after all. "Well, we both have a lot to figure out, too. Relationships aren't always what they seem like in romance books."

Certainly not the ones she'd had in the past. Not to say what she had with Grant wasn't sparks and butterflies—it was all of it and more, but if that's all she got out of this month, it wouldn't have done much good. And though she hated to admit it, she wouldn't have been ready for a serious relationship without some self-reflection first.

"What I'm trying to say is there's more to love than *falling in love*," she continued. "You don't need to wait to find someone before you experience it. Love yourself. Love the fun parts of life, love learning, and even figuring out how to get through the not-so-fun parts of life. I think forgetting that is part of why I had to come here."

"That makes sense," Renae mumbled. "Then when you do meet your soulmate, you can love all those things together."

"Yeah," she whispered.

Lightning illuminated Renae's face as her eyes shut, the sleeping bag pulled up to her nose. Their conversation faded, and the muted roar of raindrops took over. Serena blinked into the dark. The rumble of thunder clashed with the beat of her heart.

That was it. She loved Grant—and loved life *with* him. Loved deeper because of him. As soon as they were together again, she'd say it. Tell him everything.

With that thought, exhaustion finally overcame her restlessness, and she slipped into a light sleep.

It didn't last long.

Outside, wind and rain continued to shake the trees, and thunder crashed in the distance. She tossed and turned, unable to get comfortable. Something didn't feel right. Not just that she hadn't spoken to Grant or that she woke wishing he were next to her to chase away the bad dreams.

The storm hadn't let up.

Every flash of lightning felt like a signal, a warning. Was everyone else okay? What about the horses? Eventually, she made up her mind and slipped out of the sleeping bag, trying not to disturb the others. She pulled her jacket closed and braced herself for the cold, then stepped out of the tent.

Rain plastered her hair to her neck as she breathed in rich soil and minty pine sap. She could barely see in front of her feet. Searching her pocket, she found the flashlight Grant had given her and clicked it on. The forest looked gray and foreboding, opposite of the vibrant frontier they'd ridden through during the day. Wet dirt splashed on her shoes and soaked into her socks.

It wasn't difficult to find Grant's tent. He'd brought a personal one—smaller than the rest and lower to the ground. It weathered the storm better, but he must've had to fold himself in two just to get inside.

She stopped outside his door. How did one go about knocking on a tent without looking like a wild animal? What if he thought she was some kind of angry bear?

Before she figured out what to do, the zipper pulled open, and Grant's head poked through. His blond hair looked damp and curled at the ends, his shirt twisted at the hip to expose a strip of skin. If he was cold, it didn't show.

"Sunflower?" His eyebrows pulled together. He looked down as if trying to find a way to squeeze them both inside a tent that barely fit him. "I saw the flashlight. Why are you outside?"

I missed you.

"Um, I'm worried about the horses." Which was also true. "But I figured I shouldn't go alone."

The last time she'd ventured out late at night, she'd almost been turned into a roasted marshmallow. And not the perfect, golden kind that went well with melted chocolate.

Grant looked up. "You came to bring me with you?"

She nodded.

His worry lines smoothed for a moment, then he stuck out his hand and extended his hat. "Here. Take this; it'll keep the rain off your head."

A little too late for it to do much good, but she took it and tied it under her chin so the wind wouldn't blow it off. Water poured off the brim instead of into her eyes so she didn't have to blink as much. "Thanks, that's better."

He searched her face. "The horses should be fine. They've been through storms before." But as he spoke, he tugged on his boots and a waterproof jacket with a hood. "I'll go with you and check things out if you want."

She stepped aside to make room, and as soon as he exited the tent, he tucked her against his side. "I'm really glad you thought to get me first."

She hugged him back, his body heat seeping through her wet clothes and finally soothing the unease. "I hope it's not a bother."

He tipped up her face and pressed a hot kiss to her lips. "Never."

Taking her hand, they went around the tents and up to the lean-to barn. The horses stood along the fence at either side, most sleeping comfortably under the roof. Rain angled inside on the edges, but the horses getting wet didn't seem to mind. A few swiveled their ears and looked up curiously as she passed.

The storm must've bothered her more than any of them. *Relax, they're okay.*

Then, she spotted an empty space at the end. Hoping the horses had shuffled closer to each other to stay dry, she aimed the flashlight where the last horse should be. Where *her* horse should be. Her stomach dropped at the sight of a broken ring of metal where she'd tied the rope just hours earlier—and no horse.

Lucy was gone.

THIRTY-FIVE

Grant

"We'll find her, I promise."

Lightning cast shadows of the rhythmic windshield wipers and sliding raindrops onto Serena's face. Her cheeks were flushed from the cold air, streaks of drying hair curled around her neck. He hated how distraught she looked.

She hadn't said a word since he'd opened the shed behind the barn and started up the emergency ATV. They bounced along the trail, backtracking their steps in the rain. It pelted the roof with a metallic ping as wet gravel crunched under the tires.

Serena kept her eyes fixed out the cracked-open window, refusing even to blink as she shone her flashlight into the trees from the passenger seat. He gave her leg a reassuring squeeze, the cotton sweatpants damp from when she'd stood outside his tent. She covered his hand with hers and squeezed back.

Earlier, he'd laid awake for hours, wishing she were beside him tonight. Worried that her first night sleeping outdoors had to be in crappy weather like this. Or maybe he couldn't sleep because he didn't know when he'd see her again after tomorrow.

Being alone had never bothered him. After sharing a room with his brothers for most of his life, he coveted his own space. Even with Payton, a simple phone call or text had been enough.

But he couldn't stand the thought of having Serena so close and not holding her. Not keeping her body against his to keep away the cold, not sharing kisses or secrets, or whatever the fuck else she wanted to do to pass the time. For however long she wanted to do it.

The fact that she came to him—even for something as small as being anxious in an unfamiliar environment—meant everything. It meant she trusted him to take care of her. She could've easily gone out alone, could have ended up lost or hurt in the storm, and made him sick with worry, but instead, she actually asked for his help. Lord knew he'd do anything for that woman, whether it meant sheltering her from a storm or going out in one.

"What if she isn't close to the trail?" Serena whispered, breaking their silent vigil. "What if she went where we can't find her?"

He squeezed her thigh again, and she exhaled into the touch. "Wherever Lucy went, it's somewhere she senses will be safe. Horses have a better intuition about these things than humans."

Serena sniffed. "It's my fault. I must not have tied her up right. I didn't check on her before we went to sleep. I could've seen if something was wrong. I could've done something—"

"Don't blame yourself." He flipped her hand and put their palms together. It'd be no use spiraling with negative thoughts. "Lucy isn't a trail horse like the others. I should have asked her owner if anything might spook her. Even then, you can't predict how a horse will react in new situations."

"But what if she hurts herself again?" Serena turned to him with pleading eyes. "What if—"

He hit the brakes and cut her off with a kiss, wrapping a hand around the back of her neck to tug her close. She shivered and leaned into him as her lips softened. "We'll find her," he whispered. "Whatever happens, I'll take care of it."

She nodded and tried to break away with a shaky breath, but he pulled her back for more. No way was he letting her go until she understood. Until his certainty overshadowed every single one of her doubts.

Their kiss deepened as she gave in—not from lust or longing, but because she let him carry her worry. Give her strength. Because they were in this together.

He cradled her lips between his and warmed her chilled skin, entwining their fingers. The taste of her alone was enough to clear his head and keep him steady. "You're with me, sunflower. I got you."

She rested her head on his arm, and some of the tension left her limbs. "Okay, let's keep looking."

They continued down the trail for over an hour, scanning for clues and whistling into the dark. The rain would've washed away any hoof prints, but he searched for newly broken branches or strands of hair caught from Lucy running by.

She was a smart horse and, if anything, was probably waiting for them back at the barn, wondering why the heck humans wanted to sleep outdoors. But Serena wouldn't be able to rest without knowing Lucy was safe, and he couldn't stand still if either of them were in trouble.

The crack and boom of thunder filled the silence. Eventually, the rain slowed to a decent drizzle, and the forest thinned. They neared the back of the pastures, only a couple miles from reaching the main house. If they were going to find Lucy, this was their last chance.

Serena began to chew her lip and gazed across the open field. "Wait—Stop. I think I see something."

He let off the gas and leaned over.

"There—" She pointed to a spot along the fence that bordered the woods. One of the poles had been pushed askew, the wire yanked free and tangled on the ground. "See it?"

"Mhm." He pulled to the side and put the ATV in park. "Stay here."

Her hand had already gone to the door handle.

He grabbed her chin and locked their eyes. "I mean it. *Stay. Here.* Don't make me worry about you, too."

Serena pushed past his grip and gave him a quick kiss.

"That's not gonna change—"

She rolled her eyes. "Fine. I'll let you handle it, cowboy."

He sighed, but she was smiling for the first time since they'd sat down, so he let it slide. They kept a pair of walkie-talkies in a compartment by the dash, and he reached in and handed one to her. "Press this button to turn the screen on. This one to talk."

She nodded and took the device.

"Since you offered, I'll take one more for the road." He leaned in to steal another kiss along with his hat, then hopped outside.

Cold rain slid down his arms and wet grass stuck to his jeans. The air felt clean and crisp. The worst of it may have been over, but lightning strikes still lit up billowing clouds across the field. He stuck to the tree line and marched out to the broken fence.

No horse in sight.

Inspecting the damage, he found a knot of black hair snagged into the wood. Hope sparked in his chest.

The walkie-talkie crackled. "Got anything?"

"Gimme a sec."

He let out a piercing whistle and held his breath, aiming the flashlight into the field.

Nothing.

Fuck. Maybe she'd made it all the way to the barn, after all.

A snap behind him from the woods made him spin.

Lucy tentatively stepped out of the shadows and shifted on her feet. She lowered her head, ears on a constant swivel.

Thank God. He clicked the walkie-talkie on. "Found her."

Serena cheered on the other end. "Is she all right?"

Lucy's ears piqued at Serena's voice, but she hesitated to approach.

"Don't know. Can't see anything." He stepped toward Lucy and clicked his tongue. "C'mere girl. That's it. I'll bring you back."

As soon as he got close enough, he grabbed the lead rope dangling from her halter and stroked a hand along her neck. Moving his hand to her back, he did a quick evaluation. No cuts or blood stains. Her leg didn't seem to be bothering her, but the injury might swell tomorrow if she'd run too much. Back to stall rest, then. He'd call the vet in the morning.

Lucy kept shifting, obviously nervous, but poked her nose near his pockets to check for treats. He shook his head. "Broke the fence trying to get home, just to decide that waiting under the trees was better? And you think you deserve a treat for that?"

Lucy snorted.

What a handful. "Let's go."

He carefully led her to the trail, stopping at the window of the ATV. Serena reached out her hand, and Lucy nuzzled her with fuzzy lips, puffing hot air on Serena's palm.

"I'm happy to see you, too." Serena's eyes went soft and watery.

A warm, restless feeling tugged at his heart. God, he loved these two. Even with the panic and threat of danger, he wouldn't want to be out here with anyone else.

"I'll have to walk her back to the barn. Think you can drive the ATV?" he asked.

Serena's smile widened. "I've been waiting for a chance to get behind the wheel."

"You'll have to go slow."

"Yeah, yeah."

He knew better—that woman had one speed, and it wasn't slow.

THIRTY-SIX

A HALF-HIDDEN MOON BATHED THE RANCH IN SILVER LIGHT AS SHE parked the ATV beside the barn. The steady drizzle of rain tapped against the roof, wet leaves shimmering in the calm wind.

Grant said to wait inside as he finished putting Lucy in her stall. But she'd never been good at doing what she was told.

Stepping into the mist, cold droplets slid over her face and down her neck. It felt refreshing now that her worry had passed —when she'd found a way through it with Grant at her side. The heat of her pulse thudded against the chill like a live wire under her skin. A reminder of how amazing it felt to be alive.

How amazing it felt to be *here*.

She took off her jacket and left it in the ATV, walking across the path to a patch of trees and grass. The earth had soaked up the rain, and her footsteps sunk into the dirt. Her fingertips drifted across foliage that would soon turn green and vibrant from the storm. Too bad she wouldn't be here to see it.

Seasons used to pass without her noticing, the weather an afterthought—either inconsequential or an inconvenience. But the ranch changed every day, and watching it constantly adapt made her feel like she could, too.

Lightning crackled on the horizon. She watched it light up the sky, then closed her eyes and turned her face to the clouds. An accompanying wave of thunder rolled through her with a deep, resonating thrum.

She understood why Grant didn't want to leave. Why she couldn't breathe at the thought of leaving herself—this was what she needed. A place where she could grow roots *and* spread her wings.

The click of a door closing and the rustle of boots signaled Grant's approach, but he didn't say anything—he didn't need to. His hands found her arms and smoothed away the goosebumps. She shivered at his touch. Could something be more than perfect? Flawed and whole at the same time?

She parted her lips to finally say how she felt, then heard him take a small, quick inhale. "I love you."

Her heart beat right out of her chest. Their eyes met. A hot raindrop rolled down her cheek.

"It's okay if you don't—" he continued.

"Of course I love you, Grant," she blurted. Even in the dark, his expression was so clear, unfailingly genuine. He loved her, and she didn't need to question how deep that went. "I love when you're bossy and gruff. I love when you're sweet and soft. I love working beside each other and running off together. I love...this." She pressed his hand to her heart, hoping it could convey all the things she didn't have words for. "I feel like if I take my eyes off you for one second, I'll miss too much."

Her voice caught, and the next words came out in a broken whisper. "What am I going to do without you?"

He gathered her tears with a gentle swipe of his thumb and covered her mouth with his. "You're not going anywhere without me, sunflower."

And just like that, she could breathe again. It was the warm puff of his words against her lips, the way he cradled her in calloused palms. It was the scent of rain on his skin mixed with a fragrance entirely his own. The way he felt like home.

His tongue swept into her mouth, and she rose on her toes to get closer. He scorched her soul with his fervor, gripping her tight and reiterating every endearment he'd ever said. She melted into him, into their fusion of desire and vulnerability—into the mutual claim they had carved into the other.

Thunder clapped overhead and filled her with its vibration. Of all the times they could have done this, of all the moments they let pass without confessing, *this* had to be the time they chose. In the final hour, a bitter-sweet promise wrapped in the aftermath of tempest and turmoil.

"I'm going to come back," she whispered into the feverish kiss, not wanting to separate for a single second. His lips were so soft, but also hot and demanding. Her fingers twisted in his jacket and she pulled open the zipper, craving the heat of his skin. "I want you to keep learning how to ride. I want to see Lucy compete again. I want to watch you win."

"I know," he murmured while covering her face in infinite, delectable kisses. "I know. We'll do all of it. And I'm going to the city with you. I don't know when, but I'll come." He pressed his forehead to hers. "As long as we make our way back here, together."

She nodded, choking on a laugh mixed with a sob. "Yes. Absolutely. We can do it all and I'd still want more."

"I'll always want more of you," he groaned. His hands found her hips and he rolled their bodies—a slow, indulgent motion that sent sparks up and down her spine.

"Don't hold back," she begged.

"Couldn't if I tried." He grabbed the front of her sweatpants in his fists and ripped apart the center seam. She whimpered as the night air kissed her thighs, barely able to mourn the ruined clothing.

"I have more pairs," Grant said with a knowing chuckle, already nibbling on her breast through the wet shirt. Her nipples had tightened from the cold, and when his teeth closed around one and tugged with a sharp bite, she lost her mind.

"Fuck, I can't—" She didn't know what. Couldn't think. Couldn't move. Couldn't believe this was really happening. Didn't want it to ever stop.

Even though it hurt, even though it felt like she might split in two, loving him had been the best decision of her entire life—and she didn't need to look back twenty years later to know it.

"Good thing *I* can," he replied, then took off his hat and set it on her head. "You've earned this, sunflower." He sank to his knees in the mud. "Now let me have what's mine."

The absence of his touch mingled with the throb of his bite, and she tangled her hands in his hair to make him share the pain. The damp strands curled between her fingers, soft like silk. More lightning flashed behind him as the storm hovered at the edge of her vision.

He tipped his head up and met her gaze, pupils wide and hungry. A sliver of glow from the moon broke through the clouds and highlighted the angles of his face, revealing a dark flush on his cheeks. His lips were swollen, full and red.

She wanted to kiss him again—to kiss him forever—but then his thumbs hooked around her panties. He ripped them, too. Hot anticipation sparked between her legs. She bit her lip, noting the hard imprint of his dick tenting his jeans and the way his eyes devoured her nakedness.

His mouth latched onto her pussy with the sound of a man starved half to death, and it obliterated her last shred of control.

Wind and thunder carried her moan as his tongue banished the chill, sweeping through her slit in long strokes. It felt like all the electricity in the sky gathered on the tip of

Grant's tongue. His hands spread her thighs open further, fingers stretching over her skin. She buckled as he pulled her clit between his lips and sucked.

"I'm gonna fall," she gasped.

He moved one hand to her ass while the other gripped her waist, steadying them with bruising strength. "Ride my face," he panted, voice muffled between her legs.

She managed a breathless chuckle. "More riding lessons? I'm sore from camping."

He answered with a slap on her ass. She arched into the sting, making her hips roll against his mouth. Oh, *fuck*. He licked inside, and she threw her head back, rolling her hips again to take him deeper, fucking his face until his nose nudged her clit.

She tightened her grip on his hair and made him moan. His voice sounded as rough and needy as the rumbling sky.

He coaxed her into a rhythm, and she lost herself to the pleasure. It took effort to stay upright, sweat beading on her back and a burn working its way up her legs. If anything, the soreness made it better, each clench of her muscles accompanied by a twinge of pain. Cold rain continued to soak her clothes as it rolled down her chest and stomach.

When the first wave of the orgasm hit, she had to grip his shoulders and sink her nails into his muscles, feeling them flex. He kept sucking her clit with quick flickers of his tongue, and she cried out, shaking and grinding against him until her body collapsed from exhaustion.

He caught her as she fell, circling his arms around her back to lay her down. Faintly, she felt the slight give of wet earth and whispering blades of grass against her skin. His hat rolled off and let her hair fan over the ground.

Grant kneeled above her, face glistening. Lips parted. His jacket had come off, and the white t-shirt clung to his chest like a second skin. It hitched over his hips, bunched from where she'd gripped him. His pulse throbbed in a vein running from his jaw to his collarbone.

"Say it again," he rasped.

Did she say anything when she came? She couldn't remember even being able to form words. But it wasn't hard to guess what he wanted to hear.

"I love you, Grant."

His eyelids fluttered, and his hand clutched the imprint of his dick like he might come in his pants from those words alone.

A lazy smile curved her lips. She spread her feet to let him see just how wet and ready he'd made her. How much all of her yearned for all of him. "Now be a good boy and fill this pussy with your big, hard dick until you come inside me."

THIRTY-SEVEN

Grant

Sheer possession flooded his veins.

His dick throbbed, fighting to tear through his pants and follow Serena's command before he gave it a second thought. The world reduced to the raspy tone of her voice, to those breathy cries that wrote themselves into his DNA. He craved the sweet, wild taste of her, the way her thighs wrapped around his head, and her crescent nails marked his skin.

She cast him a knowing look, one that said he belonged to her as wholly as she'd laid herself out for him. Her breasts rose with each breath, rain gliding over her hips and pussy fluttering in the aftermath of her orgasm.

He wanted to see her come again. Make her say his name again and again and again and pump her so full—

He should ask if she had protection. At the least reach in his back pocket to check for a condom. But if they had a kid...he wouldn't mind. They could start a family. Build a home. Love each other through all the ups and downs.

"Please, Grant," Serena whispered over another wave of rolling thunder.

Fuck it. He was going in balls deep, and not even God could stop him.

"Dirty girl," he chastised, undoing his belt. "Wanting me to come in that pretty little cunt." Fisting his cock, he notched himself at her entrance and pressed his palm over her stomach. They both felt him slide inside as his thumb worked her clit. "So damn tight. You're perfect. Gonna make you come so many times. Gonna make you have my babies and wear my ring and ride my cock for the rest of our lives…"

Light flashed behind his eyes, and he lost his sanity, mumbling nonsense as he sank in the last, glorious inch. Bare skin on bare skin. Hard into soft, heat into heat. Pleasure sliced through his gut as he looked at her face. Shit. Had he said too much?

Serena watched with hooded eyes, raindrops glittering on her golden lashes. Then she arched her hips and contracted around his cock. "This is home. Wherever that takes us."

He let out a desperate hiss as his dick kicked, ready to burst at her command. "Yeah, this is home," he echoed. "*My home.*"

Punctuating the statement, he pulled out and thrust back in as hard as he could. Then, neither of them could speak because he couldn't stop. Being in her raw felt like heaven, like his favorite place. His holy place.

He pressed his hand over her abdomen and shuttered along with her at every stroke, in and out. Her clit swelled, and he forced himself to take even breaths as she started to shake underneath him. Every twitch and sigh pierced him to the core.

"Let me feel it," he rasped. "Let go, sunflower."

She gave him what he asked for, coming again so hard that it knocked the air from his lungs. He grit his teeth and shoved his hips forward, pushing her orgasm higher. She shook even harder, moaning into the sky and reaching above her head to claw the earth.

"More," she begged.

"Gladly."

He fell onto his hands and stole her breath with another kiss, letting their bodies move in sync. Her legs hooked on either side of his hips, and he pushed one knee up to her chest to angle in deeper. They both groaned.

Mud coated his hands, staining the sweatpants and squishing between his fingers. Reaching between them, he yanked down her shirt and plucked at one of her nipples. She gasped as the cold mud coated her breast.

He leaned down and sucked the other one into his mouth. "Mmm."

"Shit," she rasped, rolling her hips in a circle.

"That's it, make yourself feel good." His pretty little sunflower liked getting messy, and seeing her writhe in the dirt underneath him brought out a true beast. He had to mark her —claim her. Ruin them both for anyone else.

He straightened and filled his palms with her breasts, smearing mud in the process, then thrust twice as fast. She squirmed, panting, "*More, harder, yes,*" as her hands ran over his side and across his chest, hooking into his belt loops to pull them closer, even though he was already as close as he could get. The tremors for another orgasm coiled deep inside her, milking his cock, and he knew he wouldn't be able to survive a second wave.

"Give me everything," he growled.

Her eyebrows scrunched, and her mouth parted in a silent cry. He drank in the sight as pleasure rippled through them. It pulled him under, dragged him into the current. Hot, ferocious need consumed his vision.

He tipped his head back and lost all sanity. Somehow, his body kept moving on its own, each jerk of his hips leaving more of himself in her pussy. Pouring out his soul like the offering of a depraved worshiper.

She moaned and pressed her heels into his back to keep them sealed together. "Yes, you feel so good."

"So do you. Fuck, I can't even think straight." He didn't want to stop. Wanted to keep fucking with blind abandon until he unraveled, but every movement felt like it peeled away his skin, like he was splitting himself apart inside her.

He collapsed and dragged her against his chest as his dick kicked in defeat.

She giggled and took his face in her hands.

"I love you," they said in unison.

He kissed her smile, then scooped her up and stood before the adrenaline wore off. "Now that I've gotten you all dirty, I get to clean you up."

"Oh, is that how it works?" Her chestnut eyes glittered in the moonlight; legs wrapped around his waist with him still semi-hard inside.

He'd never seen her look so disorganized—hair tangled, clothes ripped, a flush running the entire length of her body— but most of all, she looked *content*. Like she'd finally found where she wanted to be.

"Wish I could keep you messy forever, all happy and sticky." He tightened his arms around her. Then his dick softened enough to slip out, along with a rush of their cum. A thrill of pride surged in his pulse.

She nuzzled into his neck. "My heart feels messy. Sticky, too. I don't want tonight to end."

"It isn't over yet." He took a step toward the house but paused. "Are you sure it was okay for me to..."

She nodded, hiding her face. "Yeah. I'm on birth control." Her voice lowered to a whisper. "For now."

For now? Shit, he shouldn't get ahead of himself, but a stupid happy grin had already appeared on his face. "Do you want kids? I guess we never talked about it."

"Honestly, I never met anyone I'd want kids with. But the

way you interact with the guests and the animals...I don't know." She shrugged. "Maybe we could start with a fur-baby?"

The image of Serena playing with a cute puppy or brushing a spindly-legged foal lit up his heart like a firecracker. "Yeah. I like the sound of that."

She smiled against his skin, and nothing in the whole world had ever felt better.

He carried her to the ladies' guesthouse, where they stripped out of their clothes, and he washed her until she sparkled. By the end, she'd gotten him hard all over again, so he laid across her bed and let her ride him like a true cowgirl—hat and all.

"Could watch you do this all day, sunflower." They'd both gotten lazy, her rocking side-to-side on top of him while he worked her clit.

She raked her nails down his chest. "I'll hold you to that."

When they both came again, she curled against him and sighed. "Grant?"

"Mm, yes?"

"Can you stay the night?" she mumbled, already half-asleep.

He chuckled and ran his hands up her sides, pulling the blanket over her shoulders. "Pretty sure it's morning by now."

Her lips pushed into a pout. "I mean, while we sleep. If that's okay."

He tucked her head under his chin. "I'll always stay. For as long as you want me to."

THIRTY-EIGHT

Serena

THE COMFORT OF GRANT'S EMBRACE LASTED THROUGHOUT THE whole night, even in her dreams. Strong arms and a steady heart. Soft lips pressing kisses into the crook of her neck...

Wait, this *wasn't* a dream.

She stretched across the bed like a cat. Warm, rough hands skimmed over her side. The slide of their bare skin sent a hum of pleasure along her nerves. She could catalog every inch of Grant's body by touch alone—from the thin, ticklish hairs on his legs to the thick erection nestled against her ass.

"Mmm, is it morning already?" she mumbled, teasing him with a little wiggle.

"Not quite." His voice came out deep and gravelly from sleep, and he trailed unhurried, open-mouthed kisses across her chest. "The sun isn't up yet."

"Good." Her sigh morphed into a yawn, and she tossed an arm over her face, turning onto her back. "I don't think I could open my eyes if I wanted to...besides, who wants to rush when we can wake up like this?"

"Agreed." He swirled his tongue around her nipple, making

her arch into his mouth. "You taste better than morning coffee —the kind you make, anyway."

She broke into a laugh, recalling their first morning together on the ranch. "Guess I'm better at serving breakfast in bed."

"That you are." He slid down the bed and lifted her leg to slip a finger inside, chuckling as she winced. "Too sore for another round?"

He tried to pull out, but she clenched around him. "No such thing."

He groaned. "I fucking love when you do that."

Lifting her arm, she managed to pry one eye open. The sight was worth it—Grant with messy post-sex-and-sleep hair, full bottom lip captured between his teeth, forearm flexing as he curled his finger against her g-spot.

She spread her legs wider and gripped his hips with her thighs. "Then come get some more."

He smirked. "How generous of you."

Her eyes flicked to the hard length he'd taken in his fist, flushed red and shiny with a fresh coat of spit. "Oh, I'm not the only generous one."

He bit his lip and wasted no time pushing in his dick, which somehow felt even bigger and harder than it had last night. They kept a slow, unhurried pace that made every thrust feel like a second heartbeat. The room smelled of clean linen and sex, early morning stillness broken only by their hushed moans and the rustle of sheets. Time seemed to stop completely.

Even though they didn't speak, she felt when he was about to break. Likewise, he knew exactly how to get her to the same place and rubbed her clit between two fingers, murmuring about how he wanted this every morning—wanted to hold her every night, and when they couldn't share a bed, she had to call him and let him watch. They came at the same time, him grunting her name and her gasping for air, feeling their pleasure mix inside her.

"You're too good, sunflower," he murmured, pulling out and cleaning them with a tissue. Then he pressed a lingering kiss on her forehead and sat up.

She watched him as sleep tugged at her consciousness. "Going somewhere?"

He sighed and looked at her with sad puppy dog eyes. "Yeah. I sent Mr. Weston a text about Lucy last night, but that won't let me off the hook this morning. Besides, I should drive the ATV to camp and ride my horse back with everyone else. Stay here and get some rest." He tucked her in. Although she wanted to help, it looked like her body wasn't giving her a choice but to let Grant have his way.

"Stay safe," she mumbled, then passed out before he even left the room.

❀

The rest of the day went by in a haze.

Renae and Richard were more than excited to tell her about the ride back—especially how Grant had been so tired he'd almost fallen asleep in the saddle. They all checked on Lucy, who thankfully only got a few scratches from her night escapade. But she appreciated some extra attention all the same, so Serena spent the afternoon learning how to wrap her leg and combing out the knots in her mane.

Some of the returning guests joined them for dinner, and afterward, everyone stayed up playing charades in the main house. Enjoying their company calmed her, and despite not being able to sleep in the same bed as Grant, she dreamed of riding across open fields and laughing together under the Milky Way. She also realized he'd stir up quite the commotion walking into the club with his hat and cowboy swagger, and that made returning to the city not sound half as bad.

"Goes by faster than you think, doesn't it?" Mrs. Weston smiled knowingly from across the table. Several empty boxes of pastries and sweating pitchers of juice were strewn between them, the picked-over remnants of their morning buffet. A few guests had gone back with their families already, Renae and Richard included, while the rest either joined them for brunch or took the chance to sleep in.

Serena quirked her lips. "Did you know I'd stay all along?"

Devious smile lines appeared around Mrs. Weston's eyes. "Oh no, I had a list of last-minute contacts in case you bailed on us."

"Wow, thanks for the vote of confidence," Serena deadpanned as Grant snorted in the chair next to her.

"Trust me, you had plenty of confidence all on your own," he scoffed. "Strutting in like a princess and just about breaking my back with your *vacation* bags."

"Don't remind me," she groaned. "I haven't finished repacking yet." Yesterday, she'd all but given up on stuffing everything in a suitcase that didn't seem the right size. Nothing she'd brought felt the same—most of all, herself.

"Ah, that's right. You might have to make room for one more thing in there." Grant stood as she raised her eyebrows.

A minute later, he brought back a gift-wrapped box and set it in front of her. "Happy belated birthday, country princess."

"Woah, hold up. Didn't we already celebrate?" She rapped her nails on the table, the clear coat from Missy surprisingly still intact. Going to the salon would definitely be on the agenda when she visited again.

"We all enjoyed sharing a treat on your behalf, but I don't think it was much of a present," Mrs. Weston commented. "This is something you can take with you...or bring along if you decide to visit again. You're always welcome here."

Serena broke out in an enthusiastic grin. "Actually, I'll take you up on that."

"Good, wouldn't be able to replace ya if we tried." Mr. Weston reached for another chocolate glazed doughnut and nodded toward her gift box. "We all wanted to pitch in, but this was Grant's idea."

She eyed the present, too curious for her own good. "It isn't gonna be some sort of gag gift, right?"

Mrs. Weston broke out in a cackle as Grant shot her a suspicious look. "Oh Lord, you're gonna keep us on our toes. Not this time. It's the real deal."

Hesitantly, she hooked a finger under the tape and peeled back the paper to reveal a brown shoe box. Classic choice—anything could be waiting inside—but the corners were crisp. The box looked brand new. A Western-style logo scrawled over the lid, and she breathed in the sweet scent of leather.

Lifting it open, her jaw dropped. A layer of tissue paper encased a pair of polished pink cowboy boots, complete with sunflowers embroidered up the shaft. In the perfect size. They weren't too fancy to get dirty but intricate and gorgeous all the same.

She looked up and found everyone smiling, then turned to Grant. His green gaze warmed straight through her chest.

"Thank you," she choked out. "I love them."

"They came out great, if I do say so myself," Mrs. Weston complimented. "Go on, let's see you try 'em on."

She hurried to toe off her shoes and slipped on the boots. "I can't wait to break these in. Aren't there barn dances around here?"

"You should probably get dance lessons first. Good thing I know a guy who won't mind if you step on his feet." Grant flashed her a dimpled smile, which did funny things to her pulse. As much as leaving hurt, the promise of coming back to be twirled in his arms more than made up for it.

Then the doorbell rang. "I'll get it," Grant said, stepping out to the entryway.

When the door clicked open, a familiar voice carried into the dining room. "Hey, remember me? I'm here to save my kidnapped sister." Lexi raised her voice. "Shout if you're being held against your will!"

Grant let out a gruff chuckle. "It's Lexi, right?"

"That's my name, don't wear it out. And *you're* the infamous Grant."

"Infamous?"

Serena rushed into the entryway before her sister blurted anything else. "Hey—you made it!"

Lexi squealed and tackled her with a hug. "You're alive!" She stepped back, then caught sight of the new boots. "Oh. My. Gosh. Those are adorable. Never seen anything fit you so well. I rushed to your rescue, but it looks like you took the place over without me."

"Something like that." Serena grinned and led her into the kitchen. "Come on, we have pastries to eat and then I'll need your help to cram everything in the car."

"Ooh, got any chocolate doughnuts?" Lexi peeked around as they joined the others.

Serena laughed. Her cheeks hurt from smiling so much. "I think you'll have to fight for the last one..."

Much too soon, she sat in the driver's seat with her life packed in the trunk and her heart standing outside the window in a leather hat and worn jeans. She'd seen him wear the same things every day for the past month, but right now, it felt like that hadn't been enough.

"Even if there's no traffic, keep your eyes on the road. Take a break if you need one and don't eat those snacks while driving," Grant lectured.

Lexi rolled her eyes. "He has it bad, doesn't he?"

Serena smacked her on the arm. "We'll be safe," she promised Grant.

"Call me when you get home?"

Right, cell phones were a thing!

Serena turned, but Lexi had already reached into the glove box and pulled out a bejeweled case. "Am I your favorite sister for nothing? Here ya go."

The phone powered on instantly. "You're an angel," Serena praised. "It even has a full battery."

Lexi beamed. "I know. You're welcome."

The notifications she expected after a month away were... nonexistent. Surprisingly, that didn't disappoint her as much as it should've. Maybe that meant getting her fresh start would be easier than she anticipated.

She leaned back and snapped a quick photo of Grant before he could protest, then handed him the phone. "Here, put in your info."

When he finished, she noticed he set the contact name to *Bossy Cowboy*. She bit her lip and slid the phone into her pocket.

"Got everything you need?" he asked.

"Yep," she replied, popping the 'p.'

His eyes flicked down to her lips. "Good."

"Mhm."

She didn't know what else to say, but looking away felt too difficult. Was it possible to drive off without breaking eye contact?

"Well, you gonna kiss her or what?" Mr. Weston called out from the porch.

The heat of a blush crawled up her face. Since when had everyone seen right through them?

"Damn right, I'm gonna kiss her!" Grant shouted, then he leaned into the car and kissed her like she stole his last breath —and did his best to steal it right back.

That boy never played fair.

Grant straightened with a wink and blush of his own. "See you soon, sunflower."

THIRTY-NINE

Grant

Fucking traffic.

He'd gotten up at the break of dawn and watched as the sun rose over rolling hills, pink-golden light reflecting off the dew and dusting the fields in tiny diamonds. Driving through the countryside had been perfect—blue skies, warm air, and open road.

Until now, that was.

It felt like a crime to roll the windows up and turn on the A/C, but the stench of exhaust and hot asphalt had already begun to infiltrate the cabin of the truck. He slouched in the seat and slowed to a crawl behind a shiny blue sedan. Only twenty-six miles left between him and his sunflower. And about twenty million other people crowding the highway.

The past few weeks were the ultimate test of his endurance. Getting to know Serena without the mayhem of regular life and commitments had been a true blessing, but they'd learned so much more about each other with all of that, too.

Her siblings commandeered their video chats on multiple occasions to bombard him with questions, which he was more than happy to answer, and the younger ones adored when he took them on a virtual tour of the farm animals. Even Lucy got in on the fun, learning to nudge his pocket for the phone and whinnying whenever she saw Serena on the screen.

After the storm, she'd been put on stall rest for a week before the vet and her owners agreed he could start riding with her again. Her impatience to get back into the action rubbed off on him, and their exercises became the one thing that took his mind off Serena.

He needed the extra practice as much as Lucy did. Going through the basics and reminded himself how much work it took to make riding look effortless—and how alive he felt while doing it. All his past competitions were in the junior rodeo, but next year, he would be gearing up for the real thing. The prospect of a challenge rekindled a fire in his spirit, and he was determined to have Serena make good on her promise.

She'd managed to get away and visit the Hollow Oak for a weekend, where he'd introduced her to his family, and they'd fallen in love with her as fast as he had. The Westons gave them their blessing, too, along with an uncomfortable talk about being madly in love *and* staying responsible. Even then, he hadn't stopped smiling the whole time.

A few days together wasn't nearly enough. Hell, this week he'd taken off work wouldn't be enough, but all that was about to change. He eyed the unopened letter on the passenger seat. Hopefully, sooner rather than later.

The congestion on the road finally opened up, and he maneuvered out of a maze of orange construction cones. Clusters of tall, sleek business buildings and billboards dotted the heart of the city, his pickup truck loud and out of place.

He took the next exit, and soon, the college campus came into view. Meticulously manicured grass and windows of classroom after classroom gleamed in the sun, students already populating the sidewalks. A small cafe with several picnic tables had attracted a crowd, and he envisioned himself taking Serena there for a treat between lectures.

Yeah, it'd be different than the ranch. It'd take some time to adjust, but he was starting to look forward to a new adventure.

Driving past the row of imposing Greek houses, he scowled at their bold letters—in particular, the frat Serena's ex had been president of. She'd heard they kicked him out following the police investigation, and the university put him on a watch list.

They wouldn't be the only ones watching.

That's another reason why he had to be here. Serena purposely chose a place on the opposite end of campus and insisted she could take care of herself, but he wasn't the kind of guy who would sit on the sidelines. He'd be here to support her no matter what.

Apartments and dorm buildings thinned as he turned onto a quieter street. The rush of the city faded with every block, and he started to admire the quaint atmosphere—tiny houses on tiny lawns that all looked the same—but it was cute. It was a place to start. A place to grow.

Your destination is on the right.

As the GPS chimed, he squinted at the house numbers but quickly recognized the Audi with an open trunk full of boxes parked just ahead. He pulled over and cracked his neck with a sigh of relief. Hours of being on the road felt nothing like hours on horseback. Still, it'd all be worth it the moment he saw Serena's face and got to kiss her lips...along with every other part of her he could get his hands on.

He left the windows cracked to let in some fresh air and shoved the letter in his back pocket, preparing to grab a box or two on his way in. But before he got out, an obnoxious engine roared down the street. A polished motorcycle swerved into Serena's driveway.

He tensed. The biker fit the description of her ex perfectly —decked out in leather, silver rings, and a dragon tattoo on his head. Worse, Serena must've left the front door open from carrying stuff inside, and Jace looked way too comfortable as he sauntered up to the porch.

Grant clenched his jaw. His fingers froze on the door handle as Serena appeared, arms crossed and chin held high. Damn, she pulled off looking thoroughly pissed while still being one hundred percent adorable.

Maybe he shouldn't rain on her parade just yet.

Jace stopped a few feet away and glanced down. "Where'd you get the boots—a Barbie cowgirl convention?"

"Where'd you get the crooked nose—a Fight Club clearance sale?" Serena pursed her lips and blocked the doorway.

"Could've moved back in with me, you know."

"Get off my lawn, Jace."

He smirked. "Nice to see you, too. Gonna let me in or what?"

"I'm gonna call the police."

"We both know you don't have the best track record with the pigs."

"This is your last warning."

Jace stepped forward—but before he could get out another word, Grant shut the truck door so hard it rattled. It had the intended effect. Both of them turned as he caught up in a few long strides. Jace scowled while Serena's eyes brightened, standing a little taller with a confident smirk.

Hell yeah, sunflower. Your enforcer has arrived.

He didn't bother walking between them and instead stepped directly into Jace's personal space, forcing him to fall back. Such a shame his ears hadn't worked when Serena told him off, but when someone bigger and stronger got in his way, he didn't put up a fight.

All offense intended—this guy looked like a pipsqueak, as easy to snap in two as a twig, and must've had a major case of little man syndrome. Not that Grant underestimated what Serena told him, but he could never be intimidated by someone who placed fear over respect.

"Who the fuck is this?" Jace snapped.

"Someone who happens to be best friends with the sheriff." Grant pulled out his phone. "Got the number on speed dial and everything. Wanna see?"

"Save your party tricks," Jace scoffed. "Or are you the kind of guy who needs to hide behind a badge?"

Grant smirked. "I'm the kind of guy that can take you any day."

"Enough," Serena interrupted. "If you fight, I *will* report it to the school. You're already on probation—think you'll get a third chance?"

Jace glared at her. "You're not worth it, anyway. I'm done wasting my time." He turned and got on his bike, revving the engine.

"Oh, and Jace?" Grant called before he drove off. "Don't ever come back here again."

At that, Jace's lips curled into a grin, and he broke out in a jarring laugh. "A whole mother-fucking cowboy..." He shook his head and shifted his gaze to Serena. "Suit yourself."

Then he peeled away. Grant followed the bike's tail light until it went out of sight, memorizing the license plate for later.

"Talk about good timing." Serena sighed and wrapped her arms around his waist. "I'm so glad you're here."

The last of his worries melted at her touch, then all that mattered was pressing their bodies as close together as possible, letting their skin and breath mingle—feeling her heart beating against his.

"Sorry I didn't step in sooner," he murmured, kissing the top of her head and burying his nose in her hair. "Were you worried?"

"Not anymore." She shook her head against his chest, then

frowned. "He seemed...different. I haven't seen him since the police pulled us over. I wonder if something happened."

"You think someone gave him a reality check?"

"I hope so." She shrugged. "Whatever it is, I'm glad to be done with it."

He hooked his thumb under his chin and tipped up her face for a kiss. *This*. Warm lips and a playful tongue, her familiar taste and scent. Everything that had become his whole world.

"Kinda liked watching you turn into a sexy boss lady," he murmured into the kiss.

Serena laughed. "Oh, but you're the one who's best buds with the sheriff. I'm pretty sure he knew you were bluffing."

Grant winked. "He doesn't need to know which department. Sheriff Gaines would play along. Might even be able to pull some strings with the locals, too." He bracketed Serena's face in his hands. "I'm giving you his number. If I'm ever not around, you call him."

She nodded. "All right, will do."

"Good. And I'm installing security cameras tomorrow." He leaned in and stole another kiss, their hands wandering farther than they should in broad daylight. "Let's get in the rest of your stuff and lock the door."

"Sounds like a plan."

A handful of trips later, they sat side by side on the floor, surrounded by a citadel of cardboard boxes. The house looked bare; white walls and laminate floor, no furniture, and nothing but the basics in the kitchen. He'd already mapped out the space and thought of a few things he could build from scraps around the ranch. Like a table, for starters. Maybe a bed frame. A *special* bed frame.

"What's this?" Serena asked, tilting her head as she noticed the wrinkled envelope sticking out from his pocket.

"Oh, I brought it so we could open it together." He took off his hat and ran a hand through his hair.

Her eyebrows rose as she plucked it out and read the sender's information. "It's from the college?"

He nodded. "I applied to go in the spring like I said I would." She opened her mouth, but he held up a hand. "They have a here I'd thought about enrolling in before. Just didn't think…" He sighed. "I guess a part of me wanted to stay bitter and lonely at the ranch, but here we are."

"Here we are," Serena repeated.

And he wouldn't want to be anywhere else.

He pulled her into his lap, and she giggled. "You can open it."

"You sure?"

"I'm sure. You're my good luck charm."

She rolled her eyes. "Okay, then."

Without an ounce of hesitation, she ripped through the seal and unfolded the letter. He watched her face instead of trying to read the typeset writing. It'd be great if he got accepted. But if he didn't, there were other ways to make himself useful.

Serena chewed her lip and pulled the paper to her nose, peeking at him over the top.

"I'll try again next year," he mumbled.

"Stop being such a pessimist," she teased.

"How about you stop toying with me," he shot back, tickling her side until she squirmed and pressed her ass into his crotch. The paper fell from her hands, and the room filled with her breathless shrieks. Fuck the letter, all he wanted was to strip her down and—

"You got in," she gasped.

He froze. "Wait, really?"

She laughed again. "Yes, really! Pre-vet school is hella impressive—and a lot of work." Her eyes shimmered as she dragged a finger along his neck. "You're gonna need someone who makes sure you don't overload yourself."

"Mhm..." He leaned back and pretended to think, but could hardly form a coherent thought as she turned and wrapped her legs around his hips. "I'll need a place to stay, too. Guess I better start filtering through potential roommates."

"It just so happens that I'm in the market for a roommate." She wiggled her ass, purposely this time. His dick kicked beneath their clothing. "But the requirements are pretty strict."

He grinned. "Is that so?"

"I'll only consider someone who can win the rodeo, who'll take me to visit my favorite place on the weekends, *and* looks hella good in a cowboy hat."

"Well, it just so happens that I fit those requirements." He slipped his hands under her shirt and lowered them to the ground.

"Is that so?" she mused, threading her fingers through his hair.

"But I have a requirement of my own," he added.

"And what's that?" A flush bloomed over her skin, devious shadows flickering behind her lashes.

"She has to be my girlfriend—until I make her my wife."

Serena pulled him closer. "You have a deal. Let's make this official."

He skimmed his lips over her smile. "Looks like going to the city won't be as bad as I thought."

EPILOGUE

Serena

Dirt sprayed in the air with a flurry of hooves.

Seconds raced by on the clock.

The cowgirl spurred her horse across the arena in a clover leaf, making a tight pivot around the third and final barrel. Her leg caught, the barrel wobbled, and the crowd gasped. Then, it settled back upright.

Cheers erupted as she grabbed the reins with both hands and leaned in to fly toward the finish line.

Serena clapped and hollered, heart pounding along with the contagious energy in the stands. Sunlight glittered on rising columns of dust while country music blasted through the speakers.

Cowboys knew how to throw one hell of a party.

It'd been a full year since she first stepped foot on Hollow Oak Ranch. A year that had turned her life upside down, but in the best way. A year of sharing a house—a *home*—with Grant, of reconnecting with friends she had once lost, and realizing having those people in her life was all that mattered.

An announcer came over the intercom to signal the end of barrel racing, with the final scores being given after a short intermission. Then it'd be time for the best event of the day, the one featuring her favorite cowboy: tie-down roping.

Serena looked across the arena and spotted the top of Mrs. Weston's bejeweled cowgirl hat next to Mr. Weston's plain one. They'd insisted on sitting on their own, using the excuse that they couldn't keep up with a group of college kids. More like they wanted to watch the show without distractions.

Missy was somewhere around here, too, working with the stock animals behind the stage. Her husband would compete in the bull riding event at the end of the evening.

"Wow, this is exciting! I'm glad you invited us," Ivory gushed, eyes alight and smile as radiant as ever. She and her fiancé, Adrian, had accepted Serena's and Grant's invitation to spend a weekend trip on the ranch, including a day at the county rodeo. After going on double dates with them over the past few months, they'd both been eager to come and see what all the fuss had been about.

"I'm glad you came," Serena replied, mirroring Ivory's enthusiasm.

"We enjoyed the ride," Adrian added, no doubt referring to how they'd ridden the entire way here on his Harley. "I think it's safe to say we wouldn't mind making the trip again."

Ivory nodded in agreement, a purple ribbon bobbing up and down in her hair. Adrian's gold rings glinted as he wrapped his hand around Ivory's shoulder, and she leaned into his side. They were the two people who understood exactly the kind of gutter trash Jace could be and had graciously offered their support if she ever needed extra protection.

Fortunately, she'd never needed it. He'd driven past her house a few times but never stepped on the property again. Maybe the threat of expulsion or a restraining order had done the trick. Maybe it was the 6'7" possessive cowboy watching through the window. Or maybe it was her new concealed carry permit and the handgun stashed in her purse at all times.

"Oh shoot, did we miss the whole round?" Nia and her husband, Caspian—the couple who completed their trio—stepped into the row carrying a precarious stack of nachos, hot dogs, and sweating cans to fill everyone's orders.

They also seemed to have picked up a few extra items. A new decorative clip sparkled in Nia's bright red hair, and the corner of a leather book stuck out of her purse, while Caspian sported a braided bracelet and a pack of hard candies that barely fit in his pocket. That's what had taken them so long, the vendors must have sucked them in.

"Yeah, but the next event is the important one," Serena mentioned.

"Oh, Grant's up next?" Nia sat next to her and started handing out the concessions.

Their relationship had been rocky at first, considering their history from freshman year, but Grant and Caspian had clicked immediately, and eventually, she and Nia became closer than ever. Their personalities balanced each other out, Nia helping her with her studies, and in turn, she managed to get Nia out of the house every now and then.

The six of them had spent several nights out at the club learning how to line dance with Grant, and on days when they wanted to stay in, they rotated hosting board game tournaments. They'd even pulled a few all-nighter study sessions fueled by Ivory's homemade cookies.

Serena nodded as Nia unwrapped the new journal and scribbled something down. "Yep. I think he drew fourth out of eight contestants."

"That means he has to beat everyone before him *and* set the bar higher for everyone after him," Ivory commented.

"No sweat." Serena crossed her legs and flipped her hair. "Obviously, he's the best cowboy here."

"I think you might be biased," Caspian chuckled, taking over when Nia got distracted. "Drinks all-around." He passed beers out to her, Ivory, and Adrian, keeping two sodas for himself and Nia.

"Not partaking tonight?" Adrian asked.

Caspian winked and popped a candy in his mouth, sharing the bag with Nia. "We have plans later."

"Wouldn't surprise me if you two were already making out under the bleachers," Ivory mumbled.

Nia blushed, and Caspian burst out in a laugh. "Sometimes, I think you know us too well."

"Too well, indeed," Adrian scoffed as he opened his beer and took a swig.

Good friends, good food, and great entertainment. A girl couldn't ask for more.

Several minutes later, Serena shifted on the bench as the third rider crossed the finish line. He'd come in at 11.4 seconds, the fastest score so far.

Grant could beat that. He'd done it repeatedly in their practice sessions. But there were factors they couldn't anticipate—the calf might be particularly evasive, an audience added to the pressure, and he'd only get one chance to leave his mark.

The one thing they didn't have to worry about was his horse. *Their* horse. Lucy made a full recovery, and her owners agreed that she and Grant made a great team. They'd signed the paperwork last month to make Lucy a part of their little family.

She'd spent countless weekends watching Grant go through every movement, shaving off a hundredth of a second in the smallest of details. When he wasn't practicing, Grant taught her the basics of riding. She'd managed to get up to a canter but had a long way to go before it felt natural.

Her favorite ride had been when they went bareback through the trails. Wildflowers were starting to bloom in the spring, and Grant took her to a rocky cave behind a waterfall. They'd fucked under the cold mountain water, then cuddled in their tent where they made out, and then fucked again until dawn.

The best part was that when they had to return home, they could go back together.

She snapped to attention as Grant rode Lucy into the roping box. He waited while a thin barrier was stretched across the opening and tied to the calf's neck. The riders weren't supposed to start until the calf ran out and broke the barrier, ensuring it got a head start. If they left the box too soon, it resulted in a ten-second penalty. Timing would be half the battle.

Lucy's coat gleamed, her mane plaited in a thick rope along the top of her neck while a tight running braid kept her tail neat and out of the way. Serena made sure Lucy looked picture-perfect this morning, and the horse knew it.

Grant looked even better—a thin piggin string clamped between his teeth, the top buttons of his shirt undone, and a shiny buckle at his waist. He swung a longer, thicker rope through the air that he'd use to lasso the calf. She couldn't wait to pounce on him as soon as they were done.

The announcer called his name over the speakers, and the clock flashed to zero.

She held her breath.

Grant gave a nod. The calf bolted out, then Lucy shot after it.

They galloped across the arena as he twirled the lasso in the air. It landed perfectly around the calf's neck. Grant leaped off before Lucy even came to a full stop, and the horse dug in her hind legs to pull the line taut. Grant ran to the calf, hooked his arm under its belly, and tossed it onto its side.

Hunching over, he gathered three of its legs in one hand, then with a blur of movement, tied them with the piggin string.

She let out a cheer as Grant raised both hands and stood. Lucy let the rope go slack.

The calf struggled, but it couldn't break free.

The others broke into a chorus of hollers beside her. She glanced at the clock—11 seconds flat. Tears of pride welled in her eyes.

Grant hopped on Lucy and searched the crowd as the announcer called his time. His green eyes glimmered with exhilaration, and when he found her at last, she blew him a congratulatory kiss. He made a catching motion with his fist and brought it to his lips.

A fever broke out under her skin, pulsing with every heartbeat. One day, that man would make her poor heart explode. Ivory elbowed her in the side with a giggle, and she didn't even bother trying to hide the smile that split across her face.

Grant rode back to the starting gate as the calf was untied, and the next rider got in position. The round ended with only one rider managing to beat his score—but taking second place here meant he'd be guaranteed a spot in the next competition.

"Before we start our next intermission, one of our cowboys has something to say to y'all..." Everyone turned to the announcer's box. Her breath caught. Grant had ridden Lucy to the side of the arena, where someone handed him the microphone.

...What on earth was he doing?

He motioned to her. "Sunflower, come here for a sec."

The crowd swooned, and her heart swooped into her stomach.

She made her way through the stands, ducked between the bars of the arena fencing, and gave a breathless laugh as one of the barrel men bowed and made a show of escorting her to Grant. Dust from his run coated his sleeve, sweat glistening on his forehead under the hat. His full lips pulled into a sheepish grin that made her knees weak. He'd dismounted and spoke as she walked toward him and Lucy. "If it weren't for you, I wouldn't be here today. And dare I say, I've never been so motivated to make a good impression in my entire life."

The crowd laughed.

"That said…" He fumbled around in his pocket. Then took off his hat and dropped to one knee.

Her jaw dropped. This couldn't be real. This couldn't really be happening right here, right now—

Lucy stuck out one leg and dropped to a knee beside Grant.

He looked up with a flush in his cheeks and those twin dimples that made her heart skip. In his hand, he held a little black box with a sparkling diamond encased in an antique ring —Mrs.Weston's. "The only prize I want to bring home tonight is you, Serena Lawson. My one and only sunflower. Will you let me tie the knot?"

She could barely hear the crowd erupting into applause, could barely process the scene in front of her. It was a miracle she could form words—but she only needed one.

"Yes," she whispered. Then, stepping closer, she covered the ring in Grant's hands with one of hers and took the microphone with the other.

"Yes," she repeated for the crowd. "You can tie me up anytime you want, cowboy."

If possible, the crowd cheered even louder. The barrel men started doing cartwheels around them, and Lucy tossed her head with a snort of approval.

Grant picked her up and spun her in his arms, claiming her lips with a kiss that sealed her fate—a kiss that she'd feel for the rest of the night as they twirled under twinkling lights at the barn dance, and back at the ranch where they made the kind of love that shattered them both—a kiss that she'd feel for the rest of her life.

ACKNOWLEDGMENTS

There's a special place in my heart for being in the great outdoors For silence that isn't silent, and for stillness that isn't still. This book is my happy place. I hope it made you smile.

Many thanks to the BEST HUSBAND EVER (all caps just like I promised), who makes sure I eat and sleep and shower every now and then. The person who encouraged my 'silly little romance books' from day one, and who reads the same scene every time I ask. Love ya endlessly.

Thank you to my beta readers, who laughed and cried and yelled at my characters. Authors need that.

Thank you to my editors—Dee, for bringing humor and empathy into Hollow Oak. Marisa, for your enthusiasm and polishing the story until it shines. Lindsey, for your meticulous work on all the edits I hate the most.

Thank you to everyone who has read, critiqued, and reviewed this book. Especially to the team of ARC readers and those who took a chance on a new author. Your reviews make all the difference.

Thank you to the artists who brought Serena, Grant, and Hollow Oak to life. The visuals make me fall in love with the book all over again.

Thanks most of all to the Creator, to the Earth, and the passion that drives us all to take our next step.

On to the next page,

Siberia

ABOUT THE AUTHOR

Siberia writes sinful romance for the soul, featuring characters who are as unapologetically smutty as they are sentimental. She's a true romantic and can often be found trying new foods, making blanket forts, and taking long walks on the beach with her husband.

Join her email list to keep up with new updates, giveaways, ARC opportunities, and more!

Author website: beacons.ai/siberia
Reader Group: facebook.com/groups/sweetsinners
Instagram: @siberiathewriter